JOHNSON

STICK HANDLING - BOOK ONE

SHAE MICHAELS

They're both professional hockey players, albeit for different teams. They're both attending the same celebrity charity golf tournament. And they both have a hotel reservation under the name 'J. Johnson'.

Or so they thought.

What happens when the hotel accidentally only holds one room instead of two? Can these two antagonistic, rival hockey players manage to share a hotel room without any sexy, forbidden, naughty hanky panky?

For Jaime Johnson and J.J. Johnson, the answer is... no.

A momentary lapse in judgment is all it can be. That's all they can let it be. But what if underneath all the sniping and squabbling, there was... more?

Jaime Johnson and J.J. Johnson know how to handle being enemies. Can they handle falling in love?

Je t'aime
J'aime!

I ♡ #14

♡ Love Me

Loverboy !

♡

♡
♡

♡

♡ LOVERBOY

Loonie

4

Loverboy

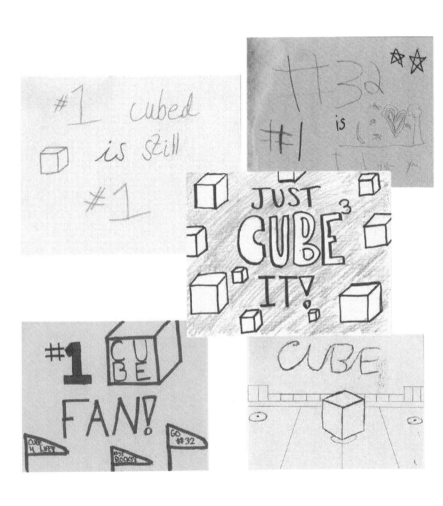

This is a work of fiction. I've yet to have any NHL teams invite me to stalkerishly attend their practices, games, stow away in their luggage to travel with them, or otherwise invade their players' lives for any first-hand knowledge of what it's like to play in the NHL. So, the depiction of the NHL in this book is derived from some research, reading other fictionalized stories, joyfully watching games, and whatever else my imagination decided to conjure up.

For helping to bring my hockey universe to life, I shamelessly pilfered the ideas and suggestions of several people in regards to team names, location, and mascots. And I would like to take the time to thank the following:

Jenny Benisch- for your suggestion of the Kansas City Snappers. As soon as I saw the name and the snapping turtle mascot idea, I knew that was the team J.J. Johnson had to be on.

Charmene Saint-Victor- I adored the team name of the Griffins that you suggested. I hope you don't mind that I ran with that idea but relocated them to the city of Phoenix. It made me giggle to give a city named after a mythical figure a team named after a different mythical creature.

Bonnie Carter- The Firebirds needed to be relocated since I stuck the Griffins in Phoenix (see the above). So, I moved them to Pontiac, Michigan, in honor of the muscle car.

Heather Wood- The D.C. Stealth seemed like such a cool name for a hockey team. I'm not sure how stealthy hockey players are, but it is a cool name.

Brei-Ayn Nichole Moscato- The Chicago Suns got such a short mention in this book. Sorry about that. I'll try to do better.

Content Warning:

On-page mention of child abandonment of a main character and related mental trauma from that event, mentions of childhood and on-page depiction of on-going emotional neglect of a main character by his parents, and some mild homophobic language relating to reactions to queer athletes coming out.

Additionally, there is some physical (non-sexual) violence between the main characters depicted on-page, before and during their relationship. However, it occurs solely within the confines of hockey game play.

This book is dedicated to the Stanley Cup.

I am so, so sorry.

(Not really)

Contents

Excerpt from an article in *The Hockey News*, 4 years ago:

With the Kansas City Snappers' recent acquisition of right winger J.J. Johnson from the D.C. Stealth, there's a possible match-up in the works to thrill hockey announcers and fans. If Jaime Johnson—a left winger who last season played the majority of his games with the Minnesota Loons' AHL affiliate—does well in this year's Loons' training camp, then it's quite likely we'll all soon be seeing frequent Johnson vs Johnson confrontations.

Instagram

snappinpete

♡ ◯ ▽   🔖

2,869 likes

snappinpete Welcome to KC, Cube! But we'll have to get you to swap out your lucky lion out for a lucky snapper!

4 hours ago

Prologue

J.J.

April

"Would you two break it up, already?" Mark or Mike or…
whatever the dude's name was… said. "I swear, you two are
worse than my fucking toddlers. I hate having to ref the
fucking games between your teams."

As the ref glided away on his skates, shaking his head in
disbelief, or annoyance, or irritation, I called after him, "It's
not my fucking fault this guy doesn't know how to play
without fucking high sticking all the damned time."

"I don't high stick," Jaime Johnson retorted back, an indignant expression on his stupidly handsome face. Fuck, someone with that many freckles should just look ridiculous, not ridiculously lickable and hot.

"Do too," I, of course, immediately shot back. Because high-sticking was, like, the guy's fucking go-to move whenever whoever he was playing against was snagging the puck away from him every chance they got. Or maybe that was just me.

"Do not," was Jaime's oh so mature response. He tacked on a shove to my shoulder. "You're just always in my way while I'm trying to get the puck."

Whatever. Like that shove even would've hurt. I was wearing padding, he had a glove on, and his shove was feeble at best.

"Do too," I sang back, giving him a proper shove to his shoulder. One that actually moved him backward a few inches over the ice. "But it's okay, Loverboy," I said, full of fake sympathy and using Jaime's hockey nickname. "One of these days I'm sure you'll figure out that, unless the puck is in the fucking air, your stick should be down. On the ice. Not waving around everywhere and smacking the other players in the face. You know... I would've assumed that everyone who grew up with the last name of Johnson, like we did, would've learned some time around puberty how to properly hold and handle their stick."

Hmm. For some reason, Jaime seemed to take exception to the pantomimed jerk-off motion I made.

"You... you... frick-fu-fu-fucking a-asshole..."

God, it was hilarious whenever Jaime swore during a game. I've watched plenty of his interviews and other media PR tape and the dude—off the ice—was the picture of saintly pure vocabulary. He danced around and substituted all sorts of ridiculousness for good old-fashioned swear words during the majority of his speaking and he always sounded so out-of-practice and as stumbling as a newborn colt whenever he did let the odd profanity or two pass through his pale pink lips when he was on the ice.

I don't know what the hell was up with that. But it was amusing.

And it sure as hell didn't stop me from jerking myself off a time or two while watching those video clips. What can I say? I did like me a little freckle-sprinkled ginger and cream, every now and then, and Jaime Johnson was the epitome of milky-white skin smattered with a heavy layer of freckles, topped off with a head of slightly wavy gingery-red hair. Plus the thought of dirtying up that too-pure-for-profanity mouth by shoving my cock into it... Hmm hmm hmm. Gets me shooting off every single time.

And then, when I was actually on ice with him, the couple of times in the preseason, the four times our teams met throughout the regular season, and the series of games we played when we were both lucky enough to reach the playoffs and got scheduled to play against each other—like we were currently doing—and being able to drive him to sullying that pretty, pretty mouth with curse words... it gave me a little thrill every time.

11

Really, it was the little things in life you had to live for.

"You're disgusting," Jaime said. "Why do you always have to act like such a... such a..."

"All-around awesome dude and hockey stud?" I supplied. Naturally, I assumed that's how Jaime was going to finish his sentence. He was probably just too stunned by my outrageously awesome awesomeness to get the words out. And, because I was a nice guy, I even left out the word "fucking" that I normally would've thrown in. Because, let's face it, I'm not just a hockey stud; I'm a fucking hockey stud.

Jaime crossed his arms and gave me what, I assumed, he thought was a death-glare. As if. "Ass," he said. "An ass. Why are you such an—"

"Hey, guys," the large, blond form of Sawyer Brzycki said as he skated slowly past Jaime and I. "You may not have noticed, but the rest of us are playing a fucking hockey game here. You wanna get with the program?"

Man, I really wished I had a thing for long-haired, bearded dudes who looked like the yummy off-spring of a lumberjack and a Viking. But, while I could appreciate that he was fucking hot, Sawyer "Breezy" Brzycki wasn't really my type. He looked like he'd be a bit too aggressive and bossy in bed for me and I liked a more even, level playing field when I played the dick hokey-pokey.

"And those Loonie assholes just scored while you and Red, here, were having your little lovers' tete-a-tete," commented my teammate Sasha "Yuri" Yuralaev. For a dude with such a Russian-sounding name, it always tickled me how

12

American he sounded. But I supposed he couldn't help it. If I remembered correctly, his parents had emigrated to Southern California a couple years before Sasha had been born.

Sasha had been skating next to Sawyer and, presumably, exchanging some chit chat with him. But unlike Sawyer, Sasha glided to a stop next to Jaime and I, instead of continuing on to our team box. "Not that I blame you for not noticing Sneets' not-at-all-celebratory celly," he commented. "The man is gloomy and dour as fuck even when he's supposed to be happy. But surely you must've noticed all the other shitheads dressed in black and blue over there whooping it up like they're about to win the fucking game? Because they are. Well, unless they rule the goal no good. Refs are currently reviewing it, so we'll see."

Sasha's smack to the back of my head probably would've hurt if I hadn't been wearing a helmet. Instead, it was just a literal nudge to get my head back in the game and off the man in front of me. But, damn, it was hard. I did wish that Jaime wasn't swaddled up in the bulky and shapeless hockey gear we were both wearing. In the photos and videos I'd seen of him, he looked mighty, mighty fine out of his uniform.

"Cube?"

Sasha's voice calling my nickname pulled my mind, yet again, out of Jaime Johnson's pants. To reassure him I was ready and eager to get back to playing, I responded, "Yeah. Yeah. We're still only down a point, we can do this. Finish this game off with a win and finish off this series so the loony

13

Loons can curl up in their beds tonight and cry into their pillows while we prepare to move on to the next round."

"What a bunch of baloney," Jaime stated, a sneer curling the corner of his mouth. "You guys'll be the ones sobbing when you load your sorry bu-asses onto your plane tonight when we send you home to Kansas City like the losers you are and *we* move on to the next round."

"Bu-asses? Basses? Really, Loverboy? If you're going to swear, at least sound like a fucking grown-up and fucking swear properly," I commented. "Or did you mean to imply that our team planned to load up a bunch of fish onto our plane with us after the game tonight? What kind of freaky celebratory shit do you get up to? 'Cause I gotta tell you, fish don't usually play a big factor in my celebrations."

"F-fuck off! That's not what I meant at all and you know it, you ass. There. Ass. Ass, ass, ass."

"Gonna stick your tongue out at me next? 'Cause you sound about three-years-old there, Loverboy."

"Would you stop calling me that?" Jaime asked and, fuck, if he didn't look like he was about to throw gloves and started wailing on me.

Awesome.

"You two are ridiculous," Sasha commented with a massive eye-roll. "I'm out. I, for one, am going to get my ass back to where it's supposed to be before the refs are done taking their sweet-ass time with this replay and get back to playing hockey. You know, that thing we're doing. And why we're wearing all this shit and chasing a tiny, black rubber

14

disk across some frozen water back and forth and back and forth for sixty minutes. You coming, Cube?"

"Yeah, yeah. I'm coming," I replied. And I would. But not before I asked Jaime, "Why shouldn't I call you Loverboy? It's your nickname, yeah?"

"Doesn't mean I have to like it," he muttered. "I'm not the one who chose it."

"Aw. Poor, little baby Johnson doesn't like his nickname. Wah, wah, wah." I was tempted to throw in a fisted eye-rub while I was at it, but figured the overly exaggerated pout and whining got my point across well enough. It was hard to make a fist wearing hockey gloves, anyway. "What'd you want to be called instead? Should I pick out some other lame-ass 80s band to call you instead? Should I call you Wham! Or the Go-Gos?"

Jaime crowded close to me and since we were roughly the same height—naturally, I was just a little bit taller—we were practically nose to nose. Close enough to kiss. If, you know, we didn't have the bulk of our padding in the way. And I wanted to throw my career out the window by inciting a fight—there's no way Jaime Johnson wouldn't punch the shit out of me if I kissed him—and facing ejection and suspension from this game and, probably, the rest of the games of the season for inappropriately and non-consensually making advances on another player and violating the league's guidelines on proper conduct.

"How have you not spent more time on the IRL?" Jaime asked me. "With as much as you tempt people to slug you... There's no way I can be the only one."

15

"Oooh. Or I could call you Red, like Yuri called you," I commented, ignoring Jaime's question. "Nah. Your hair's a little too... carrot-y orange to be called Red, I think. Although, that was kind of mean and not all that accurate. Sure, Jaime's hair wasn't red-red, Ronald McDonald-red—he should thank fuck and luck for that—but it was a lush coppery, rose-gold, glowing-banked-coals sort of light, warm red.

It was kind of unfair how well it suited him and made him ridonculously attractive.

"You... you... you..." Jaime spluttered.

"Are you two still fucking at it?" Asked Max... Mick... Mcwhateverhisnamewas. Seriously, it seemed like half of the refs in the league were named Mike, or Mark, or Milt, or Mick, or Mack, or Martin, or Matt. "The replay's over and the goal was ruled good. If you two don't go back to your boxes right the fuck now, I'm going to give you each a fucking Delay of Game penalty."

"Um. Neither one of us has the puck," I helpfully pointed out to the pissed off looking ref.

"Does it look like I fucking care?" he asked. "Puck or no puck, you're delaying my fucking game and I'll call you for fucking Delaying the Game if I fucking want to. Then you can go sit your asses in the penalty box while the last minute-fucking-forty-two winds down on the fucking clock and this fucking game is over. Understood?"

"Yes, ref," Jaime and I both mumbled. Man, all this moment needed was a note sent home to my mom and it'd feel like getting in trouble in elementary school all over again.

The ref skated off again, muttering and cursing none-too-quietly as he went.

"This is all your fault," Jaime hissed. "If we get in trouble…"

"Fuck off. This is your fault," I told him as we both started skating toward the team boxes. "You're the one who high sticked me in the first place and started this whole thing."

"I did not high stick you," Jaime declared, a mere decibel below yelling, throwing his hands in the air.

"Did too." Not like I could let him get the last word in.

I punctuated my statement with a shove to the back of Jaime's shoulder as he climbed over the boards and into his team box. He practically fell right into the lap of his teammate, George Nickleby. Both men glared at me, although Nickel did it much, much better than Jaime did. Probably because he had a face that looks like it gets regularly punched. Which it does, since he was one of the Loons' more aggressive defensemen. Even when he was irate with me, Jaime just looked… cute. Like a little cartoon character who should be having flames and steam shooting out of his ears.

The whole thing was glorious. I loved playing against him and getting the opportunity to rile up Jaime Johnson. It was a highlight of my season.

From *The Hockey News,* June:

This year, the hockey world is happy to be sending two Johnsons to the K9s for Warriors celebrity golf tournament at the Wolf Creek Golf Club in Mesquite, Nevada. Jaime "Loverboy" Johnson and J.J. "Cube" Johnson, to be precise.

The two Johnsons—who last met on the ice during the first round of the Stanley Cup Playoffs, where the Minnesota Loons managed to knock out the Kansas City Snappers in five games before they were then eliminated in the second round by the Pontiac Firebirds—will, presumably, be setting aside their on-ice rivalry as they make their appearance at this charity event.

Jaime Johnson, a left winger for the Minnesota Loons, is quoted as saying, "I'm so proud to be representing all of the other hockey players at this year's tournament. This charity, whose goal is rescuing shelter dogs, training them to be service animals, and then getting them to any American former military service members that need them at little to no cost, is one that we can all support. My hope is that my appearance in the tournament will help raise some of the badly needed funds that this charity depends upon. And, for those of you unable to come out to see me in the tournament, please consider donating whatever you can to this charity, whether that's monetarily, through your attention by spreading the word of their good works, or through your time and labor if you're able to directly volunteer at one of their events."

The other Johnson who will be swinging the sticks on the green in this tournament, J.J. Johnson, also had many positive things to say regarding the charity the two will be raising money for. The right winger for the Snappers stated that, "I get to play some golf in the fabulous deserts of Nevada with a bunch of other famous people while we raise some money to get some dogs to military vets. The whole thing is a win-win-win. Of course, I'm excited to go."

We also asked both men if they thought that last week's announcement made by Sawyer Brzycki, who plays on the Minnesota Loons with Jaime Johnson, regarding his homosexuality would bring any negative publicity to themselves or their charitable efforts.

"What the [expletive]? So the guy's gay. Why the [expletive] should that matter? Hockey is still hockey and hockey players are still hockey players, no matter who they [expletive]. And anyone who says otherwise is a giant piece of [expletive] and can go [expletive] themselves," was J.J. Johnson's response to our question.

Jaime Johnson answered more tactfully, although his sentiments seemed to echo that of the other Johnson. "I, and the rest of the Minnesota Loons organization, fully support Breezy (Sawyer Brzycki). He is an excellent player and a good friend. His sexuality in no way impacts his playing, nor should it affect his image as a player or a man. I am happy that Breezy reached a point in his life where he no longer felt that he had to hide that part of himself from our team, the league, or our fans."

As they make their way to Nevada, we at The Hockey News would like to wish both Johnsons a good weekend of eighteen *holes. And good luck swinging around a different kind of stick than they're used to.*

If you would like to check out K9s for Warriors and find out more about what they do and how you can help, please visit their website at k9sforwarriors.org.

Chapter One

J.J.

June

"What do you mean there's no reservation under J.J. Johnson?" I asked the hotel desk clerk, attempting to keep my temper and not just start shouting at the, now, nervously flushed and twitching young lady. "My personal assistant... um... *personally* called this lovely hotel and confirmed that I had a reservation for this weekend. I'm not sure if you're aware, but I'm playing in a little *celebrity* charity golf tournament that's happening just down the road, so it's kind of imperative that I have somewhere to stay while I'm doing so." I had no idea if she'd recognized me or not, although I was leaning toward not, but surely the emphasis I'd put on the word "celebrity" in my statement was sure to get me some extra sway. Right? And if it turned out that I didn't actually have a reservation, then I was going to need all the sway I could get.

"I... I... I'm sorry, sir. It's just... it's just... I don't have a reservation under your name." She hesitantly smiled at me, as though all she could think to do was fall back on her customer service training on how to best soothe irritated and annoying customers. "We do have a reservation for a *Jaime* Johnson. But not a J.J. Johnson." Then she hopefully tacked on, "...unless your first initial stands for Jaime?"

Mother. Fucker.

"It does not," I tersely informed her.

It was irritating enough having to share a last name and a first initial with that... that... *him*. I didn't need to be mistaken for the uptight buzzkill.

"Oh." Her crestfallen expression pretty much matched the unhappy feeling swimming around in my gut at that moment.

"And you don't have any other available rooms?" I asked hopefully, even though I damn well knew that with the golf tournament going on there would be a snowball's chance in hell of there being any open rooms in the hotel. Or anywhere else in this middle-of-nowhere desert town.

"I'm so sorry, sir. But... no. All of the hotels in town... and anywhere nearby... are fully booked. There are no available rooms. Anywhere. Because of... um. The tournament."

Fuck it. That's what I had figured. "Let me just... call my assistant and see if I can clear this thing up for us, shall I?"

I don't know if the relieved expression that then crossed her face was over the idea that there might be a solution to what was looking like a colossal fuck-up or if she was just glad that I was moving away from her and would no longer be her problem. But either way, as I walked away from the reception desk, her initial friendly and perky smile was once more back in place.

I just wished that I was back to feeling even remotely as happy as she looked as I fumblingly yanked my phone out of my pocket and pressed the series of icons that would connect me to my personal assistant, Greg.

"Cube! How's it going, my man? How's the Nevada desert heat treating you? Spot any hot dudes yet?" he asked, chuckling at his own, frankly, pathetic play on words.

"Shhh..." I shushed him over the line, darting a quick look around the lobby to see if any nosies looked as though they had decided to eavesdrop on my childhood best friend's overly loud greeting. "You know I'm... not really out," I reminded him.

While the pressure to stay in the closet had lessened since Sawyer Brzycki had come out in a splashy, glitzy magazine interview last week with his boyfriend, I hadn't made the leap to throwing open the doors and parading my gay self to the entire media, the fans, or my other hockey teammates.

25

It's not exactly that I was afraid to do so… I didn't give a flying fuck what anyone thought about me or who I enjoyed fucking. I just didn't really see the need to do it. Not yet. Or anytime soon. Probably.

"So, how's it going?" Greg repeated.

"How's it going? How's it going?" I asked him. "I'll tell you how it's going. I just arrived at my hotel and found out that I don't have a fucking room. That's how it's going, Greg."

"No room? But… I called and made the reservation for you, myself."

"Yeah. I know. Or, at least, that's what you'd told me you'd done. But, according to them… the only J. Johnson they have in their system is that fucking prissy, stick-up-his-ass Jaime Johnson."

"That hot red-headed guy on the Loons that you totally have the num-nums for?"

"I do not have the fucking num-nums for Jaime Johnson," I insisted. I gave the hotel lobby another sweeping glance just in case. No one needed to be listening in on this ridiculous conversation.

"Oh. You so do," Greg insisted right back. "You know if he ever gave you the chance, you would happily slather that man in syrup and gobble him right on up."

"Would you shut the fuck up about Jaime Johnson?" I hissed into the phone, ignoring the fact that my best friend wasn't *entirely* wrong about my… um… *mild* sexual attraction to my fellow—similarly-named—hockey winger. "Focus,

Greg. What the hell are we going to do about my not having a hotel room?"

"How the hell should I know?" Greg asked.

"As my personal assistant, it's your job to know these things. Why the hell do I bother paying you if that's going to be your attitude?"

"Dude. You pay me twice a year. In beer," he flatly replied. "And I do actually have a full-time job that pays me with actual fucking money and a family that take up most of my time. I mostly just act as your assistant so I can have a hobby other than knocking up my wife and for some shits and giggles."

"You sell drugs—"

"To doctors!" he interrupted, doing his part to continue our long-running joke around his career. "I supply *prescription* medication to doctors."

"And you and I both know that Crystal runs your family and your kids like a well-oiled military unit. You're basically just a fourth child for her to take care of."

"That… is a fair assessment," Greg stated.

Even though he agreed with me, it wasn't true. Greg was a giving husband and father who took his role as an equal parent and partner seriously. But if you couldn't razz your longest and bestest friend whenever the mood struck you, then what was the point of even having friends?

"But you're sure you called this hotel and booked me a room?" I asked.

"Yep. As soon as you knew you wouldn't be busy with any Stanley Cup nonsense this summer…"

"Ouch. Dude. Too soon," I said.

I wasn't entirely over being bummed about the ending of this year's playoff run and our loss to the stupid Loons and would really prefer to block out each and every one of the games of that craptastic first round. I don't know what fucking burr had gotten in the refs knickers, but it seemed like they'd had it out for us the whole time. We just couldn't get any good breaks on the calls and it had sent our team morale and momentum straight to the crapper. A fast and nasty five games and we were out of it and sent on home to wallow in our defeat for the rest of the summer. At least the Loons had been trounced in the second round. It was a bit of a consolation.

"… and you told me to book you a room, I called 'em up, told them to put the room under J. Johnson… since your full legal name is on your credit card, but you hate being called—"

"Yep. Got it," I interrupted him. "You just had them list me under my first initial like you usually do."

"Exactly. They asked me if you were with the celebrity charity golf event and I thought 'Oh, good. They must've set aside a whole slew of rooms just for you big shots.' I confirmed that you were and the voice on the other end of the phone confirmed that they had you down and that you were all set. In and out. Easy peasy. One of the fastest phone calls I've ever had to make for you."

"Yeah. That sounds a little too easy."

"In hindsight… Yeah. A little," Greg agreed. "I thought it was a little odd that they didn't actually ask for your credit card, even for any incidental charges you might rack up, but figured maybe the whole thing was just being handled on that end by the charity organizers."

"Nope. It probably just means that they found Jaime Johnson's reservation in the system, assumed you were calling for him, and simply confirmed that they already had everything they needed… for him."

"Well. Shit. Sorry about that, Cube."

Greg sounded so miserably upset that it would've felt like kicking the cutest puppy in the world—after you'd taken its favorite toy away and dumped out all its food for funsies—to keep griping at him for his mistake. So, I let my annoyance with my best friend go with a sigh. "No worries, Greg. It could've happened to anyone, I guess."

"So what are you going to do?"

"I don't know," I replied. "Make some calls to any other hotels, motels, B&Bs, or whatever within the slightest nearby area… and hope for the best." Not feeling too optimistic about my chances, I sighed again, then told him, "And if worse comes to worst… maybe keep your phone handy in case I have to call you from the pokey after the hotel calls the cops on me for camping out in the lobby."

"As long as you pay me back for any bail money I have to shill out."

"Naturally."

29

Chapter Two

Jaime

I got to the hotel a little later than I'd wanted to, but that really couldn't have been avoided due to some mechanical issue that had delayed my flight from Minneapolis to Las Vegas by almost two hours. At least I hadn't had any issues picking up my rental car at the Las Vegas airport and had made good time from there to Mesquite.

I pulled up under the awning by the hotel's front door, then handed off my keys to the courteous valet waiting there. It still felt a little weird to me, even after playing in the NHL for three full years, to be the one handing over my keys instead of the one accepting them. Not that I'd ever had a job as a valet. I just mean that I wasn't used to being catered to like some big shot rich guy. The poor valet sweating in his full hotel uniform in the hot desert heat probably wasn't all that much younger than I was.

After exchanging smiles and pleasantries with the desk clerk, I told her, "You should have a reservation for me. Under the name J. Johnson?" That's what my mom had told me she'd put the reservation under. Why she thought attempting even that little bit of subterfuge to protect my privacy was necessary, when I was attending a celebrity golf tournament where the whole point was that everyone should recognize my name… I had no idea. But I had learned a long, long time ago to never argue with my mother.

"Ah. Yes. Mr. *Jaime* Johnson?" the desk clerk questioned.

I wasn't sure what the emphasis on my first name was all about or why she was peering at me with what looked like suspicion, but I just shrugged it off and confirmed, "That's me."

"Fantastic. Your room is all set for you. And if you hand your luggage over to one of our bellhops, we'll have them brought up to your room for you. We have you on the eighth floor with a lovely view of the desert. If I could just see the credit card I have on file for your incidentals and a photo ID, I'll get you your keys."

I showed her the two things she had requested. Then she gave me my room keys, a brochure on local sights of interest, and a packet of information—including the tournament schedule that the tournament committee had assembled for its participants. We exchanged smiles again as I thanked her for her help and bid her farewell. I gave my suitcase and small carry-on bag to the waiting bellhop, then I made my way over to the bank of elevators.

If I hadn't seen his cocky smile smirking at me through a helmet on a semi-regular basis or his stupid grinning face in game interviews and magazine articles, not to mention, known that I'd be seeing him here, I might have taken one look at a roguishly sprawled J.J. "Cube" Johnson in a hotel lobby chair—with his silky, flowing, chin-length dark brown hair and meticulously trimmed long stubble, framing his refined but scoundrel-like face—and assumed he was some sort of fashion model or European social media pseudo-celebrity.

His head was tipped back against the high back of the chair ever so slightly. Just enough that the overhead chandeliers cast golden splashes of light on his high cheekbones and the bridge of his somehow still unbroken and perfect nose. It also emphasized the fine arch of his eyebrows, the long length of his eyelashes, and the plush texture of his full lips. And with his lean but strong and muscular hockey physique delightfully displayed by the tight black t-shirt and almost indecently tight jeans he was wearing, J.J. looked as though he was in the middle of a photo shoot, just waiting for some clever cameraman to forever preserve his masculine beauty.

It's too bad that such a pretty package contained such a conceited, cocky, boastful, loud-mouthed, arrogant butthead. I'm only slightly ashamed to admit that I've had the occasional fantasy of shoving a wadded-up sock in his mouth and securing it in place with my stick tape. But even shutting J.J. up probably wouldn't be enough. It wasn't just the things he said. His annoying attitude just sort of… oozed out of him.

I didn't know what he was doing hanging around in the hotel lobby and I honestly didn't care. Although, upon a second, closer, look, while J.J. might've been slouched in his chair as though he didn't have a worry in the world, he was also tightly holding his phone in his right hand and lightly and repeatedly tapping it against his right thigh in what looked like irritation or nervousness. But… again. Not my business, none of my concern. I just wanted to get into an elevator and up to my room. Hopefully, before he saw me and decided to irritate me with his attention.

I would've made it too, if two things hadn't happened. First, the chime when the elevator reached the ground floor dinged unbelievably loudly, prompting J.J. to twist his head down and around to glance in its direction. Second, J.J.'s gaze swung over just in time for him to see me bump into and nearly knock over a fake plant stuck into a planter next to the elevator, since my eyes had still been trained on him and not on where I was going as I tried to enter the open elevator car.

Thankfully, J.J. made no move to stir from his position, only raised two fingers of his left hand—his right was still occupied with holding his phone—and touched them to his forehead in a mocking salute as he winked and shot me a smirking smile. I was tempted to send him a one-fingered salute back, but decided it would be better not to stoop to his level. Instead, I just sent him my fake talking-to-the-press smile, a quick wave, then jerked my head around and hit the call button for the elevator once more.

I could feel the weight of his continued stare burning into my back as I stood there and waited. *How long was it going to take for the ding-danged elevator to return to this floor? It had just been here.* But I refused to turn back around to look at J.J. Even though I knew... I just *knew*... he was still looking at me. Finally, the elevator dinged back open and I was able to make my escape.

Once I was up in my room, I took a quick look around the luxuriously appointed bathroom, sat on and lightly bounced on the king-sized bed—it seemed to be adequately firm and comfortable—flipped on the flatscreen tv mounted to the wall to make sure it worked, then wandered over to the large window to see that the desk clerk hadn't been overstating the loveliness of the view from my room. A knock on the door some couple of minutes later heralded the arrival of the bellhop with my luggage.

After giving him a nice tip—service industry people really did deserve all the tips they could get as it had to be a pretty grueling and demanding line of work. And this was coming from someone who got paid to be hit and smashed into by huge, muscular guys on a regular basis—I spent a little more time unpacking my things. Making sure to smooth out and hang the clothes I planned to wear during the tournament. I wanted to show the organizers and the various sponsors the respect they deserved by showing up looking my very best.

When my stomach grumbled at me, I was reminded that I hadn't yet taken the time to track down some dinner. I wasn't really sure what would still be open in the area this late at night or which establishments would offer healthy enough food options that wouldn't completely throw my meal plan off track. It might be the off-season, but I still tried to stick to the same dietary regime I had to follow during training camp and hockey season. It just made things easier and I tended not to miss the foods I couldn't have quite as much if I didn't splurge on them during the summer.

I flipped through the packet of information the tournament organizers had compiled and found that they had included a list of nearby restaurants and what hours they were open. Double checking what time it was and the list of choices, I finally settled on heading over to a sushi restaurant that was just down the road. Raw fish wasn't really my favorite—actually, I didn't care much for any kind of seafood at all—but sushi was something I'd trained myself to tolerate as it was quite popular with a lot of the other guys on my team and we tended to hit a lot of sushi restaurants while we were on the road. It did also offer a lot of health benefits like lean protein, good fats and carbs, plus plenty of vitamins and minerals.

Patting my back pocket to make sure I still had my wallet, I returned to the elevators to go back down to the first floor. When I reached the first floor, I was pretty surprised to see J.J. still sitting in the hotel lobby. He hadn't even really moved all that much. Although, he now, rudely, had his feet propped up on a delicate-looking metal and glass side table that he'd dragged out from between two of the lobby chairs. And he was no longer fidgeting and fiddling with his phone. Huh. I'd probably spent about an hour up in my hotel room. So what was he still doing down here?

My inherent dislike for the man warred with the good manners my mom had instilled in me. I was perhaps one of the only other people he might know here. And if he was having some sort of trouble… or just needed somebody to talk to or to keep him company… wasn't it my duty to go over and talk to him? But. I really, really didn't want to.

After a moment of internal debate, good manners won out over my inner whiny child and I reluctantly headed over to him.

Once I was only a couple of feet away, I cleared my throat and said, "J.J. I see you're still hanging around down in the lobby. Why… I mean… Um. Are you waiting for someone? I don't imagine the lobby chairs are all that much more comfortable than the one in your room."

J.J. startled in surprise when I started speaking. But then he twisted his head up and back to look at me over the top of the chair back. With an unamused sounding snort, he commented, "Yeah. About that. Funny story. I don't have any chairs in my hotel room. Or a bed. Or a bathroom. Or anything else. Actually… I don't even have a room in my room."

"I'm sorry, but… what?" I asked, completely bewildered. I expected idiotic things to come out of J.J. Johnson's mouth, but what in the world was he going on about?

"I don't have a hotel room," J.J. said.

"Why in the heck didn't you reserve a room? Who travels out of state and doesn't reserve a hotel room in advance?"

"Oh, I thought I had," he stated. "But it turns out that the hotel employee my assistant talked to never considered that there might be two people both trying to book a room under

J. Johnson. So, they only held the one. The one that had your credit card on file. So, since you called first, you got a hotel room. And I... just got screwed."

"But... but... there's probably not a single available hotel room in the area," I exclaimed.

"Oh, there's not. I checked," he wryly stated.

"So, what are you going to do?"

"Hang out here. Try to get some sleep. Wait to see how long it takes them to find the balls to tell me to get the hell out of their lobby." He shrugged, seeming unconcerned with having nowhere to sleep for the night.

Well, that stunk. Was I a horrible person for being glad it had happened to him instead of me? Probably. And yet, I couldn't find it in myself to feel too much remorse that I'd have a snug bed to retire to tonight. And I'm sure having to spend a night or two being forced to sleep in a chair could only do wonders for knocking a little of the shine off J.J. brassy ego.

"Huh." I didn't bother offering any sort of commiserating platitudes. Even if I could force them out of my mouth, I doubted J.J. would believe that I meant them. Because I wouldn't. But, in the interest of being a helpful sort of guy, I asked him, "Did you try to contact the tournament organizers? They might be able to find you somewhere to stay."

"C'mon, Jaime. What're they going to do? Magically pull a spare hotel room out of their asses?" J.J. rolled his eyes at me when I cringed at his crude language. "There. Are. No.

Available. Rooms. Anywhere. Crashing here is the best option I've got. The AC alone makes it a better choice than sleeping in my rental car. Barely."

"You could share my room," I blurted out.

We both looked at each other in what appeared to be equal measures of shock. Yeah. I couldn't believe I'd just said what I'd said, either. Had I really just offered to share a hotel room—with only one bed—with J.J. Johnson? I know I prided myself on doing the right thing whenever I was able to. But doing the right thing was one thing. Inflicting hours of being around a person I couldn't stand upon myself, in a pathetic attempt at being nice, indicated that, unbeknownst to me, I might have some masochistic tendencies.

"Alright," J.J. slowly responded. "I suppose that would be a better option than spending the night in the lobby. At least, it has a slightly lower chance of me winding up in jail."

Holy frick, I had. I had actually offered to share my hotel room with J.J. Johnson. Heaven help me.

Chapter Three

J.J.

"I'm not sleeping on that," I unequivocally stated as I stared down at the rollaway cot the bellboy—bellperson?—had brought up to Jaime's hotel room after he had called down to the front desk and requested that one be sent up.

After his surprising and unexpected offer to share his room, proving the politeness gene was strong in him, Jaime had also invited me to join him for dinner as he'd been on his way out to grab some grub when he'd approached me in the lobby. We'd walked in a mutually agreed upon, but unvocalized truce of silence down the block in the glow of the rosy-hued desert sunset to a narrow, but deceptively large, sushi restaurant. The whole place was very warm and welcoming, all done up with a rich, dark brick floor and subtle tone-on-tone wood paneling and furniture.

From his chair two down from mine—just because he'd invited me to eat with him apparently didn't mean he'd wanted to sit to close to me or apparently talk to me at all— Jaime had watched with seemingly disgusted fascination as I'd plowed through a sizzling hot, heaped-full plate of the edamame appetizer. …What? To my midwestern-raised brain, just because they were deep-fried and liberally dusted with salt didn't make them any less of a vegetable— legume?—and thus totally allowed on my diet. Plus it was the off-season, so who the fuck cared if my team nutritionist would give me equally horrified and disappointed looks as the ginger-haired man to my left?

I may have sent him some dubious glances of my own as I watched him pick at and nibble on his boring choice of a California roll. My own combo platter of sushi—I told the waiter to just surprise me with whatever the chef wanted to pile on there, as long as it was spicy—was fucking delicious and almost enough to restore my customary good humor after the shit-show the entire afternoon had been.

With a happily sated stomach, I paid my bill—adding a sizable tip since I could easily afford it and our waiter had been awesome—waited for Jaime to pay his bill, and then we made our way back, once again in complete silence, to the hotel. I would've tried to engage in conversation with him— if only because it was fun to watch the man turn crimson with annoyance and aggravation—but I really didn't have the energy or mental sharpness left. I just wanted to crash and recharge my tired brain for the night.

When we got back to the hotel, I snagged my battered and well-travelled suitcase from where I'd left it sitting next to the lobby chair I'd nearly permanently left my ass-print on, shot a jaunty wave to the desk clerk—*see, despite your best efforts, I'm not going to be reduced to being bedless for the night*—and followed after a grumpy-looking Jaime Johnson toward the elevators. At least the visuals were a decent compensation for having to put up with the man. He might be a boring, cheerless, straightlaced killjoy, but he did have a mighty, mighty fine ass.

Had it been stupid of me to just leave my shit where anybody could've come along and taken it while we'd gone to dinner? Eh. Probably. But it's not like there weren't a shit-ton of cameras all over the hotel lobby to catch someone in the act if they'd made off with my suitcase. And I wouldn't miss any of the easily replaceable stuff I'd shoved in there. My more immediate concern had been that I didn't want to bother dragging it with me to dinner or taking the chance that Jaime would change his mind—about dinner and/or sharing his hotel room with me—and flee like the fires of hell were licking at his feet if I'd taken the time to stow the suitcase in my rental car.

He, for shit, didn't seem elated to be stuck in a small hotel room with me. More resigned than anything else. But, nonetheless, after dinner, Jaime let me get in the elevator with him and accompany him to his eighth-floor room. He even took it upon himself to call for the rollaway bed. Which was what we were doing now—setting that up.

After shoving the club chair and ottoman out of the way, we'd unfolded the thing and tucked it away in the corner of the room as far as we could get it. Sure, I'd be practically lying on top of the air conditioning unit, but it still had to beat sleeping in a chair all night.

Or so I'd thought, until I'd set my suitcase down on one end of it and the whole thing had creaked, and bent, and collapsed. I'd tried setting it back up. Even whacked on the locking mechanism to make sure it was locked in place. But the whole fucking thing was listing at an odd angle like it'd gone a few rounds with a gorilla and come out on the losing side. I just didn't trust that it would support my weight... or even anything heavier than a pillow.

"I'm not sure what other option you think you have," Jaime stated. "I suppose you could just roll yourself up in your blankets like a caterpillar in a cocoon and sleep on the floor."

"Or we could share the fucking bed," I suggested, waving a hand at the damned thing taking up a large percentage of the room. When Jaime just gawked at me, his mouth gaping open like a startled fish, I heaved a sigh and said, "Don't look at me like that. It's a perfectly reasonable suggestion."

"Why don't I... why don't I call down and explain the situation and see if they can send up a different rollaway?" Jaime said with a sharp shake of his head.

I waved a lazy hand toward the room phone and drawled, "Suit yourself. Have at it. If you're too much of a chickenshit to share a bed with me for the night..."

"It's not... I'm not a... a... chicken," Jaime protested.

And, of course, he even troubled to leave off the 'shit' portion of the 'chickenshit' I'd suggested he was. I've heard the man swear at me and others on the ice. I kind of wondered what it would take to drive him to sully his mouth with some curses when he wasn't on the ice. Now, there was a goal for the coming next few days. Forget about perfecting and improving my golf handicap. Getting Jaime Johnson to bend some of his prissy ways was a much more enjoyable prospect to occupy my time.

"I just don't want to voluntarily be that close to you if I don't have to be."

I rubbed at a muscle twitching next to my right eye with my middle finger. "Uh huh. Sure you don't," I replied. "You might accidentally catch some of my awesometude if you did. Wouldn't want that, would we?"

"Yeah. 'Cause awesometude… like that's a word… would really be what I'd catch from you," Jaime muttered. "More like some gross venereal disease."

"Oh? Were we going to be getting that kind of close enough to each other, if we shared a bed, that STDs would be a concern?" I asked him curiously.

Watching Jaime Johnson blanch and then turn fiery red when I waggled my eyebrows and leered at him, was possibly the highlight of my day so far. I wasn't too terribly concerned that he'd take my sexual innuendo seriously or think there was anything more to it than the general sort of shit hockey players generally gave each other.

"Shut up. That's not what… That's not… And why would you even…" Jaime spluttered. Then he seemed to shake himself out of his fluster, took a deep breath, and repeated, "I'm going to call down and see if they'll send up a different rollaway."

I figured that statement didn't necessitate a response on my part, so I just kept my mouth shut, idly settled my ass on the end of the one bed in the room, and waited.

An examination of my filed and buffed fingernails reassured me that I didn't need to schedule another manicure appointment quite yet. My pondering was interrupted by a huff of disgust from Jaime and the noise of him clattering down the hotel phone's handset.

I looked up at him, feeling absolutely no surprise, to see an unhappy frown gracing the yummily-full pale pinkness of his lips as he dolefully informed me, "They don't have any other rollaways available to send up. It appears this one..." He waved a hand at the wretchedly listing cot, that gave a creak, shuddered, and lurched over even further. "...was the last one they had. So, you'll either have to sleep on that or..."

"Or we can share the bed," I suggested again, giving the mattress a playful pat next to my hip. Then, I held my hand up and gave him the Boy Scout sign—I think. I'd never actually been in the Boy Scouts, so I wasn't sure I was doing it correctly—and told him, "I promise I'll keep my hands and the rest of my body to myself. This isn't some sort of ploy I concocted so I could despoil your precious little virginal body."

Even if this whole scenario overwhelmingly struck me as something resembling a dubious plot of a porno, I mentally promised myself that I would keep my hands and my other assorted body parts to myself. Then I silently told my dick to shut up when it protested that promise. Just because it wanted to become acquainted with the hot redhead in front of me, didn't mean that I didn't know that it would be a horrible idea to attempt anything. Now that I'd found a bed to rest my head in for the night, I didn't relish the thought of getting punched and thrown out on my ass.

"I'm not... I... I'm not a virgin," Jaime protested. "Why... Why would you think that I was? And what makes you think I'd automatically assume that you were trying to put some moves on me? You're not gay. Are you? Actually, don't answer that. It's none of my business and it doesn't even matter. Maybe I just don't want to spend the night squashed in a hotel bed with... Well. You. It might be a king-sized bed, but that's in hotel sizing. And we're not exactly two small guys." Jaime gestured at the both of us, as though I'd somehow overlooked the fact that we were both around the same height at 6'2" and packing plenty of muscle due to our mutual hockey careers.

"So what?" I retorted. I was going to ignore his assumption of my supposed straightness. Just because I didn't care if he knew otherwise, didn't mean I wanted to hand anything over on a silver platter. Besides what was more important was the way this stubborn jackass was pushing against the most obvious solution and the one that would get us into bed—to sleep, obviously—the fastest. "I've shared a bed with other players before. Just like I'm sure you have. A late night with plenty of drinking and celebrating a win with the guys after a game... Who hasn't shared a hotel bed with another guy a time or two? And I know I didn't really give a shit who was lying next to me as long as they didn't puke all over me or the bed."

"I'm so glad for you that you're not that picky. Somehow, I'm not surprised. But I do actually care about who I share a bed with. Even if it's just for sleeping. I wouldn't want to accidentally catch your… you-ness… through prolonged proximity."

"My *you-ness*? What the fuck is that supposed to mean?"

"You know danged well what I'm referring to," Jaime shot back, pointing a finger at me before he waved his hand up and down motioning to my entire body. "The way you're all arrogant and cocky all the time and act like you're the best player since Gretzky. For all I know, those personality traits could seep out of you while you sleep and infect me like some disgusting parasite. A douchey-personality tapeworm sort of thing."

"What the actual everliving fuck?"

I knew I wasn't exactly everyone's cup of tea and I could sometimes rub people the wrong way, but I don't think I'd ever had anyone treat me before like I was some sort of leper. Had someone pissed in his Wheaties this morning or did Jaime Johnson actually hate me? Sure, I'd always tried to get the better of him when our teams played against each other. Because that was… you know… *my job*. And it was fun. But to dislike me so much, not as a player, but as a person… I had no idea where that was coming from. I didn't hate him. Think he was straight-laced and a little boring for as hot as he was? Need some shaking up and loosening up? Pretty much. But that was about the extent of it.

"Not to mention you're also obnoxious and crude."

"No, I fucking am not. You're just uptight and... and... wholesome," I spat out. "Maybe it would be better if we didn't share a bed. Maybe I would be the one waking up like you and I sure as hell wouldn't want that. You and your 1950s-Ozzie-and-Harriet-goody-two-shoes-prissy-clean-cut manners and attitude. You don't even fucking swear."

"I do too swear. On the ice."

"Well. La-di-fucking-da. I wish you could see your face, standing there looking all proud about the fact that you let a couple damns and fucks trip out from between your washed-out-with-soap mouth when you're playing hockey. But you sound about as fucking comfortable doing it as a middle-schooler first learning the words of a foreign language. And off the ice, you're all about the dangs, and darns, and shoots, and fricks. What the hell is wrong with a good old fuck now and again when you're not on the ice?"

When Jaime rushed at me, my first thought was *Oh shit. This fucker is totally about to try to kick my ass.* My second thought was *I hope the charity organizers don't mind having their token hockey players showing up bruised and more than a little worse for wear. Although, we're hockey players, so maybe they'll be happy about it.* I was totally unprepared for how wrong I turned out to be.

Because, instead of planting his fist in my face, Jaime clenched his hands around fistfuls of my dark hair and used his handhold to keep my head steady as he crashed his mouth against mine. A move that completely short-circuited my brain for several long moments.

Fuck. *Jaime certainly wasn't boring when he kissed* was what popped in my head once my brain came back into play. His tongue fucked into my mouth with long, sweeping strokes against mine, interspersed with nips, and sucks, and licks to my quickly sensitized lips. I wasn't normally all that passive of a partner during any kind of physical contact with someone else but, in that moment, Jaime Johnson completely owned my ass and all I could do was submit to being devoured by him.

Until I suddenly found my lips caressing nothing but air as Jaime ripped his mouth away and stumbled back a couple of steps. The backs of his legs collided with the relocated ottoman, which he must have forgotten about, his arms windmilling around and his torso contorting this way and that as he fought to keep his balance and remain upright. Once he was stable, he wrapped his arms around his stomach and stood there looking at me with wide eyes and a shocked expression on his face. His breath came in fast, panicky pants.

"I'm sorry. I'm sorry," Jaime blurted out. "I don't... I don't know why... Why did I do that? I shouldn't have... I shouldn't. I'm sorry."

"Don't be sorry," I told him. I was feeling about as shell-shocked as he looked. Holy fuck. "Outside of some of the shit you do on the ice, kissing me like that was probably the most interesting thing I've ever seen you do."

"You... you... but you... Are you...? Does that mean...?" he spluttered.

"Yeah. I'm gay."

For some reason, I felt absolutely no qualms about admitting my gayness to Jaime. Even if I didn't *like* him, and wasn't exactly ready to leap out of the closet waving a rainbow flag for the whole world to see, I did trust him. I might not exactly know Jaime very well, since we only saw each other the couple of times a year that our teams played each other, but he struck me as the type of Dudley Do-right, moral goody-goody that would rather gnaw off an arm than betray a secret. Besides, based off of the way he just attacked my mouth with his, Jaime Johnson was likely somewhere on the queer spectrum himself. But just to double check, I asked, "And you?"

With my admission, some of the nervous agitation left Jaime and he unwrapped his arms around from himself and his shoulders relaxed and eased from their tense bunching.

"Oh. Um. So… so am I," Jaime said, then nibbled on his lip as he pointedly did not look at me to see how I reacted to his pronouncement.

His gaze quickly snapped back to me when I responded with, "Well. Thank fuck for that. Or else it's going to get really awkward in the next two seconds when I ask you if you'd like to fuck." I paused a beat and ignored the taunting and little victory dance my dick was doing as I quickly abandoned my plan to keep my body parts away from Jaime Johnson. There's no way I wasn't going to ask him what I was about to ask him. "So, you wanna fuck?"

Would having sex with Jaime Johnson, another hockey player—a rival hockey player—who didn't really like me and that I didn't much care for either, be a bad idea? Yep.

Undoubtedly. Would it wind up making our sporadic games against each other even more fraught with animosity and friction? Again. Yep. How could it not? But I'd never prided myself on my wise decision-making capabilities and I wasn't about to start now. So what if a night spent fucking each other's brains out came back and bit me in the ass— metaphorically speaking, as I wasn't at all opposed to that literally happening—and what little professional politeness between us completely crumbled away until it was just the size of a small speck of dust that got lodged in your eye and irritated the fuck out of you?

All of that would totally be worth it if it meant that I got another taste of Jaime Johnson's mouth. Which tasted oddly of strawberries even though we hadn't had any at dinner. Was that a redhead thing? Tasting like strawberries? That brief taste I'd gotten of him as his tongue invaded my mouth wasn't enough. At. All. I wanted more.

And here we were stuck together for the weekend sharing a hotel room. A hotel room with only one bed. ...One pretty good-sized bed, sure. But what the fuck. Why not? We might as well take advantage of the situation we found ourselves in.

Regrets could be tomorrow's problem.

Chapter Four
Jaime

"Well? What do you say, Loverboy?" J.J. asked in a completely normal tone of voice, as though what he was suggesting wasn't totally preposterous. But had he intentionally used my hockey nickname to remind me of who we were to each other and how potentially scandalous and career-wrecking being intimate with him could get? Not to mention, possibly personally disastrous. Or was he just using it to be irritating? "You wanna get all naked with me and do the nasty? Rugby thump? Bang bananas? Bump uglies? Although, speaking for myself, what I've got going on in my pants is pretty much about as far from ugly as you can get."

What in the holy heck was happening here? First, we were sniping at each other—no big surprise as J.J. Johnson was exactly the kind of brash, egotistical, jerkhole athlete that I can't stand and he seemed to delight in annoying me at every turn when we faced each other and fought over the puck when our teams played against each other. And then… and then… something inside of me snapped and I suddenly had my tongue shoved in his mouth like I was examining how good of a job he had done the last time he'd brushed his teeth.

It seemed stupid to even think it, but I could've sworn that I was able to taste his flashy, cocky personality when I kissed him. It tasted silky and musky and left me with the same sort of static-charge-y feeling in the bottom of my stomach that I got just before a massive thunderstorm.

And now. Now… J.J. was casually suggesting that we have sex with each other.

Against my better judgment, I was tempted.

It had been almost a year since I'd last had sex with someone. It had just always seemed smarter to constrain my amorous activities to the off-season when I went to visit my family in Illinois. As I hopped from suburb to suburb, visiting different gay-friendly bars in the Chicago area— which was more of a football, baseball, and basketball town—it was easy for me to be just some random, nameless white guy looking for a hookup. There was a decent-sized Suns fanbase in the Chicago area, but they were far outnumbered by the bulk of the population who wouldn't recognize one of their own city's players even if they came and smacked them upside the head while telling them their name and that they played professional hockey. So, for me, who didn't even play for Chicago, going unrecognized had yet to be a problem.

But it was more than my customary long dry spell that was pulling at me to seriously consider J.J.'s proposition. It was the fact that this wasn't just any man. It was the stupidly, outrageously attractive J.J. Johnson. I'd seen his gracefulness, his agility, his athleticism, his confidence, his fierceness, his determination as well as his less-than-endearing qualities up close and personal before. And the idea of all of... that... unleashed on me... It was dizzying in its tantalizing possibilities.

I glanced at J.J. Then at the lone bed in the room. The one I'd already invited J.J. to share with me for the duration of the golf tournament. Or, at least, for tonight. My eyes swung over to the rollaway cot deathtrap. Back to J.J. To the bed. The cot. The bed. To J.J.

"Well?" J.J. demanded.

He couldn't just take my silence as an answer and drop the whole thing? Because... heaven help me... I was tempted.

I didn't want to be.

I wanted to insist he sleep on the rollaway, despite its broken condition, and rely on it to kill him in his sleep so he would no longer be my immediate or long-term problem.

It's what I should do. Even if it would make me a jerk. That's what I *should* do.

So, I was not prepared for the word that left my mouth. "Okay."

What. The. Heck?

If J.J. was surprised by my acquiescence, he didn't show it. Except perhaps in the slight widening of his eyes and the sudden bob of his Adam's apple as he swallowed.

"What... uh. What do you want? To do?" I managed to squeak out, my voice cracking slightly in a way it hadn't since I was a gawky pre-pubescent.

The corner of J.J.'s mouth quirked up just a little, but he, thankfully, didn't outright laugh at the clear evidence of my nervousness. He laconically ambled the few steps needed to bring him back within touching distance. J.J.'s strong, capable, and callused hands came up to cup my cheeks, forcing me to meet his dark gaze as he stated, "It doesn't matter. I can fuck you. You can fuck me. However you want. As long as there's a cock and a cock equaling fucking and coming, it doesn't really matter to me which side of the plus sign I'm on."

My own cock—which hadn't really calmed down from its hard state one bit in the intervening time since my lips first made contact with his—gave an aching throb each time the filthy words cock or fuck passed through J.J.'s lips. My own lips suddenly feeling dry, I swiped my tongue across them. Which caused J.J. dark eyes to somehow get even more impossibly darker. Until I could barely distinguish where the chocolate-syrup-brown of his irises met the inky black of his pupils.

I still couldn't believe we were actually going to do this. That he had suggested it and I agreed. But. I knew what I wanted.

"Do you... do you have condoms? And lube?" I asked. I was desperately aware that I hadn't thrown any into my suitcase or carry-on bag. I was just going to be in Nevada for a long weekend and certainly hadn't planned on needing sex supplies while I was here. I was more than used to just using hotel-provided body wash for my jerking-one-out-in-the-shower needs.

"Of course," J.J. replied. "No offense to American Express, but *those* are the two things I never leave home without."

Of course he didn't. One more swipe of my tongue over my lips. "Then. I want you to f-fu-fuck me." As a predatory, wolfish grin of delight curled up the corners of J.J.'s mouth, I tacked on, "This time. You can f-fuck me this time. Next time, though, I'll fuck you." There. That ought to put him back in his place.

"Oh, babe. I am more than okay with that. And look at you. Dropping the f word and everything to tell me how it's going to be."

J.J. threaded his fingers through my hair and brought our mouths together in another kiss. It was nice being the same height as him. Although, if compelled, I might begrudge him an extra half inch on me. It meant that our mouths, and the rest of us, were perfectly aligned with each other and each and every single millimeter of the front of my body was mashed flush against his as we pressed together. This time it was his tongue exploring the interior of my mouth, languidly stroking and teasing.

After a minute or two of kissing, J.J. pulled back with a hum and remarked, "After the second time, we'll... what? Keep taking turns? Flip a coin? Or. I know. We can play rock, paper, scissors and the winner gets to bottom."

"What makes you think we're going to have sex more than twice?" I asked him. Wanting to knock his cocky attitude down a little, I stated, "I only said there'd be a second time, with us switching positions, in the interest of fairness. If the sex is bad, I won't even want to bother."

"Pfffth," was J.J. unsubtle response to my statement. "Since I'll be there, the sex will be stupendous. Even your possibly mediocre sex skills won't be enough to drop the level below that. I'm just that good."

God. He was just so annoyingly arrogant. But somehow, perhaps because his statement was made with such over-the-top confidence and a teasing twinkle in his eye, at that moment... J.J.'s cockiness was almost... cute.

Ungh. Trying to shake off the momentary gross and confusing feeling of liking, I scoffed, "Whatever. Just shut up already, take your clothes off, and fuck me. Before I come to my senses and remember why this is a bad idea and why we shouldn't be doing this."

"You're going to have to let go of me, first, if you want me to undress," J.J. said, causing me to realize that I had a death grip on the belt loops of his ludicrously tight jeans and had been using them to pull his body as tight against mine as I could get it.

"Oh. Right."

I uncurled my fingers, jiggled my hands a little to get rid of the tingly feeling in them caused by having had them clenched so tightly, and leaned back enough that we each had room to set to work on removing our clothes. My fingers were still a trifle clumsy as I fumbled open the buttons on my palm tree patterned ecru shirt, which I had purchased thinking it would be a whimsical nod to the desert locale but, instead, made me feel like a stupid poseur next to J.J. in his simple, understated black tee and jeans that somehow still managed to look stylish.

Once I got the buttons undone, I shrugged the shirt off my shoulders and let it slide down to the carpeted floor, glancing up at the sound of J.J.'s low whistle and muttered, "Nice." Only to nearly choke on my saliva as my brain completely forgot how to swallow... or breathe... as I took in the sight of a now-shirtless J.J. Johnson wriggling his snug jeans down over his hips and freeing his delicious-looking, long and hard cock.

"Gnghf," I choke-gasped. "You. You weren't... you weren't wearing underwear?"

At my question, J.J. paused in shoving his pants down and stood back up to look at me—he should have looked ridiculous with the way they were now slumped and bunched around his calves as he stood there but, of course, he didn't—and answered, "Nah." He gave his hard cock a leisurely stroke, then stated, "As long as you tuck it away all nice and easy and you're careful of the zipper, I've never found the need to bother with skivvies. Off the ice, anyway. I'm all jocked and cupped when I'm suited up, though. Forgot to once when I was little and took a puck to the nuts once. Peed blood for a couple of days. But I learned my lesson and I haven't forgotten to wear one since."

Part of my brain processed what he was saying and I gave a small gurgle of laughter at the thought of how painful that particular lesson must've been. But most of my attention was firmly fixed on the way J.J. was still stroking his cock.

"We still doing this?" he asked. "'Cause it seems to me you've stopped taking your clothes off. It's okay if you've changed your mind but, I must say, that's *not* the usual reaction I get once a dude gets a look at my cock."

This was still such a *bad* idea. I knew it was. But. Fricking hell. Against my better judgment and with no clue in the world why… yeah. I still wanted to have sex with J.J. Johnson.

In no way was I about to hand over the ammunition that I'd only stopped disrobing because his near-nakedness had rendered me stupid, so I shrugged his comment aside and just told him, "Go get your supplies. I'll meet you on the bed."

Chapter Five

J.J.

So. This was really happening then. Jaime Johnson was actually going to let me fuck him.

When I'd thrown the suggestion out there, I'd totally expected to get a punch in the face. And that was the best worst-case scenario. The worst worst-case scenario would've been finding myself thrown out in the hallway on my ass, locked out of the room, and back to the necessity of sleeping in the hotel lobby. After being punched in the face.

But instead of a busted lip or slammed door in my face, I was treated to the sight of Jaime Johnson tortuously slowly revealing miles and miles of pale, creamy skin. And what glorious skin it was. A lusciously lickable shade similar to melted vanilla ice cream which served as a gorgeous backdrop to all of his cinnamon-colored freckles. Jaime's shoulders and upper arms were liberally sprinkled with them. The freckles were also scattered across his pecs but became scarcer and scarcer the further down his torso my eyes traveled. Until they seemed to peter out altogether somewhere above his belly button.

My cock twitched in my hand—I was still lazily petting myself since it felt good and Jaime seemed to be enjoying the view—at the thought of getting close enough to explore those freckles with my fingers. And my lips. And my tongue. Until I investigated each and every single one of them and found them all.

I wondered if he had more freckles hiding underneath his pants.

Right. Finish undressing. My stupid jeans were still tangled around my legs. I needed to get those off.

And fetch my stash of condoms and lube out of my suitcase.

Then I could have my opportunity to get my hands, and other body parts, on Jaime.

When I saw Jaime arch an eyebrow at me, I realized I hadn't actually made any move to do what he'd told me to. I mentally smacked myself upside the head and told myself to get with the plan already, before he did change his mind.

Don't blow this, dumbass.

I let go of my cock and balanced on one foot and then the other as I finished shoving my pants off, thankful that I'd already toed my shoes off when we'd gotten back to the hotel room. Knowing me, in my haste to get naked and naughty with Jaime, I'd probably have tried to take my pants off with them still on and fallen over on my ass.

Once I was fully naked, I glanced at Jaime to see if he was still watching me but saw that he'd turned his attention to getting his own pants undone. Was I disappointed that his gaze wasn't riveted to my stripping act or glad that he was moving on to get the rest of his clothes off? A little of both?

I allowed myself a brief glimpse of what looked like boring old tighty-whities under his olive-green khaki pants, then turned around to rummage through my suitcase still precariously sitting on top of the half-collapsed rollaway bed. I wrapped my hand around the soft leather Dopp kit that contained the handful of condom packets and a mostly full bottle of lube I'd stuffed into it before I'd left for this trip. Might as well take the whole thing over to the bed with me. Hopefully, we'd put a decent dent in both items by the time this long weekend was over.

Fuuuuuckkkk.

When I turned around once more, I had to literally pinch myself to make sure that I was awake and seeing what I was seeing. The brief, sharp sting on my forearm assured me that I was actually conscious and in the same room as a completely naked Jaime Johnson, on all fours on top of the king-sized hotel bed, his ass in the air. Waiting for me.

Holy fuck.

"What's taking so long? For Pete's sake, this was your idea."

An apparently impatient and naked Jaime Johnson.

God, he was a stunning sight. Logically, I'd already known that the man had to be built. Even the boring touristy clothes he'd been wearing couldn't manage to hide that. Not to mention, since we were both wingers, I figured he was probably on a similar training regime that I was. And I'd certainly felt his strength and solidity the times we'd smashed into each other against the boards. But actually getting to see it... that was something else.

From where I was standing, I could see that his shoulders were broad and his arms were roped with well-defined muscles. His strong, lean back tapered down to a narrow waist. Then there were his slim hips, thick thighs, and a firm, round ass that was currently sticking up and out. Just waiting for me to come and lay claim to it. I was sure that the front of him was as equally as delectable. But I'd have to wait to flip him over to find out.

Later. I'd do that later.

If he let me.

I strode across the room to stand at the foot of the bed, thrilled with the knowledge that momentarily I'd be touching, and licking, and rubbing against all of Jaime's spectacular body. It's just too bad that his freckles didn't continue further down his body and were limited to only the back of his neck, his shoulders, and upper torso. Except. Was that... was that...?

I canted my head a little and peered closer at the back of his right thigh. Was that a small patch of freckles there? And it kind of... resembled the Nike swoosh logo. A shape I was incredibly familiar with as it also adorned the good luck sign

Greg had made for me in high school. The one that had a permanent place in my locker room cubby along with the stuffed lion—for our high school mascot—Greg had glued the sign to. It was my good luck charm and even went with me on all of my away game trips.

Huh. Seeing that familiar shape emblazoned on Jaime's skin, even if it was just a giant coincidence, made me feel like this was meant to happen. That I was meant to see Jaime Johnson naked and make him mine. It was a stupid idea. I didn't really put much stock in things like fate and destiny. But…

I ran my hand over that small swath of skin. To make sure it was actually there, and not a figment of my imagination, and for that first thrilling touch of Jaime's soft skin. I couldn't help but feel smug as even just that small touch caused Jaime to shiver and goosebumps to break out across his skin.

"Seriously. If you don't get on with this, I'm going to change my mind. About the sex and the sharing of my room," Jaime said. Although, the way he sounded out of breath and turned on made me doubt the validity that he was going to be changing his mind any time soon.

Still, I had a feeling he was as much of a contrary bastard as I was and there was always the chance that Jaime would back out of this just to spite us both. So, I delivered a sharp smack to his ass—not a hardship for me to do at all—and gently reprimanded him with the reminder, "Hey. Stop being impatient. You're the one who asked to get fucked first, which means I'm in charge this turn. We'll get to the fucking when I decide we get to the fucking."

He tried to stifle the groan he made, but I still heard it. And delighted in getting that sort of a reaction out of the uptight Jaime Johnson. Hmm. The thought of getting firsthand experience of just how much of a tightass he was and possibly forcing more of those sorts of noises out of him, had me scrambling to rip open a condom packet much faster than any of his begging had done.

My dick now suitably covered and happily raring to go, I uncapped the lube bottle to the accompaniment of Jaime's muttered "About danged time" and deposited a healthy dollop onto my fingertips. What? I'm a gentleman, I wasn't going to just glob some onto Jaime's hole without warming it up first.

"Oh, Jesus fuck," I groaned as I used my other hand to spread apart the hockey-toned and rounded globes of Jaime's ass and got my first glimpse of his pale pink and tightly furled hole. I smeared the now-warm lube across his hole and enjoyed the visual treat of the way it glistened and turned the light furring of gingery hair around his opening a darker red. "How... uh. How long has it been? Since you last bottomed?" I asked with a gasp as I tried to wriggle just one of my fingers inside him and, even with a generous amount of lube, it didn't want to slide in.

"None of your business."

"Except it is my business," I replied. "Since I'm the one who's trying to fuck you and you're clamped up tighter than Ebenezer Scrooge at a fundraiser for widows and orphans."

"Shut up. I just… I just need to relax and it'll be fine," Jaime insisted.

"Uh huh. Relax. 'Cause that sounds sooo much like you. Are you sure you want to do this?" Fuck knew *I* wanted to do this, but I didn't want to feel like some creep fucking a guy who wasn't really down to fuck.

"Yes," Jaime stated petulantly. "Just do it."

"But. It doesn't really…"

"Just do it," Jaime repeated impatiently. "And… it's been a while, okay."

"Okay," I quietly echoed.

It shouldn't really matter… how often Jaime has or hasn't been fucking other people. But… for some reason… it kind of did. To me. It made me want to not just fuck him, but be gentle with him. Take care of him. Make sure he enjoyed himself and not just to live up to my boasting or stroke my ego.

So, with that in mind, instead of just pushing or wiggling my finger into his ass and getting right to the opening-him-up-enough-for-my-cock stage of things, I started slowly teasing him with soft touches, over and around his rim. Down along his taint and toward his heavy-looking balls. More goosebumps erupted along the length of Jaime's back and I could see the muscles along his spine relax infinitesimally. It wasn't much, but it was a start.

My hard cock brushed against the curve of Jaime's ass as I leaned over him and placed slow, open-mouthed kisses to the freckle-specked hard curves of his shoulder blades. Those freckles looked like they should taste spicy or cinnamon-y or something. But, instead, all I could taste against my lips—and with each little licking sample with the tip of my tongue—was man, and a little bit of sweat and soap, with the faintest hint of cotton and laundry detergent from the shirt he'd been wearing.

I really wished I hadn't already covered my cock with the condom; it would've been so much better to feel the heat and silkiness of Jaime's skin directly against my skin. But the little bit of friction from rubbing against him and the knowledge that it was so close to ultimately being where I wanted it to end up, made my dick a happy camper.

"What... what are you doing?" Jaime gasped out. "Just... just get on with it. I'm not gonna break. Shove your fingers in me, shove your dick in me, and let's get this going and over with."

I know Jaime was trying to sound impatient and annoyed with me and the way I'd slowed down our frantic impulse fuck to something... a bit too slow, gentle, and caring for two guys who didn't really like each other. But the faint trembling of his large body under mine, the way he leaned and arched into each soft brush of my mouth over the skin of his back, and the hint of vulnerability threading through his voice told me to keep doing what I was doing. I could take him hard and fast, like Jaime said he wanted me to. But I doubted either of us would enjoy that all that much. Not this time. At least, not as much as we could if I took my time to ease him into this and prep his body the way it needed to be so that it was ready and begging for me to finally sink inside of him.

"I'm in charge," I reminded him with a quick snapped flick of my fingers against the back of his thigh. "So just shut up and let me do this how I want to. We'll get there. And you'll fucking love it once we do."

The tips of the fingers on my right hand continued to make teasing passes around and over Jaime's opening while I went back to exploring the cascade of freckles on Jaime's shoulders and back with my mouth. One particular spot, about half-way down his back and just to the right of his spine, caused Jaime to groan and start thrusting his delightfully round ass back against my hand when my lips brushed over it. I redoubled my efforts and tickled the tip of my tongue against that spot, then scraped the edges of my teeth as best I could over it, followed by soothing licks by the flat of my tongue.

"Aa-aaah," Jaime gasped.

Ooh. That was a good sign. As was the way Jaime's hole fluttered and relaxed open enough that I could finally slip my middle finger inside of him.

Fuck. The feel of that hot tightness wrapped around my finger about had my eyes rolling back in my head. It was going to take a bit until he was loose enough for me to get my cock in there but, holy fuck, it was going to feel so good once it was.

"Ah. Babe. That's it," I murmured in encouragement. Now that it was in there, it felt like Jaime's ass didn't want to let my finger escape. Fine by me. My finger was in no hurry to go anywhere other than exploring. "Let's see if we can find…" I pumped my finger in and out a little, rubbing and twisting and feeling around for…

"Fuck! Gaah. Fuck. Fuck fuck fuckfuckfuck fucking hell!"

Theerrre it was.

Chapter Six
Jaime

Oh, God. I didn't even care that filth was now spewing unheeded from my lips. Thoughts of my mother and the disappointed and chiding expression that overtook her face whenever my sister and I would use profanity growing up—which was why I didn't swear other than on the ice, where it was an expected and secondary, common language between all players—were unsurprisingly nowhere present as J.J. unerringly found and stimulated my prostate.

Holy fucking hell. How had he managed to find it so easily? It was my prostate and even with my routine use of a dildo, it often took me a little finagling to find it as perfectly as J.J. Johnson had done within just a few thrusts of his finger.

If he kept it up and his dick wound up being just as accurate as his fingers were, I might actually have to concede that some of his cocky attitude might just be warranted.

Shit.

"Oh, yeah. Let's try a second finger, now, m'kay?"

It stung and burned as J.J. pressed a second finger into me alongside the first one that had been delighting me so much. But, holy crap, it was totally worth it as there were now two firm, strong fingers stroking and rubbing over my prostate.

"Oh, fuck. Yeah. Yeah. Fuck me. C'mon, J. Fuck me. I want it," I babbled. More words that would've gotten me a trip to the dictionary as a child to look up and list better words than swear words tumbling out of me.

"You do, do you?" asked the frustratingly annoying man playing with my ass.

"Yes. Do it. Fuck. Just. Do. It."

I started to tense up again when a brief snicker came from behind me, but J.J. immediately said, "Ah ah ah. None of that. I wasn't laughing at you. Um. Not really. I'll... explain it to you later. After. Right now... Yeah. Right now, I'm gonna open you up a little more..."

The feel of a third finger breaching me caused me to catch and hold my breath and I had to sternly remind myself that I needed to breathe and let him in. J.J.'s fingers in me felt fantastic, but I'd agreed that I was going to let him fuck me and... God. I really wanted him to fuck me. I wanted his long, hard cock in me, pounding away until I made a complete mess of myself and the sheets under me.

"Fuck, you feel so good," J.J. said as he moved his fingers in and out of my opening. "So tight. So good. Fuck, my cock's gonna think it's died and gone to heaven once I get it in you."

"Now. Now. Get it in me and fuck me now, J," I begged.

"Fuck, yeah," J.J. replied.

My hole felt empty and frustrated when J.J. pulled his fingers out of me. But that only lasted for a few seconds before the blunt head of his latex-covered dick nudged against me and started slipping in.

J.J. and I groaned in unison as his cockhead breached my hole. I was desperate for him to fill me. I wanted him to just plunge in and shove his whole length into me, even if, rationally, I knew that'd be a bad idea.

While it'd been almost a year since my last sexual encounter, it'd been much longer than that since I'd been fucked. Much longer. A couple years, easily. My hookups last summer, during the off-season, had mostly been quick and furtive blowjobs or jerks. Although, the one guy I'd picked up at a bar had had an apartment over the bar and he'd invited me up to his place. But he'd wanted me to fuck him, so that's what we'd done. Because of my size and build, most guys I ran across either just assumed I was a top or assumed I wouldn't be interested in bottoming—both of which were such bullshit, stupid stereotypes.

So, I knew it was a good thing that J.J. was making careful, shallow thrusts of his cock, gradually stretching my channel open until he could go all the way in and bottom out.

But that didn't mean I was happy about the situation. I wanted him to fuck me into the mattress and to do it fucking now. C'mon. Of all times for him to not act like his usual arrogant, aggressive, doesn't-care-who-he-has-to-go-through-to-get-to-the-goal-and-score self, now was *not* the time.

"Do it. Fuck me. Fuck me harder, you asshole," I ordered him. "What do I have to do to get you to—AaaaghhAAH!" I cut off with a groaned shout as J.J. finally plunged all of the way into me with a hard shove.

"There. Better, you impatient fuck?" he asked.

"Oh, God. More. Gimme more."

J.J.'s fingers dug into my hips—and was I horrified or thrilled that I knew my fair skin was going to definitely bruise from that?—as he thrust in harder and faster. I could hear myself making the most embarrassing whimpering and whining noises as he fucked me. But, J.J.'s cock was just as marvelously skilled as his fingers had been. Because, even though his movements seemed hurried, he was still accurately pegging my prostate with each in and out pounding stroke. So, it wasn't my fault that I sounded pathetically eager and cockhungry.

"Ah, shit, Jaime. Your ass is fantastic. And… fuck. Love how my cock looks in you."

"Uhnnnn…"

"Fuck, I'm not gonna last long. I'm about to blow like a fucking geyser. You?" J.J. asked. "Are you… Can you come like this?"

Shit. Could I? Zings of pleasure were shooting through my body. The fast, steady rhythmic pass of his cockhead over my prostate had my balls drawn up tight and my own cock was rock hard and dribbling pre-cum. Yeah. Yeah, I could definitely come like this.

I shifted my weight so that my upper body was resting on one elbow and a shoulder, although that gave me a face and mouth full of pillow, and reached my right hand down so that I could wrap it around my aching cock.

Oh, fuck, that felt good. I groaned in relief, then remembered to answer him when J.J. asked again, "Babe? Can you come like this?"

"Yuhn. Yeah. Fuck, yeah, I can."

"Ungh. Thank fuck."

J.J.'s fingers dug into my hips so hard, it felt like he was trying to break something. But, while it kind of hurt, it also felt really, really good. So good. I liked knowing my body had made him desperate and worked up. So worked up that he couldn't control himself.

Me. I'd done that.

The man J.J. had always mocked for being dull and boring.

Look who wasn't so boring now.

"That's... that's... Fuck. Coming. I'm... Fuck!"

J.J.'s shout was accompanied by one last hard thrust and the complete collapse of his body on top of mine, throwing off my balance and making me crash fully onto the mattress.

I couldn't really breathe now that my face was shoved down so far into the pillow underneath me. But who the hell cared about that, when I was only a few fast and stuttering thrusts of my cock through the narrow channel of my fist—smushed tighter by the press of my own body, J.J.'s body from above and the mattress from below—from coming?

"Shit. Shit. Ugh. Oh, yeah. Fuck, me too. Coming," I said as I felt my cock spasm and twitch as spurts of cum shot out.

The heavy weight of J.J. Johnson, who was just as tall and built as I was, the sticky, cooling puddle of cum coating my hand and smeared all across my stomach and groin, and the ache in my ass from the vigorous pounding it'd just taken were annoying and I probably wouldn't want to stay being smushed into my wet spot for much longer. But they were all minor concerns compared to the overwhelmingly pleasant glow I had from a truly stupendous orgasm. Even the added irritation that the orgasm had come at the hands—and dick—of the detested J.J. Johnson wasn't enough to diminish the cloud of satisfaction I was floating on.

"Fuck. Now, that's how it's done," J.J. proclaimed with a stinging smack to the side of my ass. "Told you it'd be stupendous. You'd better bring your 'A' game when it's your turn to fuck me."

Well, there went my cloud of contentment. Vanishing like wisps of fog on a hot, sunny day.

"Really? Really?" I said. "You couldn't not be an ass for a little longer? Actually, never mind. I suppose trying to contain all that ego would be like shoving a cork in a teapot.

Too much pressure for too long and you'd probably explode. Although…"

"Shut up. It's not ego when it's the truth," J.J. replied.

"Ugh. Get off me, you cocky jerk," I told him, wiggling and trying to roll his body off of mine.

"What? Get off on you, you say? Well, alright. Might need to give me a couple minutes to recharge, but I'd happily shoot my spunk all over your creamy skin if you want me to." I made a scoffing noise of disbelief and J.J. stated, "If you use your mouth on my dick, I'm sure it'd go faster."

"Get off," I grunted again. And, this time, I either used enough force to dislodge him or J.J. cooperated with my request. But, either way, his weight shifted off of me as he flopped over onto his side on the mattress next to me. I turned my head to look at him, glared, and told him, "If there's anyone in this room who needs something shoved in their mouth, it's you."

J.J. smirked at me and replied, "Meh. I love sucking cock. You want me to suck you, I will. And that'll probably get me going enough, too, that I'll be able to paint your pretty, freckly skin with my cum. Either way is good for me. Er. Again, just give me a couple minutes and I'll be good to go again."

I opened my mouth to reply… something. I'm not sure what. But, on second thought, having J.J.'s mouth full of my dick so that he can't talk and then watching him jerk himself until his sexy cock spurted all over me… That wasn't a bad image at all.

So, once again… against my better and smarter instincts… I found myself agreeing with J.J.'s suggestion of sexual activities between us.

"Yeah. Alright. Here or in the shower?" I asked.

Who was I and what was happening to me? Why was I going along with this preposterousness? Yeah, J.J. was hot. Ridiculously hot. And the sex had been surprisingly good. Really good. Dang it. Stupendous. Just like he'd said it'd be. But that didn't make it any less of a truly terrible idea.

"Let's not get the bed any messier than we've already gotten it. There's still only the one bed and we still have to sleep in it tonight. Shower," he answered.

What the heck? We'd already done the terrible idea once, might as well make it twice.

"Shower it is," I concurred.

Chapter Seven

J.J.

We certainly hadn't been utilizing any forethought, but at least Jaime and I had been too eager to fuck to move the hotel's duvet out of the way. That was a stroke of good luck, I thought, as I watched Jaime roll it up with our mess of cum and lube ending up on the inside of a neat little fuck-fouled log, a grimace of distaste marring his square-jawed good looks. Actually, it was sort of similar to the snarl he usually sported whenever he and I came face-to-face on the ice. Honestly, since today wasn't the first time I'd found my eyes drawn to Jaime and found him more than acceptably attractive enough to fuck, it was apparently a look that did it for me.

And since someone had to tackle the post-sex cleanup duty, I was more than okay with turning that over to him.

"Ugh. Gross," Jaime commented as he stuffed the discarded roll of bedding into the unused bottom corner of the closet. The other side was occupied by the folding suitcase stand, which Jaime was actually using to hold his suitcase.

Weirdo.

I usually just tucked my suitcase under the pointless hotel room desk—did anyone actually do any work while they were staying in a hotel room that would necessitate wasting floor space with a desk?—or flopped open on the floor next to the side of the bed I didn't sleep on. I wondered if Jaime actually used the dresser to store the clothing he'd packed that didn't need to be hung up. I'd caught a glimpse of some of his clothes hanging on the provided hangers in the closet above his suitcase, so odds were… yeah, he probably did.

Like I said. Weirdo.

But at least he was a hot weirdo.

Jaime's freckle speckled shoulders were broad and rounded with muscle. The muscles of his arms were lean but well-defined. His pecs were gently rounded firm mounds, topped with pale pink nipples, and were located above a rippling, cut six-pack. He didn't have a lot of body hair, but there was a fine tracing of gingery hair leading down from below his belly button that disappeared below the band of the white bath towel wrapped around his narrow hips.

And, of course, I now hand first-hand experience with how those narrow hips felt gripped in my hands and just how deliciously firm and round the ass was on the other side of what was also a fantastically pretty cock.

A cock that tasted just as nice as it looked.

Mmm. That had been fun.

I hadn't really expected Jaime to go along with my suggestion of a blowjob followed up by jerking off on him in the shower. Maybe... sixty-forty odds. Against, not for.

But I have to say, he surprised me. Just like he'd surprised me by going along with us fucking in the first place and not just punching me in the face and throwing me out on my ass when I'd thrown the idea out there.

Maybe Jaime Johnson wasn't quite as boring and uptight as I'd thought he was.

Now there was a scary and disturbing thought.

What else would I have to rethink? That the earth was round? That dogs were better than cats? That peanut butter and jelly were a match made in heaven? That hockey was the greatest sport in the world and that Tyler Seguin had the greatest hockey ass in creation and that Alex Wennberg should be slathered in chocolate syrup and slowly licked clean... by me?

Nah. There's no way my judgment could be that far off-base.

I'm sure Jaime was just as straightlaced as I'd thought he was. Maybe he'd just been smacked too hard in the head during one of his more recent playoff games and that had scrambled his personality a little bit. Enough to make him not so… him. I mean, holy fuck, he'd actually been dropping f-bombs while I'd been fucking him. Something had to have been shaken loose. Like the must-behave-dull-as-fuck clamp he had firmly locked around the part of his brain that controlled fun-ness. That last series the Loons had played against the Pontiac Firebirds had looked pretty rough and physical. Even for hockey.

"Eh. Not like we would've needed it anyway," I told him, referencing the duvet that he'd just consigned to the closet for the night. "If it gets too cool in here, we can always turn the AC off and crack open a window."

"We're on the eighth floor. Not sure the windows open this high up. I think they're just to provide a view of the desert," Jaime commented.

"Eh. Just as well. One or the other of us is bound to be tempted to toss the other out of a window before the night's through. Not really in the mood to end up in the morgue or jail for homicide, so that should cut down on those odds."

"Why am I not surprised that your mind immediately jumps right to murder?"

"'Cause you just recognize and understand how smart I am?"

"More like twisted and depraved."

"Hey, you seemed to have no problems with my depravity level when I was fucking or sucking you."

"I still can't believe we did that." Jaime's hair had a bit of curl to it after our shower. Nice. Made it so I didn't even mind so much that he was continually shaking his head in disbelief. "We still have to play hockey together."

"Well… not together," I corrected him. "We don't play for the same team. That would be awkward. It's about the only reason I've never gone there with Sasha."

"Yuralaev?"

With as shocked as Jaime looked, I might as well answer his question with "Baron Cohen"—the only other Sasha I could think of off the top of my head, although I think the two men spelled their names differently—or told him that 'Sasha' was some nickname I'd bestowed on Santa Claus.

"Yeah. Sasha Yuralaev."

"You… you… he… what…" Jaime spluttered.

"Nope. That's the point I was trying to make. He and I… haven't. Because we're on the same team. Not that he hasn't offered and I haven't been tempted."

"So, he… he…" Jaime cast a quick look around then lowered his voice down to almost a whisper for some reason. "He's gay?"

"Nah," I responded. "I've never asked him how he identifies, but I don't get the sense he's faking anything when he goes home from bars with men or women or, more than once, both. I'm guessing he's bi or pan."

"Huh. And you and he…"

"No. Like I said. I don't fuck teammates. That'd make things too weird."

"Oh. Yeah. No. I… I can… I don't… um… f-fuck teammates either."

"I assumed," I told him. Because I had. He didn't seem like the type.

"You're… uh. The first other hockey player I've had sex with. As far as I know."

"Really?" I thought for a minute, then decided… yeah. That tracked too. "Who do you normally fuck? What kind of guys do you go for?" Obviously, Jaime had been attracted to me enough to give in to my idea to fuck for a night. But I was curious as to whether I was a complete aberration for him or if I did fall within his range of what he usually looked for in a guy physically.

Unfortunately for me, Jaime Johnson was completely the kind of guy I was usually attracted to. Physically fit, around my height, clean-cut and handsome. Plus, there was his vivid coloring of red hair and blue eyes. And the freckles. The *freckles*. I'd never get enough of his freckles.

It was probably a job for a shrink to figure out if being physically attracted to Jaime had anything to do with how much I liked to aggravate him.

I just knew I liked doing both.

Annoying him *and* looking at him.

"Uh. You know… the usual kind," Jaime unhelpfully answered.

"Uh. No. I don't know," I told him. "That's why I asked. C'mon, Loverboy." Fuck, I loved the pinched, sour face he made when I used that nickname. "When you're out at a bar... Fuck. You do go to bars, right?"

"Yes, I go to bars. What the heck?"

"Well, I wasn't sure. You seem like the kind of guy who'd spend a night out on the town at the opera or a museum or... a poetry reading or something. I wasn't sure if your aversion to all the fun vices in life extended to avoiding all the places where fun lives."

"I have no idea where you got this idea that—"

"Would you get over here?" I held up the edge of the blankets on the bed. "You look like you're getting cold and it's kind of creepy having you hovering by the end of the bed like that. Climb on in here next to me. I won't bite. Unless you ask," I added with a leer and an exaggerated, comical snap of my teeth.

Jaime's gaze seemed to snag on the bit of bare leg I'd revealed when I'd lifted up the sheet. I hadn't bothered to put anything on after we'd showered, since I usually slept in the buff and I hadn't seen any reason to change that up now. Why fuss with putting on a pair of briefs or pj pants when I was hopeful Jaime would put his mouth, hands, or ass on my dick again at some point during the night? Already being naked would cut out a couple of wasted moments where my dick wasn't getting attention.

Did I even own any pajama pants? I wasn't sure. But I was pretty positive I hadn't packed any for this long weekend. And the couple pairs of undies I'd packed were reserved for wearing on the golf course underneath my golf pants.

So, Jaime was going to be treated to the joys of a naked me whether he liked it or not.

He seemed to like it... At least, until he shook his head and said, "No. I'm not getting into that bed until you tell me why you seem to have this incorrect impression of me that I'm some sort of fun-killing, stick-in-the-mud."

"Uh. 'Cause you are?" I responded, bewildered. Didn't he know that about himself?

"No. I'm not. And, before today, we've spent a grand total of zero time alone together and perhaps only a couple hours over the past few years interacting with each other. And that was while we were in the middle of hockey games. So, what makes you think you know me? Or have the right to form any opinion whatsoever about my personality?"

"I figure," I slowly drawled. "That I gained my impression of you from the same place you seemed to have gained your impressions about me. From the sort of shit you throw at me on the ice. The things you say in your interviews. The kinds of stuff you post about and share online. It's not like you really know me, either, but that certainly hasn't fucking stopped you from deciding that I'm some full-of-myself, egotistical ass."

Two could play this game. If Jaime could be annoyed with me for forming first-impression opinions about him, then I could do the same. Who was he to not like that I didn't like him when he didn't fucking like me either?

84

"That's because you are!" Jaime yelled. "All you talk about is you, you, you. How great you are. How awesome you play. How the Snappers couldn't win without you."

"Of course I say those things," I yelled right back at him, bulldozing right over his comments. "If I don't say it, who the hell else will? And then why the hell would the Snappers want to keep me on the first line, or on the team at all, if they didn't buy into the thought that they'd be nowhere without me? All that 'I'm just a part of the team, we work as a unit' bullshit you're always spouting just makes you sound like another generic cog in the machine that could easily get replaced by some other generic hockey cog."

"I spout all that 'part of the team' stuff, as you put it—"

"Pretty sure I said 'bullshit', not 'stuff'."

"Because it's true," Jaime insisted. "There's no 'I' in team."

"Oh my fuck. You seriously just pulled out the oldest, lamest sports motivational cliché of all time. You seriously fucking did."

"It's not a cliché. It's the truth."

"Cliché."

"Is not."

"A boring, stupid, stick-in-the-mud cliché. Do you have it on a poster hanging above your bed? Do you jerk off to those words at night?"

"It's not a cliché. You're just a selfish, puck-hogging, attention-hungry—"

"It's not selfish to look out for yourself."

"That's the very definition of selfish!"

Jaime's last word seemed to echo off the walls of the hotel room as we both paused our rants, panting as we tried to catch our breaths.

"Fine. If that's the way you feel about me," I said. "Then I'm not going to share the bed with you." I huffily flopped the blankets back down over my legs. The one had been getting chilled anyway.

"It's. My. Bed," Jaime said through gritted teeth.

Huh. Technicalities.

"Fine. In that case, I guess the non-selfish thing to do… because I'm *not* selfish," I insisted. "Is for us to share the bed. Which was the original plan."

"Fine."

"Fine. But because I'm angry at you, don't think I'm going to be putting out anymore tonight."

"Fine."

"Fine."

sigh What a perfectly good waste of climbing into bed naked. And Jaime was still just wearing that fucking skimpy and barely-big-enough-to-cover-the-good-stuff hotel towel. At least, the last of the water droplets adorning his creamy-with-cinnamony-freckles chest had evaporated, reducing my urge to lick him to its usual low simmer.

"Get in the bed, Jaime," I repeated, flopping over onto my side and presenting my back to him.

And I didn't feel an insatiable need to take a peek to witness him discarding the towel. Which I could imagine as I heard the fwump of the towel hitting something. Probably not the floor. Jaime was far too neat and persnickety to leave a used, damp towel on the floor.

I stayed strong and kept my back to him. Even as I felt the weight of the blankets lift as he raised them, then the dip of the mattress as Jaime finally settled onto the other side of the mattress. I meant what I said. I was mad at him and I wasn't going to give him any more sex tonight. He could just wait until he apologized for being a jerk to me.

Or until I really, really wanted him to take his turn at fucking me and get his incredibly attractive dick in my ass.

It was going to be a toss-up, really.

Actually since I couldn't envision Jaime backtracking on his opinion of me any more than I planned to alter my opinion of him… I'd definitely cave before holding out for an apology from him. But a guy had to at least pretend to have some backbone.

My irritation with Jaime was only amped up even further since us being angry at each other also meant that I couldn't roll back over and scootch my naked body over until I was snuggled up next to the guy. What a waste of a perfectly good only-one-bed situation. There might as well be an invisible barricade of pillows between us formed by our anger and heated words for all the space there was between his body and mine in the bed and for all the unwillingness I felt to bridge that gap. Even if I normally did enjoy some after-sex-cuddling. That wasn't going to happen now.

"Just as well," Jaime quietly and hesitantly said. "We should probably get a good night's sleep so we're ready to go for the start of the tournament in the morning."

"Yeah. Probably," I petulantly agreed.

Another moment passed in which the only sound was the soft shush of our breathing, the faint rustle of the sheets, and the rumbling whoosh of the air conditioner.

"Did you… Did you… Am I still going to take my turn um… f-fucking you?"

Huh. Looked like I wasn't going to be the one to cave first. At least, as far as being willing to set aside our animosity for the sake of fucking, Jaime was showing me that he might not be quite as rigid and unbending as I'd believed. I allowed my body to relax and melt a little bit, backward in the direction of Jaime's body. We still weren't touching, but the empty space between us no longer felt like such an inhospitable chasm.

"Oh, hell yes," I responded. I was nowhere near done with having sex with Jaime Johnson and I wasn't about to let him get out of taking his turn at my ass.

"Oh. Okay, then. Tomorrow night? After the tournament stuff and dinner?"

"Tomorrow night," I agreed. "It's on."

Chapter Eight
J.J.

Golf pants sucked ass.

99% of my life when I had to wear pants was spent in sweats, track pants, jeans, or compression pants under my hockey gear. You know, stuff that was comfortable. But even though I'd attempted to find the most relaxed, stretch, athletic-fit, whatever cut of golf pants I could find, each and every single one of the damned things were stiff, irritating, and felt like they were trying to choke and strangle my ass, legs, and junk. Golf pants just weren't designed to accommodate the average hockey-honed physique.

It didn't help that I was wearing briefs under them. Going commando was by far my preference and, practice and game times aside, that was my default status under my pants. But for the sake of trying to minimize any possible wardrobe malfunction situation at a televised charity tournament and because I knew that the stiff fabric of the pants would leave my dick horrendously chafed after tromping up and down and around eighteen holes, I'd made the necessary decision to don skivvies for the day. My dick might not be thanking me now, but it would later when it wasn't all sore and scraped raw.

At least my ass did look awesome in my pants. I'd even tracked down a pair of golf pants that came in something other than boring black, beige, or gray. Sure, the close-to-fluorescent swirls of green, blue, purple, and pink on a darker blue background might be a bit of a bold choice. But I felt absolutely positive I could pull them off. And with the way the close cut of the fabric cupped my ass, I was hopeful that Jaime would be tempted to pull them off of me later.

But first we had to get through the rest of the day, clomping around a golf course while we were forced to endure the company of people rich enough to splash out for a couple of days of company with a bunch of middling- to moderately-well-known athletes, some C and D list actors, and a couple of former Disney pop stars. I know the whole thing was to raise money for charity. But I would've been much happier to just cut a check and pop it in the mail— which I also did—without having to schmooze and play nice so the non-celebrity I was matched up with wouldn't demand their money back.

Jaime emerged from the bathroom with a swirly cloud of steam, which was about the only steamy thing about the basic, boring golf attire he wore.

"Oh, look. You're wearing beige. How incredibly unsurprising of you," I said.

I decided to neglect to mention how hot he managed to make a boring pair of beige slacks look. Or how the light blue of his golf shirt made his complexion look even more like melted vanilla ice cream—totally lickable—and set off his blue eyes so that they appeared luminously bright.

"At least my pants don't look like an obnoxious explosion of the worst of 1980s fashion trends."

Despite his critical words, I definitely caught the lingering glance Jaime gave to my dickprint in these pants. Did I, perhaps, tilt and tip my hips forward to make that dickprint even more visible? Yes. Yes, I did. It never hurt to remind a dude about the equipment I had and had used on him to great effect.

"C'mon, Malibu Golf Ken. We might as well make our way downstairs, board whatever shuttle they've got set up to ferry us to the golf course, and find out what too-loaded-for-their-own-good idiots they've paired us up with for the day."

Jaime rolled his eyes at my comment, but I noticed he didn't refute it.

And my pessimism proved well-founded when I found myself partnered up for the tournament with a loud-mouthed, obnoxious Chief Marketing Officer for some pharmaceutical company from New Jersey. Oh goody. Just because I had a best friend in the same general industry and wasn't unknowledgeable about it, didn't mean I wanted to be stuck talking about it with this blowhard.

Rounding out the foursome I was expected to spend the bulk of my day with, shooting the shit while we shot golf balls, was a baby-faced tech genius—one of those wunderkinds who made a billion or so dollars before they were even old enough to legally drink—and a generically handsome dude with a square jaw, gelled hair, and an obvious spray tan that I sort of recognized from a reality tv show. One of the ones where he was trying to win the heart of some desperate woman or had to survive the wilderness by eating bugs and shit, maybe? Either way, the guy seemed about as interesting as pocket lint.

Jaime Johnson might be slightly boring, but he was at least the interesting sort of boring. I had the feeling that if I dug hard enough or irritated him enough, I might find hidden layers to him underneath his boringness.

Mr. Reality-TV Lint Guy was the sort of soggy boring like a bowl of Cheerios overflowing with too much milk and left to sit on the counter for too long.

If I was stuck with these three yahoos for the day, I just knew I was going to find myself either running over one of them with a golf cart or chucking them into a water hazard before too long. And I had the feeling that the charity organizers, Sylvie, my agent who'd arranged for me to come and do this event, and the powers-that-be for my hockey team probably wouldn't appreciate that.

I might not like Jaime all that much, but I knew I could at least tolerate him. And I haven't been tempted to commit homicide on him yet. Want to punch him in the face—within the sanctioned confines of a hockey game, of course—yes.

But no outright homicide. Besides, I had added incentive to put up with Jaime and not kill him. The promise of more sex. And this time it would be my ass on the pounding block.

So, it was out of the goodness of my heart and general goodwill toward my fellow man... and not just because I'd rather have the dubiously better company and definitely better eye-candy of Jaime Johnson close by... that I stealthily rearranged things for my benefit.

"Oi! Johnson," I called out, last-naming Jaime so as not to divulge or even allude to the fact that our private parts were intimately and happily familiar with each other. "Who all's in your foursome?"

Did I care that I was yelling across the immaculately groomed—and improbably green for the Nevada desert—grounds surrounding the clubhouse? And garnering the attention of... everybody? Nope. Not a bit.

Even from this far away, I could see Jaime's blue eyes widen and the blush sweep across his face as my hollering prompted everyone to pause their conversations and focus in on the two of us. Because we were separated by several hundred yards, I saw more than heard his, "Uhhhh..." A quick gulp of nervousness and a squaring of his shoulders preceding Jaime's answering call back of, "I'm partnered up with Mr. Jason Teague and we're playing against Delia Darling and Ms. Constance Channing-Lee."

The two non-celebrities standing near Jaime looked wealthy, but otherwise unremarkable. And Delia Darling looked a bit rougher around the edges, but still recognizable from her days of starring in and churning out released-straight-to-the-Disney-Channel movies.

Nope. I had absolutely no qualms in dishing up a former child actress and foisting her off onto my unwanted Silicon Valley billionaire and reality-tv star duo. And based on the way Ms. Channing-Lee was ogling the tv stud standing near me, she wouldn't be too upset about the switch I was about to pull.

"Awesome," I yelled over to Jaime. "But how about we shake things up a little? My partner for the day is a huge hockey fan..." I have no idea if he was or not. Probably not, since he hadn't seemed to recognize me. But I didn't give a flying fuck one way or the other. "So, I was thinking we'd give him an extra thrill by letting him play a round of golf with two hockey stars. You and your Mr. Teague against me and Mr. Kirby. And the lovely Miss Darling and Ms. Channing-Lee can play with the other gentlemen from my foursome."

A quick glance at the other people involved in my golf re-shuffle showed that Jason Teague and Constance Channing-Lee looked happy with this idea, my golfing partner, Edwin Kirby, looked confused, Jaime looked nonplussed, and the other three looked like they could care less.

"Good. That's settled," I loudly declared. "Come on over and we can get our pairings rearranged. Then we can play some golf."

"What are you doing?" Jaime hissed at me under his breath, once he and the three others walked across the lawn to join me and the three other people in my group. "You can't just rearrange things on your whim. The tournament organizers had us all… organized already."

"Yeaaahhh. I didn't really care for who they stuck me with, though," I told him. "If I'm gonna be stuck spending a whole day with some people, I'd like at least one of them to be someone I want to spend time with."

Jaime looked at me, doubt and surprise clear on his face. "You want to spend time… with me?"

"Rather you than him," I replied, nodding my head in the direction of Mr. Reality TV, who was clearly preening under the attention of the older-but-incredibly-well-preserved Ms. Channing-Lee.

"Oh."

I tried not to read too much into the quick flicker of, what looked like, disappointment that flashed across Jaime's face. He didn't want me to want to spend time with him, did he? Nah. Couldn't be.

"Besides, it's not like it really matters who we're playing with," I told him. "They're only keeping track of which groups score the lowest to advance to the championship round on the last day. The rest of us aren't going to matter. At least, I assume you're not going to wind up in the top four. Unless you're secretly much better at golf than your Instagram posts would lead me to believe. And while I'm not half bad at golf, I don't have the patience or ambition to be the next Dustin Johnson. I'll settle for being J.J. Johnson." My mind going off on a tangent, I asked, "Hey. Do you suppose that guy's related to either one of us? How many Johnsons do you suppose are involved in sports?"

Our octet was slowly ambling over to the practice green, where the club had assembled the caddies they were supplying for the tournament. And as we walked, I peeked out of the corner of my eye and noticed Jaime giving me a WTF look. Other than his pissy expression, that was a pretty common countenance for him to have in my presence, so I disregarded it and continued, "Let's get this over with and then we can go enjoy some alcoholic libations in the clubhouse. And then... later..."

Jaime shook his head like he was annoyed. But I caught the slight quirking of his supple lips. And he quietly murmured back, "Yeah. Later."

"C'mon, Johnson. You can do better than that. You're some sort of athlete, aren't you?" The pompous voice of Edwin Kirby stridently proclaimed his disbelief and disappointment in my, yet again, failing to make par.

I could, indeed, do better.

I just didn't want to.

Much to my amazement, both Edwin and Jaime's partner for the day, Jason Teague, were actually really good at golf. So good, they were off-setting Jaime's and mine matching moderately-acceptable playing so much that, if they kept on track with how they were scoring, we'd be close to making the cut for the championship round.

I liked winning. I did. But that didn't mean that I wanted to play more golf than I was obligatorily expected to play. I didn't want to have to play an extra day of golf when I could spend that last day of my stay in Nevada doing something much more pleasurable. Like Jaime.

So, while I could play better... I, intentionally, wasn't.

"I play hockey, Edwin. Not golf," I replied as I purposely aimed my golf ball just to the left of the hole. Oh, look. It didn't go in. Oopsies. Looked like I was going to get a double bogey on this hole.

Edwin might want to look into cutting down on his sodium and cholesterol intake if the red state of his face was any indication. He looked like his ticker was going to burst at any moment.

"That's okay," he said, clearly lying through his teeth as he stomped his way off the green and on to the next hole. "You might want to take some lessons though, son, if you plan on taking this up as a hobby."

"Didn't you post pics of you and some teammates playing golf in Fiji during the All-Star break?" Jaime asked me as he sidled up next to me as we both watched our golf partners leaving the green.

"Yep."

"And boasted about how you kicked all their asses?"

"That does sound like me," I answered.

"So, why are you playing like crud now? I thought you were trying to avoid homicide today. Causing your partner to drop dead in frustration is kind of skirting those lines, don't you think?"

"I have no idea what you're talking about."

"There's no way you'll be able to convince me that you aren't playing badly on purpose," Jaime stated. "I don't know how you think nobody's going to call you out on it."

"Clearly somebody is," I muttered.

"You're going to get in trouble and for what?" he asked. "I don't get you. We might've just met these people but, no matter what our personal opinions of them are, they deserved for us to play our best. They donated a lot of money to the K9s for Warriors and all you had to do was show up and act like a decent human being and put forth some effort. But you can't even manage that, can you?"

I didn't immediately have the opportunity to answer Jaime, as Edwin called back to us, "Hey, catch up! We're ready to tee off on the next hole!"

Jaime was still huffing with indignation and I was tempted to walk away without giving him any sort of justification or explanation. It was none of his business why I was throwing my game. And it's not like my play was impacting him negatively in any manner. Er. Unless he actually had wanted to make the championship round. But this was just some silly tournament to make the donors feel like they were getting something for the money they'd donated. Although, if you asked me, getting support dogs to veterans was its own reward and the tournament was just eating into the profits the charity could've banked.

I tried pointing that out to Jaime, in somewhat of an attempt to understand why I wasn't taking this round of golf at all seriously. "Everyone who's here has already paid their donation, right?" I asked him.

"Yes. So?"

"And do you think they're going to ask for their money back if they're unhappy with who they're partnered with or what the scores wind up being?"

"No. Of course not," he replied.

I dared to place my hand on his elbow and nudged him to turn and start walking so we could catch up to the other two members of our foursome.

"So, what does it matter if I'm intentionally playing like shit?" I asked him. "I'm having fun. Despite being stuck with an obnoxious windbag for a partner. Jason seems like he's having fun. Despite being stuck with you. And if you managed to dislodge the golf club you have shoved up your ass and loosened up a little, I bet you'd be having fun too."

As we drew closer to the next tee, I let the subject drop. If Edwin overheard us talking and found out that I was purposely fucking up, he probably would murder me.

We arrived at the twelfth hole just in time to watch Jason send his ball in a long, graceful arc with a perfect trajectory to have it landing neatly in the middle of the fairway and with a clear shot toward the green. I gave a soft whistle under my breath in appreciation of his beauty of a shot.

"Nice," I commented once Jaime and I had drawn close to Jason.

Edwin gave me an unhappy frown over his shoulder from where he was placing his own ball on the tee and getting ready to take his own shot. I sent him a smirk of non-apology in return. I honestly didn't give a fuck that I was getting on this guy's last nerve. Just because he'd laid down a good chunk of money to get to play golf with some celebrity of the tournament's choosing, didn't guarantee him my pleasant disposition.

"Hmm. Thanks," Jason commented.

We were all appropriately quiet as Edwin took his shot. Not a terrible shot, but nowhere near as pretty as Jason's had been.

Then, because he had better manners than I did, Jaime asked Jason, "So, you mentioned that you were an attorney in… Phoenix? What kind of cases do you usually work on?" He still sounded a little perturbed, but since that wasn't all that unusual when he was around me, hopefully Jason and Edwin wouldn't think anything of it.

"Yeah, I'm from Phoenix," Jason said. "I'm actually a huge Griffins fan, so I was kind of stoked that I wound up getting paired with you for this tournament. And it was really awesome how I somehow wounded up in a foursome with yet another NHL player." Jason sent an amused look my way because he was well aware that I was the one who'd finagled that move, even if he didn't know my reasons behind why. "And you really don't want to hear about any of my cases. They're all boring as fuck squabbles over contracts and money and trying to either pick apart loopholes or work in loopholes we're hoping the other side never catches on to… I find it boring as all fuck so I can't imagine it'd be at all interesting to anyone else. Pays fuckton amounts of money, though, so there's that." With a nod toward the tee, Jason commented, "You're up Jaime."

Watching Jaime stride up to the tee and shift his hips as he adjusted his stance was a beautiful compensation for the tedium of a day spent golfing in the dry, desert heat.

"So… contract law, huh?" I asked Jason, trying to flex my seldomly used politeness muscles.

"Seriously, if it weren't something I was strangely good at and that made me enough money I plan to retire by the time I'm forty, it's not something I'd be at all interested in," Jason reiterated. "I have no interest in discussing it when I don't have to and it's not a topic I'd wish on my worst enemy."

"Weren't you detailing something about what you were working on for a client to Edwin a couple of holes ago?"

"He's not my worst enemy," Jason responded with a smirky look. "And I was merely repaying him for his kindness in sharing the overages and unders from his last marketing campaign for some drug that has more side effects than actual medically proven benefits. You, however... I've nothing against you. So, instead of forcing me to talk about a job I hate, how about we talk about that goal you scored against the Griffins last season?"

"You saw that?" I asked.

"Saw it? I was in the fucking arena for that. Man, that deke you pulled to get by Holtzhauer..."

"That guy's always falling for that move. Every single fucking time."

"Yeah? Why don't you take your shot and then you can give me some more inside info. Anything else I should be noticing about some of the players on the Griffins?"

"Yeah. Alright," I agreed.

By the time our foursome had finished out the eighteenth hole, Jaime and I had given Jason enough fodder on players throughout the league that he should have no trouble filling out and then kicking ass with his fantasy hockey bracket for the upcoming season. Edwin had been reduced to unhappily grumbling while shooting us nasty glares, apparently not appreciating that his golf game had been co-opted by hockey talk.

And I was sporting more iron in my pants than my golf bag was from watching Jaime's ass in his form-fitting golf pants tromp all over a golf course all day. Then there was all the flexing, bunching, and twisting of those fine, fine glutes as he, naturally, executed a picture-perfect swing on each of his turns. Don't even get me started on all that flexing, bunching, and twisting. The way Jaime Johnson's body moved as he played golf was something worthy of the finest poetry.

I'm sure I could figure out some words that would rhyme with suck and fuck if I needed to.

Which meant that, while I'd had an unexpectedly nice time getting to know Jason Teague, attorney at law from Phoenix, and wasn't dreading spending some more time with him the next day during our second round of golf, I was also more than ready to give him a fast and hearty handshake in farewell. And then promptly drag Jaime Johnson back up to our hotel room so I could get him as naked as possible, as fast as possible.

"Good round today, guys," Jason said.

Edwin merely grunted in annoyance as he shoved his scorecard for the day and his golf bag at his caddy. Then he stomped off, headed toward the clubhouse.

Jaime and I had both already turned our score cards and bags over to our caddies for the day—I'd also slyly snuck mine a couple folded up hundred-dollar bills as a tip—and had been hanging around and waiting for Jason and Edwin to turn theirs over as well.

"It was," Jaime agreed. "It was nice that the weather provided us with a little cloud cover to keep the sun from scorching down on us all day."

"Here's hoping tomorrow's weather cooperates just as much. Or else my play's liable to get worse and then Edwin probably will blow a gasket," I commented. I was mildly intrigued by the thought of how poorly I'd have to play to make the other man reach his breaking point. We'd have to see how much of an experimenting mood I was in tomorrow.

"Hmm. Don't take this the wrong way," Jason said. "But both of your games would probably improve if you focused more on the game and less on eye fucking each other."

I have no idea if Jaime's face showed as much shock as I know I was feeling, because all of my stunned attention was narrowed in on Jason after his comment.

"Wha... Wha... Tha... Wha..."

Huh. So, Jaime could at least get out portions of babbled questions. Good for him. I was knocked speechless, personally.

"Oh, come on," Jason stated. At least he seemed amused and teasing and not disgusted or horrified at what he thought he'd sussed out about Jaime and I. "Were you two trying to be subtle about it? 'Cause you weren't. At all. It was actually kind of hot watching you two watch each other all day. I could practically see the clothes mentally flying. But you might want to fuck it out of your systems before tomorrow. Or I'm liable to get some sort of contact high from all the sexual tension and pheromones flying between you two. Or don't. No skin off my nose, either way."

With that, Jason touched two fingers to his forehead in a teasing salute and made his own ambling way toward the clubhouse.

"Did he... Did he... Was he saying..." Jaime stuttered out, waving a hand at the empty air that Jason had just been occupying.

"Did Jason just guess that we were either fucking or that we should be fucking? Yep. Looks that way," I told him.

I sort of assumed that having someone know, or think they knew, that Jaime and I had fucked would send me directly into panic mode. After all, I'd both grown up with the unwritten rule, the unspoken understanding, that hockey players weren't gay. And they certainly weren't gay with other hockey players. And rival ones, at that. Sleeping with the Enemy was supposed to be a film title, not a life goal.

But if I'd assumed that I was going to freak out because Jason had guessed at our impulsive couple-of-nights-stand, I was wrong. In fact, I felt kind of... okay about it.

"I'm panicking," Jaime gasped. "I'm panicking and I can feel myself panicking. Why aren't you panicking?" he asked. "And why can't I stop saying panicking? Oh, holy frick. I'm panicking that I'm panicking."

"Hey. Babe. Calm down," I told him.

Jaime's glare probably would've incinerated me on the spot if his eyes weren't also twitching and flashing all over the place.

"Did it seem like he was going to hunt down the nearest reporter and sell an exposé about us? Was he pulling out his phone to blast our business all over the internet?" I asked.

Jaime took a couple slow, deep breaths. "Nooo?" he hesitantly answered.

"Exactly. No," I said. "He seemed amused by us, not eager to tell everyone and their uncle that J.J. and Jaime Johnson were desperate to get in each other's pants."

"But… but… What if he…"

"Look. Why don't we talk to him tomorrow and make sure he knows we don't want anyone to know about…"

"Or we could tell him he was wrong?" Jaime asked with a hopeful expression on his face. "Tell him nothing was going on between us?"

I ignored the brief pang that went through me at how quickly Jaime was to start pretending we hadn't fucked each other, even when it was just the two of us.

"Sure. We can do that," I told him. "I'm sure he'll believe us when we tell him that he was seeing things."

That was such a lie. Jason Teague didn't strike me as an idiot. There was no way he was going to buy that Jaime and I weren't fucking when we so clearly were throwing off fucking-each-other vibes. But I sold the lie with as much conviction as I could to make Jaime feel better. His breathing was finally returning to normal and he no longer looked like he was about to keel over.

"Okay. Good."

"Good." We stood looking at each other. I finally broke the strange silence by asking, "So… what now? It's a little early to just head back to the hotel room."

I was hoping that Jaime would fall back on his natural inclination to always disagree with me. I couldn't find any fault with us going back to his hotel room already and getting the fucking filled night started.

"We could go get dinner?" Jaime asked in a sweet, shy voice. It was fucking adorable.

"Yeah. I suppose we should eat," I allowed. We probably should get some sustenance before we burned up a zillion calories being sweaty and rolling around in bed—or elsewhere in the hotel room—all night.

"I... uh... don't really feel like eating in the clubhouse," Jaime said. "You want to order up room service or find someone nearby to go to?"

Hmmm. Room service was a nice idea. Food and the chance to get Jaime naked around some food was a hot thought. But he'd just barely gotten over his freak out about Jason sort of guessing about what we were doing, I didn't need some nosy room service person seeing us together and saying something or giving some sort of look to send Jaime back into a panic-spiral.

So, I answered, "It's not too late yet, we can find somewhere nearby to eat."

"Okay. Maybe somewhere that makes a good steak, this time," Jaime said. "No seafood places. I don't really care for seafood."

"Then why the hell did we go to a sushi place last night? A place you picked out," I felt the need to add as I turned to follow Jaime off the golf course.

Jaime's grunt wasn't much of an answer. But then he said, "We can talk about it over dinner." And then surprising the fuck out of me, he commented, "Just make sure you don't stuff yourself during dinner. Because I fully intend on taking my turn to stuff you after dinner."

With promises like that, who the hell cared what the fuck we had for dinner?

"Oooh. Those are some big words, Mr. Johnson. Big words. I guess we'll have to wait and see if you can deliver."

"I guess we will," Jaime replied.

Chapter Nine
Jaime

Why had I boasted about how I was going to stuff J.J. tonight after dinner? What had possessed me to spew those words? Big words, indeed. And now it was time for me to live up to them.

Except I had supreme doubts that I'd be able to.

I wasn't a complete novice to topping. When I'd had anal intercourse in the past, I was almost exclusively expected to top by my partners. But that didn't mean that I had scads of experience. Because I didn't.

During the off-season, when I went back to Illinois to visit my parents, I'd go once or twice a week to hit up a gay bar and to find someone to blow off some steam with for a little while. But those were usually limited to fast hand jobs or blow jobs. Even though the odds of being recognized and outed against my will seemed low, I was too cognizant that they weren't nonexistent to feel comfortable spending too much time with a random stranger. Like the kind of time it would require to go back to his place or some other neutral location to engage in full anal intercourse. I'd chanced it a few times here and there with guys I'd felt particularly drawn to but it hadn't been a regular occurrence. And not one that I'd done all that recently.

But now I was going to have to put my money where my mouth was and try to top J.J. as well as, or better than, he'd topped me last night.

And that was a fricking high bar he'd set.

Holy frijole, the man was good at fucking. I guess all that confidence and attitude he carried in spades really did pay off. In the bedroom at least. From the way he'd known to ease me into taking his dick, to the way he'd nailed my prostate just right and at the perfect tempo—not too fast, not too slow—to get me to where I needed to go to climax…

There was no way I was going to win the Who's the Better Top contest between J.J. and I. Not that it was a contest…

But it kind of was. Come on. Of course, it was.

I was going to fail as a top and J.J. Johnson was never going to let me live it down that I wasn't as good at fucking as he was.

"And this just officially turned into the worst pep talk in the history of all pep talks," I told my blurry-looking reflection in the steamed-up hotel bathroom mirror. "Goodness knows, you've been on the receiving end of enough pep talks over your fifteen years of playing hockey. Surely, you can draw upon some of those to find something to pep yourself up." I glanced down the length of my naked body and grimaced at my flaccid dick. My confidence wasn't the only thing that needed some pepping up.

"Are we doing this or what?" came J.J.'s impatient voice through the bathroom door. "You'd better not be backing out of taking your turn. You got to bottom last night, it's my turn tonight. I even gave you the time to yourself in the bathroom that you'd asked for so that you could get yourself ready. Although, since I'm the one who needs the prepping this time around, I'm not sure what the fuck you needed all that time in that bathroom for."

I looked back down at my dick in confusion and amazement. Was J.J.'s annoyance actually… getting me hard? What the heck? It was.

I emerged from the bathroom as J.J. petulantly whined my name. "Jaiiimmmeee…" And, just like that, I was fully hard.

Huh. I wasn't aware that aggravation kink was a thing, but I seemed to have it in regards to J.J. Johnson.

God, the sight of him spread out naked on the hotel room bed was the stuff of about half of the fantasies I had about him. The other half involved a lot more clothes and a lot more punching and shoving than I assumed was about to happen tonight.

I have no idea what came over me, but I stalked over to the side of the bed, grabbed onto his shoulder, and flipped him over, saying, "If you're going to act like a whiny brat, I'm gonna have to spank you."

It was muffled by the pillow, but I could easily hear J.J. happily reply, "I'm good with that. Bring it."

Leaning over him, I whispered in his ear, "Or maybe I'll put you in a time out until you learn to be a good little boy."

"I don't know what the fuck is going on right now," J.J. said. Frankly, neither did I. "But I like it. Good game strategy. Keep it up."

I delivered a sharp smack to J.J. left butt cheek and told him, "That doesn't sound like what a good boy would say. You should stop talking or you're going to get another."

"See, that sounds kind of contradicting there, babe. Why would I want to stop talking if that's going to stop the slaps to my ass?"

"So, you want to be spanked, is that it?"

"Fuck, Jaime. Yes. How much clearer do I need to be?"

"I'm going to spank you so hard your ass will be red for days."

J.J. pulled the pillow out from underneath his head and shoved it under his hips, raising his firm, round ass in the air. He gave me a wink and said, "I am more than okay with that." Then he rested his head back down and stretched his arms out so that he could curl his hands around the edges of the mattress.

Mmm. The thought of getting to deliver a smack to that gorgeous behind for every shove on the ice, every cocky smirk at the camera, every conceited, boasting comment to a reporter, every attention-grabbing, grandstanding moment where J.J. Johnson acted like the universe's gift to hockey... His ass really was going to be red for days.

That was a thought that prompted me to ask, "Do you want some sort of safe word? Just in case I get carried away?"

J.J. peeked at me over the rounded muscle of his shoulder. His silky dark hair tumbled over his forehead and almost obscured his single raised brow. "How about if I want you to stop, I just tell you to stop?" J.J. said. "Or I'll just reach over and punch you in the head or something."

I never envisioned being in bed with someone where the threat of violence didn't faze me in the least and was, almost, sort of expected.

"Alright," I told him. "You say 'stop' and I'll stop."

"Duh," J.J. muttered as he resettled into position. "Now get on with it. My ass isn't going to spank itself."

That second smack to his butt was just as thrilling as the first had been. And the mottled pink splotch left behind, blooming across his skin, was fantastic. I wanted every square inch of J.J.'s ass to be that bright, raspberry-red.

"You can go a little harder than those little love taps, babe," J.J. said, wiggling his butt at me. "I'm not gonna break. I can take it."

"Stop. Being. A. Brat. And. Giving. Me. Orders," I said, delivering a stinging blow to his left cheek and then his right, alternating between the two with each of my panted words.

"Better. Keep going," J.J. said, his own words starting to come out in little gasps.

Because it seemed to be what we both wanted, I let the blows rain down and across his ass. One right after the other. With the barest pause between each one, only long enough for my brain to calculate and decide upon where it wanted my hand to land next.

"Are you ready to be a good boy yet?" I asked him. J.J.'s butt was an angry-looking red that had to be hurting him. My hand was definitely stinging and burning from its repeated sharp impacts to his ass.

J.J.'s knuckles were white from gripping the edge of the mattress so hard and his biceps were taught and bulging with how much he'd tensed up, but he still managed to sound impudent as he choked out, "Make. Me."

Was it because it now resembled a bright, juicy cherry? Or because I wanted to convince him of how serious I was about teaching him a lesson? I'm not sure. But something drove me to place my lips against the spank-reddened, hot surface of his butt and sink my teeth into the firm flesh.

"Oh. Ow. Fuck. Stop. Stop," J.J. cried. Which caused me to immediately remove my teeth from his butt cheek and sink back down until I was, once more, kneeling next to him. My own bare butt resting on my heels.

"Oh my God. I'm so sorry. I'm so—"

"Stop. Fuck. I need you to fuck me. Now. Or else I'm going to blow and I'm going to be done before you even get your dick in me." Wait. What? "Now, babe. Fuck me now. Please," J.J. begged.

Relieved that he wasn't mad at me for spontaneously biting him, I quickly scrambled to grab the bottle of lube and a condom packet that J.J. had set out on the nightstand next to the bed. He must've done that while I was dithering in the bathroom.

Before I got my fingers all gloopy with the lube, I ripped open the condom packet and rolled the condom down my flushed and aching dick. Ungh. It was so engorged and ready to burst that it was almost as red as J.J.'s ass. The lube was next and J.J. let out a whimpering hiss of breath as I drizzled the viscous liquid down the crease of his ass.

"I'm not gonna need as much prep as you did," J.J. said as I started rubbing the lube in and around his opening. "And my ass hurts so much, I'm not even going to notice it if you go in a little rough."

"Oh, God, J. I'm sorry," I started to apologize.

I'd been completely winging it with the spanking thing. It wasn't something I'd ever done with a partner before. And I certainly hadn't set out to cause him any physical pain. Kind of an ironic thought to be thinking in regards to spanking somebody, but there it was. Although, there was also a trickle of annoyance threading through my feelings of remorse. He'd told me he'd tell me to stop if I was going too far. But he hadn't done that and *now* he was complaining about it?

J.J. turned his head to look at me over his shoulder. "Don't apologize," he said. "It's a good kind of hurt. I'm good. Be even better if you got that cock of yours in me right the fuck now, though."

Hurting butt or not, I couldn't let that comment go without another stinging smack to the meaty roundness of J.J. ass.

"Dude," J.J. choked out with a chuckle, shaking his head from where it hung between his shoulders. "That wasn't an invitation to do it again. Not right now."

"No. That was you opening your smart mouth and continuing to be the naughty boy you are." I lined the head of my latex-sheathed dick at his opening and nudged in the smallest amount, mostly to get his attention and to let J.J. know I was about to breach him. "But you can make it up to me," I told him. "By being a good boy and taking my dick."

I could see J.J. settling himself more comfortably and stably on his hands and knees on the mattress. And, on his next exhale, I pushed in until the entire head of my cock was snugly nestled inside of his tight, hot ass.

"Give it to me, Loverboy. You know you want to."

What was it going to take to shut up J.J. Johnson? To reduce him to nothing but wordless sounds and moans?

"Would you. Shut. Up?" I asked as I shoved my cock the rest of the way inside him, bottoming out. And, oh God, it was a tight, hot squeeze of perfection around my hard cock.

"Make me," J.J. moaned, echoing his order—request?— from earlier.

A small part of me was tempted to take the time to pull out of him and find something I could shove into his mouth as an ad hoc gag but the rest of me was too firmly enthralled with the tight grip J.J.'s channel had around my dick. So, I decided to shut him up the best way I could. By fucking him as hard as I could until all he could do was moan and whimper.

I pressed down on J.J.'s back hard enough that he collapsed forward, his chest and face now resting on the mattress. Then I grabbed hold of his hips as I drew my cock most of the way out of him and then slammed back in hard.

"Urghnpf," J.J. groaned with what sounded like approval. "Oh, yeah, babe. Like that."

My fingers dug into his muscular flesh with enough force that I had the feeling that he'd be wearing marks on his body, in the shapes of my fingertips, for at least a day. Maybe he'd even still have them by the time it came for the two of us to leave here.

Now there was a thought that sent a renewed surge of lust through my balls. Not like I needed another. Not with how good J.J.'s ass felt around my dick. But the thought that there'd be no way for J.J. to immediately forget what we'd done—forget me—as soon as he strolled out the hotel doors, awoke some primeval part of my psyche to find as many parts of his body to leave little imprints of myself on.

My eyes tracked over J.J.'s body as I continued to pound into him, shoving and jouncing his body so hard that, even with my firm grip on him, he was starting to slip and lurch forward on the bed. The redness of the surface of his butt, from the spanking I'd given him, was bound to fade to a softer pink before dissipating altogether. The reddish abrasion from where I'd nipped at his tender ass might last a little longer, although I hadn't bitten him that hard. I was happy with the marks I was currently bruising into his hips and flanks with my hands. But I wanted more. I wanted J.J. to see me all over him every time he looked in a mirror for at least a week.

I wrapped an arm around J.J.'s ripped abs and hauled him backward, shifting my own body back until my ass was resting on my heels and the tops of J.J.'s thighs were pressed along the length of mine and his groin and hips were cradled in my lap.

"Jesus Christ, Jaime," J.J. gasped out. "Whatever workout routine your trainers have got you on, tell 'em to keep you on it. I didn't realize you were so strong. Holy fuck." And then he started laughing.

Granted, it was a snorting, snuffling, hysterical, disbelieving sort of laughter. But the man was still laughing while I was fucking him.

And that was something I wasn't going to tolerate.

I hammered into his ass with short, fast strokes and hauled his torso up closer to mine so that I could get my mouth on the back of his shoulder. Then I sank my teeth into his skin along the ridge of J.J.'s shoulder blade. I wasn't trying to break any skin, but I was definitely digging in and bruising that delicate, soft, smooth skin.

There. That ought to leave a nice, long-lasting mark on J.J.'s body. And it had the added benefit of cutting off his laughter, mid-chortle, as J.J. let out a surprised, rough bark of noise that quickly morphed into a moan.

"Can you get a hand on your dick?" I asked him. I really needed J.J. to be close to coming because goodness knew I was teetering on the brink of it myself. Manhandling him and aggressively fucking him the way that I was had gotten my balls drawn up and tight, ready to burst, in a surprisingly short amount of time.

J.J. groaned out a noise that I took as an affirmative, so I commanded him, "Do it. Get yourself off." We were pressed tightly together from shoulder to knee and my chest was plastered to his back, so I felt it when J.J.'s whole body shuddered with pleasure as he, presumably, did what I told him and got his hand on cock. "Now."

The whimpers and gasped cries he made were music to my ears. And the way his channel spasmed and clamped down around my aching dick was pure ecstasy.

Knowing that he'd come, I let my own orgasm take control. Not that I was very positive that I would've been able to stop it, even if I'd wanted to. I slammed into J.J.'s ass a few more times. Then my cock pulsed inside of him as my cum spurted out of me and into the condom.

Taking advantage of the fact that my grip on him had loosened while I was orgasming and was trembling too hard from the pleasurable after-shocks to keep him upright anymore, J.J. toppled forward bonelessly onto the mattress.

Probably directly onto the mess of his own cum, not that he seemed to care.

I was lightheaded from the physical exertion of fucking J.J. as hard as I had, having held back my orgasm for as long as I'd managed, and from how strongly I'd come. That didn't stop me from getting annoyed with J.J. when he started laughing again.

"What the frick is so funny?" I asked, certain he could hear the scowl in my voice.

"You," he replied, continuing to laugh. "What the fuck was that?"

"I don't know what you're talking about."

J.J. gracelessly flopped himself over, no doubt now smearing whatever bits of his cum that hadn't already soaked into the bedding across more of himself. His eyes tracked all over the front of my body, from the tips of my sweaty and sex-rumpled hair, down across my flushed face and chest, down to where I had my hands propped on my hips in annoyance, and landing on my softening, condom-covered dick. When J.J. arched a brow at me, I hastily removed the floppy, cum-filled, lube-coated latex from my dick, tied it off, and gently deposited it on my discarded bath towel sitting on the floor for me to deal with in a little while. He was already laughing at me, I didn't need to look any more ridiculous than I probably already did.

"I don't know where the hell you've been hiding that Jaime Johnson all this time," J.J. said. "But bring him on all the fucking time, babe. Although…" J.J. paused to scratch at a bit of drying cum on his stomach. "I know we said we'd flip a coin or something to decide who got to bottom next, now that we've each had a turn. But I think I might need to pass on bottoming again next time. It just might kill me... or at least make me unable to move properly... taking your dick again any time soon."

J.J. grinned at me like the possibility of a death by dick was the greatest thing he'd ever thought of. The dark stubble covering his jaw and surrounding his smirky mouth made his teeth look stupidly white and gleaming.

I felt an answering smile tugging at the corner of my lips. The fact that I apparently had managed to wreck J.J. Johnson with my dick, and that he was happy about it, was kind of a cause for smiling.

And it's not as though giving J.J. a break and bottoming for him when—if—we had sex again was any sort of hardship.

"Oh. Um. Yeah. Okay," I mumbled, feeling slightly awkward now that the haze of lust was clearing.

"C'mon, babe," J.J. said, flicking a smack to my flank with the back of his hand. "Let's clean up the righteous-level of mess we just made and we can commence with the non-cuddling cuddling."

"Wha...?" What the hell was non-cuddling cuddling?

"You'll see. C'mon." J.J. flung himself off the bed, taking the sheet he'd been lying on with him because it had glued itself to his back with his cum. He peeled it off of himself with a grimace, wadded it into a crumpled lump with any other bits of bedding that looked as if it might've gotten any lube or cum on it, and threw it all into a haphazard pile in the far corner of the room. "Did you happen to notice if there was any extra bedding in the closet?" he asked. "'Cause I think we're going to need it. This stuff is *wrecked*," he gleefully declared.

"Maybe? I can look," I offered.

"You do that. I'm going to get all this cum off me before it's permanently stuck on," J.J. said. "After that, the bathroom's all yours. And then it's time for the non-cuddling cuddles."

"Yeah. Okay."

Chapter Ten

J.J.

Was it some sort of conspiracy? A special training course that all hotel purchasing employees need to go through for their employment? I'm not sure what it was but I've yet to stay in a hotel where the spare blankets provided in the rooms were actually big enough for the size of bed they were supposed to be blanketing when called into service. Or rather... they'd be big enough to cover the very top of the mattress but nothing else. And only as long as there were no people attempting to lay underneath and be covered up by the blanket. Because once you added a person, or two in this particular instance, the blanket fell far short of its blanketing duties.

The light gray blanket Jaime had located, tucked on the top shelf of the closet, was just barely wide enough to cover my and Jaime's bodies if we happened to be lying very, very close to each other on the bed. If either one of us moved as much as an inch away from the other, somebody's ass was going to be hanging out in the AC-cooled air.

Good thing I had no intention of allowing any space between our naked bodies.

"So, what exactly makes this non-cuddling cuddling?" Jaime asked. "Like that's even a thing." His voice rumbled beneath my head, which was nuzzled against his firm and freckled pecs. "This just seems like regular cuddling to me."

Pretty much the entirety of my life as a sexually active gay dude had consisted of hookups. Not that I'd really known to call them that when I was in high school. But throughout high school, and college, and, definitely, once I'd been drafted and started playing pro hockey—first in the AHL for a year and a bit and then moving up to the NHL—I'd never wanted to get emotionally attached to someone enough to consider them a "boyfriend" or "partner" or what have you. Being a closeted pro athlete didn't really lend itself to being in a serious, emotions-attached kind of relationship.

But that didn't negate the fact that after being naked and physically intimate with someone, I felt an insatiable urge to continue being physically close with them. Especially when I was the one who'd done the bottoming. Not to be emotionally schmoopy with them or anything. But just to continue whatever high I was riding from having an orgasm with another person and to feel some sort of connection to the person I'd just swapped bodily fluids with. To me, it was weird to go from having a dude's dick inside me and to then ceasing bodily contact once the lust and cum cooled off.

So, unless I was participating in a particularly fast and sneaky bathroom hit-it-and-quit-it encounter, I'd started instituting a period of post-fucking that I'd coined non-cuddling cuddling with the guys I hooked up with. Whether it lasted five or ten minutes or a couple hours, that time spent being in close physical contact with whatever guy I'd just fucked satisfied some need inside me.

I wasn't about to open myself up to Jaime Johnson more than I already had and expose what might be a possible vulnerable spot, but I supposed he did deserve some sort of explanation. Or at least a rationale behind why I planned to spend the next however long firmly plastered to his naked body.

"Ah. But you see…" I said. "Cuddling by its very definition involves using physical touch and closeness to convey affection and love. That's not at all what we're doing. Just because we fucked doesn't mean I'm feeling affectionate and/or loving to you."

"Ew. Gross. No," Jaime agreed.

"So, while it may *seem* like we're cuddling… we're not. We're just being physically close to each other because being pressed up against another naked dude is fucking awesome and we'll be conveniently situated for when we're ready to go again."

"So… non-cuddling cuddling."

"Exactly."

"We didn't do this last night, though," he pointed out. Damn him.

"No. We didn't. Because you acted like a dick and called me a selfish asshole."

"I didn't call you—"

"You might not have called me an asshole," I allowed. "But you did call me selfish. Which is pretty much the same thing. So, no, I wasn't in the mood for non-cuddling cuddling last night. I was mad at you." I sighed and drew an invisible doodled swirl on Jaime's pec with the tip of my finger. "And... even though we'd had sex, I was worried you'd change your mind and kick me out of your room," I admitted.

"I wouldn't have actually... Even though you drive me crazy... You have nowhere else... I'm not going to kick you out," Jaime finally settled on saying. "I said we could share the room and I meant it. I'm not going to change my mind or back out on that."

I didn't really want to start up another fight with the guy. Not when I was wrapped snuggly in his warm, strong arms and draped across his equally warm and strong body. But I just couldn't seem to help the cynically skeptical "Really? You sure about that?" that came out of my mouth.

Thankfully, Jaime must not have wanted to lapse into another verbal fight with me either. Instead of snapping back with an angry retort, he let the subject drop, just offering a non-committal hum. And then he cooperated beautifully with my desire to be snuggled up to him by using the arm he had wrapped around me to press me more firmly against him and slowly stroking his other hand over my left arm.

"Hmm. Cubes for Cube, I assume?" Jaime asked as his fingers began tracing the lines of the series of interlocking cube shapes I had tattooed around my left bicep.

Assuming he was looking as well as touching, I flexed that muscle as I confirmed, "Yep. Got it in college when it became apparent that my high school nickname was going to stick with me." I rolled off Jaime so that I could hold up my right hand, which had been tucked between my body and his, and show him my other tattoo. A simple black outline of a bucket resting on the lower segment of my middle finger. "This one I also got in college. And it was because I always wanted to have my fuck-it bucket handy." Jaime made some sort of noise. I wasn't sure if it was an aborted laugh or a non-verbal request for more info. But, either way, I decided to explain further. "It's where I mentally consign anything and everything I don't give a fuck about. Bad practices, shitty teammates, bad games, shit comments by the press… whatever. It all goes in the bucket and I move the fuck on."

"Does that… does that work?" Jaime asked.

"Eh. Sometimes," I answered. "It is fun to flash at particularly annoying teammates, opponents, and reporters. Not that my coaches or the team's PR people are very happy with me when I do it. But… boom." I waved my right hand in the air as if I was conjuring some magic. "That also goes right into the bucket."

This time I definitely got a laugh out of him.

Jaime sighed as he said, "I'm not sure if I'd ever get a tattoo. I've thought about it but…"

"Eh. You get drunk enough some time and you'll wind up with one."

"That sounds like a horrible plan," Jaime commented.

"Nah. Drunken tattoos are the best tattoos," I told him.

That was about enough talking for now. I wanted to get back to the non-cuddling cuddling.

I flung myself back on top of Jaime's naked body, snugged the blanket back around us so that we were encased in a comfy cocoon of warmth, touch, and man-smell, and resettled my head on his chest. The steady thump of his heartbeat under my cheek was a peaceful lullaby ready to send me drifting toward Pleasant Dreamland.

Jaime secured his arms around me once more, one angling along the length of my back with his warm hand naturally falling on the curve of my hip—the skin there a little tender and sensitive from the firm treatment it'd gotten from Jaime's hands earlier—and the other wrapped around my shoulders.

I was getting all set to take a short power nap before pouncing on Jaime again and I assumed Jaime was going to do the same. But before I was able to drift off to sleep, Jaime quietly asked, "J… What are we doing here?"

"Non-cuddling cuddling," I mumbled. "Told you that."

"Not… Yeah, I know that. That's not what I was asking. What… What are we doing? We can't stand each other. We play for rival teams. Having sex with each other is a really horrible idea. So, why are we doing it? Are we just supposed to spend a couple days fooling around with each other and then forget all about it and pretend it never happened when we see each other again?"

I tilted my head back. Not that I could see anything much besides the underside of his chin when I did so. And I told him, "Uh. Yeah? I didn't think I'd need to explicitly lay out the 'What Happens in Mesquite, Stays in Mesquite' nature of us fucking for the couple days we're here. Apparently, I did."

"Isn't that 'What Happens in Vegas'...?"

"Ne-vaada, Nuh-vahda," I replied. "We're close enough to Vegas and I'm pretty sure the whole state's covered. So, to answer your question... Yes. We're going to spend the rest of tonight... after a restorative nap... fucking. And any spare time we find ourselves alone and somewhere secluded... more fucking. And then some more fucking on top of that. Then, after the trophies are handed out, the giant novelty check is handed over to the charity that brought us here to Mesquite, the hotel kicks our asses all out, and we depart for the airport and our respective planes taking us to... wherever... Yes. We forget about it and pretend it never happened so we can go back to being the awesome nemeses we are."

"Oh. Um. Okay. Makes sense, I guess."

I had to be imagining the underlying hint of disappointment in Jaime's voice, right? Right. There's no way he could be feeling something other than relief that we'd both get to indulge in a couple days of glorious, string-free, non-stop sexing, right? Of course not.

"Well. Good napping then," Jaime said.

"Yeah. Night, babe."

"Goodnight, J."

"Don't think I'm going to let you sleep for too long, though," I reminded him. "There's plenty of night left and I want another turn with your ass. Or you could blow me this time around."

"Go to sleep, J.J."

"I'm serious," I told him, flicking one of his pale pink nipples.

"Yeesh," Jaime hissed. "I get it. No need to be such a brat about it."

"You like me bratty," I teased him. Good thing, too, as that was pretty much my factory default setting.

"Not when your butt can't take any more spanking."

"Pfffthft. You obviously aren't aware that my superior ass has magical restorative properties. You want to deliver another spanking? I can handle it."

Jaime shoved my head back down until it was once more resting directly over his heart.

"Go to sleep, J."

"Y'alright. Night, Jaime."

Chapter Eleven
Jaime

I knew I really shouldn't, but I found my hand slowly reaching out and grabbing yet another barbeque-slathered chicken wing from the platter conveniently located in the middle of the table J.J., Jason Teague, and I were sitting at in the course clubhouse. The plate had been a towering mound of hot, deep fried, saucy goodness when the waitress had set it down on our table after J.J. had ordered it. But ten minutes and three full-grown men later, there were just a handful of sticky, messy wings left waiting to meet the same fate as their predecessors.

"Look at those poor schlubs," J.J. commented, waving his bottle of beer at the large tv the tournament organizers had set up so the participants who hadn't made the final round could watch the presentation of the tournament trophy to the foursome that had battled it out and scored the lowest over the three days of the tournament. And, more importantly, the handing over of the novelty check to the representative present from K9s for Warriors in the amount of how much the tournament had raised for that charity.

"I don't know. They look pretty happy that they won," Jason commented in regards to the two celebrities—an Instagram fitness model and influencer and a former Miss America—and their non-celebrity partners that had wound up winning the tournament.

J.J. made a rude, scoffing noise. "Pfffth. They would. They seem the sort." Whatever that meant.

"You know… We could've been up there getting a trophy… or at least we would've had a better chance at getting it… if *someone* at this table hadn't decided to intentionally play like poo yesterday, ensuring that we wouldn't make the cut for today's final round." I was still annoyed that J.J. had purposely played poorly. It wasn't at all good sportsmanlike and I couldn't shake the feeling that J.J. had swindled Jason and Edwin—especially Edwin—from getting their money's worth out of this tournament.

J.J. turned wide, mock-innocent eyes toward me. "I have *no* idea what you're talking about."

Gee. I wonder where Jason and I would've gotten the idea that J.J. was throwing his golf game. Was it when he'd accidentally, on purpose kicked his own ball off the tee and incurred a penalty stroke by replacing it on the tee instead of playing it from where it'd fallen? Or when J.J. scoffed when we politely reminded him that a putter probably wasn't the best club to use when driving down the fairway? Or when he lined up his putt toward the hole and then turned forty-five degrees and blatantly hit it away from the hole?

Granted J.J. hadn't played like this on each of the eighteen holes yesterday—Edwin, J.J.'s non-celebrity partner, would've, for sure, murdered him right there on the golf course if he had. But he'd clearly intentionally played poorly on enough of them to drop our foursome's score for the second day of play far enough that we'd wound up sixth for the tournament. A half-dozen strokes behind the top two teams that had gotten to move onto the final round this morning.

Jason apparently decided to give J.J.'s statement the indubitable disbelief it deserved. "Oh, you noticed that too? I thought maybe it was just me. But you know J.J. better than I do. If you also think he was tanking his game on purpose…"

I rolled my eyes and said, "Uh. Yeah. Clearly."

Since his act had obviously not fooled either Jason or myself, J.J. stopped proclaiming his innocence. Not that his innocent act had been any more convincing than his I-completely-forgot-how-to-play-golf-overnight act had been. "You should both be thanking me for getting us out of an additional day of having to play golf," J.J. stated, pointing at Jason and me and then giving us an expectant look as if he seriously expected us to proffer our gratitude.

"I know you two were here to raise funds for charity, or for PR purposes, or whatever," Jason said.

"I also just like playing golf," I told him.

"But I actually paid a decent amount of money for the privilege of playing golf this weekend," Jason continued. "And I wouldn't have minded getting more bang for my buck by making the finals and getting that additional day of golf. Plus, with even as tacky and fake-silver-plated as that trophy looks, I could've had plenty of fun showing it off to the other attorneys at my firm and letting them choke on their envy every time they spotted it in my office."

Hearing that, J.J. did look momentarily guilty. But then he, literally and figuratively, shrugged the emotion off and told Jason, "Meh. I'll make it up to you. Give me your address and Jaime and I will send you some autographed swag and I'll make sure you get comped VIP tickets for the next time the Snappers are in Phoenix."

Jason took a contemplative sip of his mojito and replied, "Yeah. Alright. There was no guarantee we would've made the finals or won, even if you hadn't intentionally tanked us… so a bunch of free hockey stuff sounds like it'll soothe whatever disappointment I've got from not winning a trophy this weekend."

"Good. And I promise not to be a weird stalker-dude just because you're giving me your address," J.J. promised with a cheeky grin before he drained the last of his beer.

"Wouldn't care if you did," Jason told him. "I'm sure there'd be worse things in life than to have a pro hockey player be obsessed with you." Jason flagged down our waitress and waved his empty glass at her, signaling that he'd like another—his third or fourth for the afternoon. Then he pointed his empty glass at the tv and said, "Now, that guy…

That guy looks like a miserable schlub. He doesn't look at all happy to be part of today's festivities."

J.J. and I both turned our attention back toward the large tv screen and I immediately zeroed in on the person that Jason must've been indicating. Behind a middle-aged couple, whose appearance screamed moneyed and smug about it, stood a guy in perhaps his early twenties. I didn't recognize him as somebody who fell into the category of somebody I *should* recognize, but the banner across the screen read "Houston Family Presents Check to K9 for Warriors Organization". So, presumably he was a member of the Houston family, who owned the large golf ball manufacturing company that was the main underwriters behind the charity tournament weekend.

And the poor guy did look incredibly miserable. Staring off blankly into space, his face might have been carefully neutral but his slumped shoulders, the way his body wag angled away from the other people clustered around the giant, person-sized novelty check, and the periodic twitch of his legs, like he was holding himself from sprinting away as fast as he could, all radiated his unhappiness.

"Yeah, he definitely looks like he'd rather be anywhere else but here," J.J. agreed. "Wonder what his story is."

"Speaking of stories… What's up with you two?" Jason asked.

He glanced between J.J. and I, waggling his brows with a look of curiosity stamped across his face. His liquor intake must've turned off his brain's center for Don't Ask About the Thing That's Blatantly Right in Front of Your Face.

From the comment Jason had made after our first round of golf about J.J. and I spending way too much time eye fucking each other, I'd known that Jason had figured out that there was something going on between J.J. and I.

I know I had freaked out about that. Just a little bit. An additional day spent in Jason's company, as we completed our second round of golf, had assuaged that panic. For the most part. Jason really did seem trustworthy and, as a lawyer, I figured he knew how to keep private things private. So, I was uncomfortably okay with Jason knowing J.J. and I were involved with each other.

But he wasn't supposed to outright ask us about it! That's not the sort of thing you just up and ask virtual strangers!

And it was something I didn't want to talk about. Or even think about.

Especially as, what J.J. and I were doing was just a brief moment of stupidity that we'd both move on from after this long weekend was over.

Jason's question had made my mind turn into a frozen, slushy mush and I sat unmoving in my seat, completely befuddled.

Thankfully, J.J. was a bit more with it than I was and he told Jason, "I have no idea what you're talking about."

I'd certainly noticed J.J.'s large personality before. His brashness. His ego. His incorrect, persistent insistence that I often high sticked opposing players during games. But this weekend, spending time with him, I was also learning that J.J.

Johnson had absolutely no compunction about lying. He was just really, really bad at it.

Jason gave J.J. a skeptical look that flat out stated *Who are you kidding?* He opened his mouth to, undoubtedly, express his incredulity and repeat his question. But J.J. just held steady eye contact with Jason and slowly and emphatically restated, "I. Don't. Know. What. You're. Talking. About."

A quirk of the corner of his mouth, a tip of his head, and Jason tacitly acknowledged that he would let the question go and changed the subject. Well. Sort of.

"So, you two are headed for home tomorrow?"

"Yeah," I managed to croak out. "HUhhmm." I cleared my throat and said, "Well, actually, I'm going to go visit my parents for a couple weeks in Illinois. And then I'll be heading back to Minneapolis."

Jason took a swallow of his newly delivered mojito refill and asked, "And you, J.J.? Are you going to go visit your folks this off-season?"

J.J.'s smile was a perfunctory movement of his lips. It contained absolutely no happiness, or pleasure, or... any other emotion usually associated with a smile. "Nah. I don't see my folks that often," he said. "We're not all that close."

Seeming to realize he'd misstepped somehow, Jason gave a weak laugh and attempted to joke, "Well. At least you guys get the next couple months off before you have to head into work. I'm expected back in my office bright and early tomorrow morning. My flight from Vegas to Phoenix leaves tonight." Jason glanced at his drink glass. "Actually, I should probably lay off these things. I still have to throw my stuff in my luggage and get myself to the airport in a couple hours."

The weekend spent golfing had been enjoyable, of course. I did find the sport of golf to be both challenging and relaxing. But the other nice thing that had come out of my appearance at this charity tournament had been meeting my non-celebrity partner.

Jason Teague seemed like a cool guy. And he hadn't freaked out or tried to use his discovery of my sexuality against me to garner any favors. He'd just accepted it as being part of who I was and moved on. Even J.J.'s offer to get him VIP hockey tickets was done because he liked the guy, not because Jason had pressured J.J. into anything.

The end of almost a year's-worth of abstinence with anything other than my own hand or the dildo I had stashed in the bottom of the cabinet under my bathroom sink, plus getting to work out some of my frustration and annoyance with J.J. Johnson through some furious, sweaty sex had also been pretty nice.

But I really was going to be sorry to say goodbye to Jason. I'd have to make sure to get his contact info from him too, so I could also keep in touch with him. I think he'd make a pretty good friend. And I didn't really have many of those, outside of my teammates.

The broadcast of the award ceremony over, the crowd gathered in the clubhouse started dissipating. J.J. and I swapped our contact information with Jason, then we all vacated our table so the staff could start cleaning up. Jason meandered out of the clubhouse, in a mostly straight line, off to catch a shuttle to the hotel he was staying in—a different one than J.J. and I were in—so he could pack up and head to the airport to catch his flight home. And J.J. and I...

Well. We strolled out of the clubhouse to find our own shuttle back to our hotel so that we could enjoy one last night together. And based on the heated glance J.J. and I gave each other, we seemed pretty much in accord that any sleeping could wait until morning, when we were on our separate planes headed for separate locations. If the window of opportunity, proximity, and happenstance for J.J. and I to be hooking up was drawing to a close, then we were going to try to cram in as much filthy, frantic, sure-to-be-regretted sex as we could while we could.

And come the morning, as we'd discussed, we'd forget all about this ill-advised and foolish, lust-crazed weekend and J.J. and I would go back to our normal status quo of being adversaries.

Chapter Twelve
J.J.

Kansas City was so boring.

Okay. So, it actually wasn't all that bad. I've certainly been to worse places. I mean, fuck, I grew up in rural, dullsville Iowa. I'd long since mastered the art of finding my own fun no matter what boring as hell location I was stuck in.

And there were plenty of things to do in Kansas City. It was a city of over half a million people. At least the part over on this side of the river, in Missouri. The Kansas City in the actual state of Kansas added another hundred and fifty or so thousand people. Combined, the two identically named cities, separated by a river and a state line, had plenty of bars, restaurants, and theaters, and all sorts of indoor and outdoor activities. And since it was July, outdoor activities were actually an option. It was a little hot and humid out, but that normally wouldn't stop me from enjoying a night out on the town.

Hell, I could spend the whole day at the zoo, gawking at the critters behind the glass enclosures if I wanted to. Get a taste of being a spectator and watching the antics of wild creatures instead of being one of the observed for a change. Well... not right now. It was too late in the day for that. I'm sure the zoo closed sometime in the afternoon so the zookeepers could go home and do whatever zookeepers do when they're not shoveling up elephant poop.

So, there were plenty of things I could be doing. Plenty. If I wanted to.

Actually, I could hear the sounds of a concert going on by the Crown Center, just a few blocks away from my apartment. And, most of the time, when there was a concert going on, there'd also be food trucks loaded with some of the best barbeque I've ever shoved in my mouth. And other entertainers and pop-up shops selling unique stuff that you didn't know you needed until you saw it for sale. So, a small stroll in the balmy evening air and I could be surrounded by tons of fun.

But it didn't even matter that there was fun to be had. It didn't change the fact that I was stuck at home with nothing to do. Because, who wanted to go to a concert by themselves, and I had nobody to go with.

Alright, I admitted with a sigh at my own patheticness. That wasn't true either.

I wasn't the only guy on my team who was still in Kansas City even though it was the off season. Some guys didn't want to or had no reason to head back to wherever it was they'd lived before moving to KC. Other guys had other obligations—in the form of girlfriends, charity work, or families—that kept them here all year-round and not just for the nine months we were contractually obligated to live here so we could train, practice, and play home games.

So, if I'd gone through the roster and made my way down the list, I would've been bound to reach *someone* who was still in town and might've been interested in going to a concert with me. Especially as I wasn't the only person who appreciated food truck dining. But even if I had called everyone I had a phone number for and struck out with all of them, I normally wasn't the type of guy who hesitated at going out and finding new friends—even if they were one-night-only friends—whenever the mood struck me.

And even if I didn't feel like going out alone, for once, there were other things I could do around my condo to keep myself entertained.

I'd, naturally, sprung for the new PS5 when it'd come out and I was currently making my way through one of the Resident Evil games. Normally, blasting through hordes of infected zombies was a fun way to pass a couple of hours. Or I could get my sports groove on conquering opponents on the virtual basketball court. I wasn't a fan of NHL 23, mostly because it was a bit of a mindfuck to see people I actually knew digitized on a tv screen like that and being portrayed as the utmost caricature of themselves. And, also, because they, once again, didn't pick me to include as one of the player choices. A dumb move on their part, in my opinion. I would make the bestest caricature of myself. But at least they hadn't picked Jaime either.

Besides video games, I could also catch up on some of the shows on my DVR that I had set to auto-record but never usually got around to actually watching. Or I could work my way through the recipes I had flagged with post-it notes as wanting to try in the dozen or so cookbooks I'd purchased this year. Or I could scroll through social media. That was always a fun way to kill off a couple hours. Especially when I used one of my burner accounts to playfully harass and jab at my current and former teammates.

Although, I had learned the hard way that informing a dude that his new kid resembled his current team's mascot— the bizarrely hideous California condor—was a good way to get him to not talk to you for several months. I'd had to let him punch me in the face when our teams had met on the ice to get him to forgive me for that online comment oopsie.

But I wasn't doing any of those things because... because... my goddamned head was still stuck on a certain goddamned redheaded freckled guy that I'd spent only a couple of pleasant—*exceedingly* pleasant—days with almost three weeks ago. How had those couple of days managed to edge out and negate all the other unpleasant interactions between the two of us over the past couple years? I don't know. But for some reason, I couldn't get fucking Jaime Johnson evicted from my brain.

I dreamt about him at night. Especially what he looked like naked, how he tasted, and how he felt against my fingers, my mouth, my tongue. But even when I was awake, the sounds he'd made echoed with a delightful symphony in my ears.

And that was completely not counting the way I was bewildered and enthralled with the man he turned out to be when he fucked. How beautifully he'd submitted when I fucked him. Then how he'd become all aggressive and domineering and demanding when he'd fucked me. Who the hell was that Jaime Johnson, where the fuck had he come from, and would it be like that again if he had the opportunity to fuck me again?

I didn't even blame myself for being obsessed.

Some things were just. That. Good.

Weirdly, though, it wasn't only the sex that I missed.

I'd always enjoyed aggravating Jaime Johnson and I wasn't going to deny that aggravating him was even more enjoyable when it was followed up with him punishing me with pleasure. But I'd also enjoyed *not* aggravating him. When we were getting along and engaging in pleasant conversation about hockey, golf, food, tv shows, or anything else that struck our fancy. When we quietly coexisted, side-by-side as we non-cuddled.

I know. Weird, right?

In an attempt to get my mind off the sexy times we'd shared and to try to remind myself of why I didn't actually like the guy, I'd even gone online and downloaded footage of the games we'd played against each other. The moments where we fought over the puck or outright fought with each other, I watched over and over again. I rewatched his interviews. Any little bit of quoted statement or brief mention of Jaime Johnson by the media, I gobbled up. Desperately trying to recapture my previous impression of him as a guy I had nothing in common with, couldn't stand, and would gladly drive over with a Zamboni.

Anything... anything at all... to stop this weird and puzzling craving for the man I'd caught glimpses of during our couple of days and nights together. The guy who was quietly not as stuffy as he seemed, once you got to know him. The Jaime who put up with—and sometimes seemed amused by—my ridiculousness, as long as it had nothing to do with hockey or stretching the rules.

It was tantalizing to wonder if there were even more facets to Jaime that I could discover... if I only had the chance. That had to be why I couldn't seem to be able to make myself get on with the forgetting and moving on portion of the hookup plan. *My* hookup plan.

I was starting to think that I might actually be a little bit in like with Jaime Johnson.

Blurgk.

It was a problem.

One that had the potential to ruin my whole fucking summer if I couldn't figure out a way to eliminate it. Eliminating Jaime Johnson would probably do it, but murder wasn't really part of my wheelhouse. So, the solution would have to be something else.

In theory, sleeping on it could be considered a viable avenue to pursue in the hopes that the correct course of action would come to me. But in reality, I knew that any nighttime thoughts would be full of what Jaime and I had done and an imagining of all the things we hadn't had the time to do.

So, before night fell and I fell into still more erotic dreams, like the ones I've had every night for the past nineteen days, I pulled out my phone and opted for an impulsive, rash, last-ditch idea.

If Jaime was the one doing the biting again, I wouldn't even mind if my actions came back to bite me in the ass.

But there was the very real possibility that, as soon as the door only a few inches in front of my face was opened, I would have the cops called on me. And that would turn my so far okay day into an annoyingly messy one. I'd have to deal with my agent, my coaches, and my team's PR people when word got back to them, which it would. Plus the actual hassle of being questioned by cops... Being handcuffed could be fun. But I'd give it pretty low odds that being handcuffed by cops would lead to an orgasm. Maybe 10% at best.

The shocked and slightly horrified expression on Jaime Johnson's face when he opened his apartment door made the whole thing worth it though. I couldn't help but laugh in delight as he spluttered, "Wha? How? Why? How? J? What?"

"Surprise!" I gleefully declared. Yep. This was totally worth whatever PR or legal messiness I may have just launched at myself. "Did you miss me?"

"Ye—no. No. Of course not," Jaime replied, his wide blue eyes still sweeping up and down my body in complete disbelief.

Uh huh. Sure. There's no way I missed him starting to admit that he'd missed me too.

"What are you doing here in Minneapolis? And how the heck did you get into my building?" Jaime asked. "It's a secure building."

I scoffed because I've seen public libraries harder to get into than Jaime's building was. "You gonna let me come in?" I asked him. Jaime didn't *seem* like he was about to leap for his phone to call 911 but I'd feel better for my chances of ending the day not in jail if he let me into his home.

"Uh. Sure. Yeah. Um. Come in."

Jaime swung the door open wider and stepped to the side so that I could enter. Looking around, I wasn't terribly surprised by what I found inside Jaime's apartment.

The building itself was located in a neighborhood on the southern end of Minneapolis in a fairly residential area, although I'd driven past a fair number of shops, restaurants, and a decent sized lake with a park around it. And while it looked like it was built sometime in the 1970s or 1980s, the interior had clearly been remodeled much more recently.

Jaime's apartment had golden oak hardwood floors running throughout it, generously sized windows that let in the July sunshine, the walls were painted a creamy, warm white color, and I could see the hint of dark cabinetry in the kitchen a little bit off of the living room I was currently standing in. And all of the furniture and decor looked like the kind of generic, blandly impersonal stuff that was probably in the apartment when he toured it with his realtor. Lots of beige on beige with only some subtle patterns and textures to add any small amount of interest.

Not that my apartment was all that much better. Short of tearing out all the carpeting and cabinetry and changing out all the wall colors and tiling—which I doubted my landlord would appreciate—I was also stuck with a bland generic canvas in my place. But at least I'd gone to the trouble of moving out all the show-model furniture—if you could count throwing money at some buff college-aged movers to do it for me as trouble—and hiring a decorator to replace it with stuff that was colorful and interesting to look at. My soul couldn't flourish in a garden of banality.

Still, the couch was comfortable when I flopped my ass down onto it and Jaime's coffee table was the perfect height and perfectly situated to provide a nice support for my kicked-up legs. So, it wasn't a complete disaster. I'd just have to close my eyes and picture his place as being snazzier than it was.

"Gee. Make yourself at home while you're at it."

"Don't mind if I do," I told him as I crossed my arms behind my head.

The flight from Kansas City to Minneapolis hadn't been horrible—only about an hour-and-a-half—and I'd only had to sign a couple of autographs as I'd made my way through the airport and obtained my rental car. Navigating the freeway around Minneapolis had been a piece of cake. But a day of travel—a couple hours getting to and waiting around the airport before my flight—my nerves over what I was doing, and what Jaime's reaction would be had left me more than glad to get off my feet.

Jaime settled himself in the armchair—also beige—adjacent to his couch and looked at me. The bewildered expression on his face, like I was a strange bug he had no hope of understanding, was a bit annoying. But it was better than the yelling and anger I had sort of been expecting, so I'd take it.

"How did you get here?" he asked.

"Well…" I said. "Once upon a time there was a man and a woman living in Iowa…"

"For Pete's sake. I didn't mean—I don't need to hear about your conception, you jerk." Jaime and I gave matching shudders. "What are you doing in Minneapolis, how did you find me, and how the heck did you get in my building?"

"Ahhh. Why am I not surprised you want to get right to the point?" I asked hypothetically. I let my eyes linger on Jaime's athletic shorts and t-shirt clad body. Then I admitted the obvious. "I came to Minneapolis to see you. And I was able to get into your building by smiling at a woman exiting it and telling her I was here to visit someone who lives here. She held the door for me, wished me a pleasant day, and let me waltz right on in. I could've been a serial killer for all she'd known or cared."

"Ugh. Why am I not surprised? It seems like every other month, there's a notice posted in the lobby reminding people to not let strangers into the building. But it doesn't seem to stop it from happening."

"That darned Midwestern trust and politeness," I mocked.

"I know, right? That still doesn't explain how you found me, though," Jaime said. "Minneapolis isn't that small of a city. I never gave you my address. And I can't think of anybody who knows it who would have given it to you."

"Hmm. That's a bit of a longer story," I told him. And one that would reveal my desperation to see him again and the stalker-ish lengths I'd gone to in order to find him. "For some reason, I don't seem to have the personal phone numbers for players on the Minnesota Loons."

"Shocker."

"And I knew calling up the organization wouldn't get me anywhere. Other than put on some list that would see me banned from ever stepping foot in your arena again. *That* would be fun to explain to my coaches. 'Yeah. Sorry. I can't play in any games against the Loons, 'cause I'm not allowed within a hundred feet of their facility.' So, I had to resort to basic, old-fashioned methods to find you," I said. At Jaime's inquiring look, I explained, "I called around to all the J. Johnsons living in Minneapolis that were listed in the White Pages."

"Good gracious," Jaime exclaimed. "How many people did you have to call?"

"Not as many as you might think," I told him. "The White Pages only include landline numbers, so there aren't as many as there probably used to be."

"Still. Johnson's such a common last name, there had to be dozens of people listed," Jaime said. "You went through all of those people to try to find me?" He leaned forward in his chair, with a little pleased smile on his face.

I hated to disappoint him, because it did sound like more of a Herculean effort than it'd actually been. So, I decided not to tell him that I'd only had to call a couple of possibly-correct J. Johnsons. Instead, I opted to regale him with one of the more humorous outcomes from my calling up randomly listed J. Johnsons.

"I almost thought I got lucky and hit pay dirt with the third person I called," I told him. "The woman who answered the phone confirmed that there was a Jaime Johnson living at that address. Which threw me for a little bit as I couldn't recall you mentioning living with a woman. But then she explained that the Jaime Johnson who lived with her was her son and he was only two. The woman... whose name turned out to be Janine Johnson," I said. "Was very insistent on telling me that, while she named her son after the famous hockey player, Jaime Johnson, it wasn't because he was his kid. And it wasn't because she was delusional enough to think that he was. She said it was just because she's a really big fan of yours and thought it was a cute name."

"I'm not sure if I'm flattered by that… or creeped out," Jaime stated.

"Be creeped out," I told him. "Be very creeped out. I wasn't sold on her claim that she wasn't delusional. But if there ever comes a time where you'd like to meet your namesake, I can give you her address. I'm only a little bit certain that she wouldn't hogtie you and not let you leave before you become one big happy Johnson family and tack on a Junior after her kid's name."

"Kinda weird to know that there's another Jaime Johnson living in Minneapolis," my Jaime commented. "What about St. Paul? Did you run across any other Jaime Johnsons in St. Paul?"

"St.—Oh, crap. I forgot all about St. Paul," I said. "I always forget that Minneapolis has a second city smushed up right next to it."

"You… They're called the Twin Cities for a reason, J."

"Well, it's a good thing you live in Minneapolis then, isn't it?" I muttered.

"I guess so," Jaime replied. "What would you have done if I had lived in St. Paul? Or, shoot. One of the many suburbs? There are tons of places besides the actual city of

Minneapolis that are within a decent driving distance of our practice facility and arena. You really did luck out that I live in the one city you looked at. Heck. You're lucky I even still have a landline and that I'm in the White Pages at all."

"Yeah. I know. Why do you even have a landline anyway? You know what? It's not important," I said. I didn't want to get sidetracked by my thoughts on Jaime not ditching a landline like, I assume, most of the people under the age of senile have done. Besides, it'd enabled me to get the result I wanted. So, I just told him, "I knew the whole thing was kind of a long shot. And I was fully prepared to have to turn around and fly back to Kansas City without successfully tracking you down. But. Here you are. At the second of the four places I planned to check out in person."

"Yeah. Here I am," Jaime agreed, still looking shocked but pleased that I'd gone through as much effort as I had to try to find him. "And I've got a landline for emergencies. In case my phone isn't working or I can't find it and I need to make a call. Or just in case the woman who comes in to clean my apartment needs to use a phone and doesn't have a cell. That sort of thing."

Wow. That sort of overly cautious, ensure-for-all-contingencies attitude of Jaime's didn't surprise me in the least. I bet the batteries in his smoke detectors were swapped out every six months on the dot and his fire extinguisher was fully charged, functional, and easily accessible, too. Did I even own a fire extinguisher? Probably not. Jaime probably also had AAA and renter's insurance and all sorts of other responsible adult-y type stuff.

"You know…" Jaime said. "You could've just sent me a DM through Instagram asking me for my address. I would've recognized your account and opened it. Or… We each gave Jason Teague our contact information before we left Nevada. You could've contacted him and asked him to pass along my phone number and you could've texted me."

Huh. That would've been a more logical thing to do. Why did my brain always leap to the outlandish, most convoluted and improbable ideas and fixate on those instead of searching for a more reasonable direction?

"That would've ruined the surprise," I told him. It also would've given Jaime the opportunity to tell me not to come if I'd been able to let him know ahead of time that I wanted to see him again.

"Well, I am surprised," Jaime said. "So… now what? Now that you've come all this way and found me… Why are you here, J.J.?"

I didn't really know. I was still trying to figure out why I'd wanted to see Jaime again so much. And there was no way in hell I was going to let the man know that I'd apparently become obsessed with him or might *gasp* be feeling feelings for him. Fuck me sideways with a shovel, no. There was no way I was going to admit to that.

But there was one thing I was willing to admit to him.

"I brought a lucky coin," I said as I reached into the pocket of the shorts I was wearing and pulled out a random quarter I had jingling around with some other change. If it was getting me sex, any coin was a lucky coin. "I figured we could use it to flip and see who's turn it was to get fucked."

"You're telling me you flew four hundred miles and tracked me down... for sex? Weren't there any available gay guys in Missouri or Kansas that were willing to have sex with you?" Jaime asked. "Oh, wait. This is you. You've probably slept with all the guys willing to have sex with you in both of those states. So, you figured you'd see if the last guy dumb enough to sleep with you was still dumb enough to do it again?"

"One... Fuck you. I could fill a swimming pool with the number of guys who'd be more than happy to have sex with me. At any time. In any city I'm in. Any state I'm in. And, two. You do realize you just called yourself dumb, right?"

"For having sex with you? Yes. Pretty sure that qualifies me as dumb. I already knew that."

"Ah. But are you dumb enough to do it again?"

Please let him say yes. Please let him say yes.

"Uggghhh," Jaime groaned, dropping his head into his hands. "I can't believe I'm going to say it but... yeah. Okay." He pointed toward the hallway on the far end of his living room. "Bedroom's that way. Get your ass and your coin in there. If we're going to keep being stupid and have sex with each other again, we might as well make it fair to decide who's bottoming this time."

"You know... you don't have to sound so excited about it," I said.

"I thought we agreed, when we were in Mesquite, that us having sex with each other was a horribly bad idea and that we weren't going to do it again after that weekend. And now, here you are, unexpectedly suggesting that we continue doing the incredibly stupid thing by having sex again."

"And again. And again. And again." I pulled my shirt up over my head and flung it onto Jaime's couch—a splash of teal against the ocean of beige he had going on everywhere in his living room—and leered at him. "I've got plenty of time before there's anywhere I need to be. Days and days and weeks and weeks of time. Think of all the stupid fucking we can do in that amount of time."

"That's... Are you staying that long?" Jaime asked as he followed me out of the living room.

"Eh. We'll see," I told him. "I figured I'd stay until we got our fill of each other. Or we aggravate each other enough that someone winds up dead."

"So... probably less than a day?"

"Yeah. Probably. We'll see," I repeated.

We did tend to get along better when we were naked. So there was that. And since I was hoping to fuck the guy out of my system and out of my brain, I planned to keep us as naked as often as possible.

I stepped into Jaime's bedroom, which was also decorated in shades of—you guessed it—beige, with the occasional dark green accent. "Heads or tails?" I asked as I held up the quarter in my hand.

"Hmm. Both of those things sound good," Jaime said as he wrapped his arms around me from behind and pulled my body firmly against his. He nuzzled the back of my neck and then grazed the skin with his teeth. "Tell you what. Since you're probably tired from all the traveling you did today, why don't you lie down on the bed and I'll give you some head before I take your tail. We can flip for it next time."

"I think we might have to revise your assessment of you being dumb. Because that sounds like a genius idea," I told him.

"I must be dumb," Jaime said. "Or else I never would've invited you into my home. Or I'd have kicked you out when you told me you were here so we could continue the truly moronic decision to fool around with each other. But I didn't do either of those things. Instead…" Jaime's hands dropped down to the waistband of my shorts and nimbly loosened them. Then he removed his arms from around me, placed his hands against my bare back, and shoved me face-first down onto his bed. "Instead, here you are in my bed and I'm about to strip you naked," he said as he gripped my shorts and efficiently pulled them down and off. Per usual, I was going commando, so my bare ass was now all his for the playing with.

"Yeah, you are."

"This is such a bad idea," Jaime muttered. I was just about to contradict him and offer up any number of reasons as to why our fucking each other some more was an excellent idea, when Jaime climbed on top of me and quietly spoke next to my ear. "But for some reason, I don't care that this is a bad idea. I'll worry about that later. Right now, I'm going to allow myself to be dumb and fuck you into the mattress until you're begging me to let you come."

Based on how horny I was for him and how thoroughly he'd wrecked me the last time he'd fucked me, Jaime's goal of reducing me to begging was pretty much a sure thing. However, I wasn't about to admit that to him. "You wanna bet?" I asked once I was done whimpering in desperate need.

Jaime ground his hard dick against my ass, the silky nylon fabric of his athletic shorts swishing against my skin, causing me to groan. "Why would I bet on something I already know I'm going to get?"

"For fun?" I suggested. "And if I say you're not going to be able to get me to beg, then you're not going to get me to beg." I was bluffing. Bluffing so hard. So, so hard. Even harder than my dick was hard. And that was saying something because my dick felt like it was encased in cement, it was so hard. I was about ready to beg right now and Jaime hadn't even started fucking me yet. Fuck. He was still wearing his damned clothes.

Jaime's warm hand gripped my ass and spread my cheeks apart, his cock slotting perfectly into the valley of my crease. The thin fabric barrier of his shorts was a frustrating tease keeping his cock from where I wanted it. Where I needed it. I wanted him inside me, fucking me. The sooner, the better.

"I'll get you to beg," Jaime stated confidently. "You're going to take my cock and you're going to beg me to fuck you hard. And then you're going to be a good boy and beg me to let you come. Even if it takes all night."

Oh, fuck yes. Pretty, pretty please.

"You think you can do it, then you'd better get your clothes off and fucking do it," I told him. As hot as it was being completely naked underneath Jaime while he was still fully clothed, I really needed him to get naked. Or at least get his shorts out of the way so he could sink his cock into my ass.

"I hope you got some sleep on the plane. It's going to be a long night."

This. This right here. The commanding, confident, bossy motherfucker underneath his staid, uptight exterior... This was why I couldn't get Jaime Johnson out of my fucking head. Fucking him out of my head had to work. It had to. Or else I was going to be doomed to a fate worse than death. Hopelessly hung up on a guy who couldn't stand me.

"Bring it."

Chapter Thirteen

Jaime

Theoretically I should be happy that my trainer was pleased with the progress I was making. I'd regained the five or so pounds of muscle mass I'd shed through the course of last season. My core was strong. And I'd managed to shave some time off of the usual running program he had me do. So, all in all, a month and a half into the off season and I was well on my way to maintaining and improving upon where I was last year.

But it was the sneaking suspicion that I owed a fair amount of that progress to having J.J. staying with me for the past three weeks that spoiled any satisfaction I felt over my improved physical conditioning.

Because we realistically couldn't spend all of our time in bed, and I needed something to keep us occupied so we didn't get on each other's nerves, J.J. and I had spent a fair amount of time enjoying the summer weather of Minneapolis and exploring the various parks and hiking and biking trails in my section of the city. We'd even discovered that we both enjoyed paddle-boarding and had spent many long, sun-filled hours on the waters of Lake Nokomis.

Besides all this physical outdoor activity, J.J. had taken to working out at the same time as me and accompanying me to the gym. And each side-eyed glance and smirk as J.J. added another plate to what he was lifting... Each mocking "No wonder I'm faster on the ice than you" as he upped the speed or incline of his treadmill... Each squat, and lunge, and crunch... All of those pushed me to put my all into my workouts. To try just that little bit harder. To run just a little bit longer. So that I could shut him up and show J.J. that I could be equally matched against him. That I *was* equally matched against him. That I could be better than him. Fitter than him. More driven than him.

I was not going to go into the next season getting shown up on the ice by J.J. flipping Johnson.

All the sex we were having was definitely giving me a good workout, too.

Whether it was me topping or him topping... sex with J.J. was definitely a good cardiovascular work-out that got my heart beating, my blood pumping, and my lungs panting until I was dizzy.

All of this had left me in, possibly, the best shape of my life. And I owed most of it to J.J. Which was kind of peeving me off. I couldn't even bask in the congratulations of Tomas, the personal trainer I'd worked with for the past couple of years, as he'd patted me on the back and told me, "Keep doing what you're doing. Whatever it is, it's working and you're going to kill on the ice this year." Ungh. Would he still be saying that if he knew that what I was doing was... J.J. Johnson?

Actually, knowing Tomas, yeah, he probably would.

But I couldn't keep having sex with J.J. because... because... Why couldn't I keep having sex with him? Oh. That's right. Because I can't stand the guy and we're rival hockey players whose involvement with each other would be an unmitigated horrific scandal if it ever got out.

Or, at least... definitely that second thing. Because after having lived with the guy for a couple weeks, I wasn't sure how much I didn't like him anymore. I think I actually... kind of *liked* having him around.

It was not at all what I would have expected—not that I'd expected J.J. to show up on my doorstep on a random Tuesday afternoon in the first place—but, once he got the boasting and cocky competitiveness over with, J.J. was actually sort of easy-going and fun to be around. I was actually starting to view him as a human version of a terrier. He was much less likely to be attention-seeking and overly annoying if you gave him some attention, praise, and affection before he got himself wound up.

Viewing J.J. as a needy, little puppy quelled some of my tendency to get irritated with him. Particularly when I pictured him with a muzzle and leash.

And the man could definitely cook. Holy cow, could he cook. Maybe there was something to that whole hangry thing. I don't think I've ever eaten so well in my life and it definitely left me in a much better mood.

Speaking of... when I got home from my session with my trainer, I walked into my apartment to the amazing smell of charring steak being cooked by my... boyfriend?... unplanned visitor that I was also having sex with? What the heck was J.J. to me?

I had no idea.

He'd been here for three weeks and we'd been spending all our time together and having obscene amounts of sex. Was J.J. my boyfriend? Is that what boyfriends did? Sometimes it felt like that's what we were doing. But other times I was still sorely tempted to tie him up and chuck him in the nearby lake or back onto the first plane going anywhere that wasn't here. Just because I found myself liking J.J. more than I'd thought I would, didn't mean he didn't still get on my nerves and aggravate me more than any other person on the planet. Those times just came and went in short bursts and my aggravation was usually easily soothed away with a cuddle, a slow, lingering kiss, a blow job, or J.J. happily bending over and letting me paddle his ass.

But we sure as shooting hadn't had any sort of relationship discussion. As far as I knew, J.J. was just here until he got his fill of me and then he'd be gone just as suddenly as he'd arrived. Like a loud summer storm that brought sex.

It certainly felt relationship-y when J.J. heard me open the apartment door and called out a cheerful "Hey. You're right on time. Dinner's almost ready." He poked his head out from around where the kitchen separated itself from the living room, the freshly trimmed stubble on his cheeks sending a ghostly prickle through me as I remembered how it had felt rubbing and scratching against the inside of my thighs when he'd given me a good-morning BJ sendoff before I left. "That butcher around the corner was having a special on steak," J.J. said. "So, that's what we're having tonight. That and a grilled veggie salad and some couscous."

However, my ruminations on whether I'd somehow fallen into a relationship with J.J. Johnson, and the unexpectedly warm and content feeling that prompted, was halted smack in its tracks when I was greeted with more than the tasty smell of dinner and the warm welcome of the man who was making it.

Walking into my living room, I was also greeted by the sight of an electric blue couch that I didn't recognize.

"Jaaaayyy… where's my couch?" Ah, the things I never thought I'd find myself saying since J.J. Johnson had invaded my life.

J.J. came into the living room, walked over to where I was standing stock still and staring at an unfamiliar couch, bussed a kiss to my cheek, and replied, "It was boring. Did you even pick it out or did it come with the apartment? Actually, I take back the question. A decorator would've never picked out something with so little personality and so much beige. That must've been all you."

That wasn't really an answer, yet, at the same time, it was all the answer I needed. But, to make sure I really understood what was going on, I asked with, what I thought, was a calm voice, "You replaced my couch without asking me?"

"Yuh huh. I knew you'd say no, so I didn't ask," J.J. stated with the complete cluelessness of a man who had absolutely no idea how strange it was to redecorate somebody else's living space.

"You replaced my couch. Without asking me."

"You already said that," J.J. said. He smiled in the face of my befuddled blinking, brushed a kiss to my mouth and ordered, "Go get showered and change out of your workout stuff. I know you want to. Then come into the kitchen and I'll feed you your dinner. Okay?"

I was annoyed that J.J. had replaced my couch without any say-so from me. But, adding to my bemusement over what he'd done, was the fact that I was only *mildly* annoyed. I couldn't even seem to find enough anger in me to properly yell at the man. Which meant that without a negative repercussion for his actions, it would never occur to J.J. that he'd done something wrong and he'd continue to do stuff like this. And I... couldn't find it within myself to be bothered to care.

Because, yes, I was the one who'd picked the danged thing out when I went shopping for furniture for my apartment when I'd moved to Minneapolis. And, despite what J.J. had thought about it, it was a perfectly comfortable and functional couch. So what if it was a completely non-descript shade of oatmeal and had so little style to it that I couldn't even recall what the thing looked like. And I'd been sitting on it this morning.

But it was just a couch. I hadn't been emotionally invested in it and J.J. did look so pleased with himself over replacing the thing. His actions were irritating but that was pretty much par for the course for J.J. So, I wasn't overly surprised or upset by what he'd done. And I did find myself pleased that I could make the man happy by sacrificing a piece of furniture to his impulsive and audacious personality.

Oh, God. What did it say about me that I not only accepted this self-absorbed cluelessness of J.J.'s but also appreciated that it was simply part and parcel of his personality and finding it... annoyingly and adorably charming? Nothing good, I'm sure.

I'm not sure what I was hoping to accomplish by walking closer to the new couch I hadn't asked for. Was I hoping that it was a mirage that would disappear and reveal that my old, perfectly acceptably beige couch was still sitting in my living room? It wasn't. It was all too real. But it was comfortably squishy with deep cushions, I discovered when I sat down on it to give it a try. And it appeared to be a little bit longer than my old couch, which would probably make it nice to lay down on for naps. Assuming the vivid blue color wouldn't sear through my eyelids.

"Gah! What are you doing?" J.J. shrieked as soon as I sat down. "Get up, get up, get up. You're going to get your nasty exercise sweat all over the new couch."

I grunted in annoyance as I heaved myself off the couch. "You plonked a couch in my house without my say-so but I'm not allowed to sit on it?"

"Not until you shower and change. I don't want it getting all nasty."

"Fine. What'd you do with my old couch, anyway? And how'd you manage to move a couch in here by yourself?"

As far as I was aware, the only other people J.J. knew who might be in Minneapolis were the other players on my team. And I couldn't see him calling any of them up to help him move furniture. Even J.J. wouldn't have been so foolish as to let any of my teammates know that he was in town and visiting me. Right?

"There's this thing called money," J.J. answered. "And, strangely enough, when you throw enough of it at the people at the furniture store... it's bye-bye crappy, unwanted couch and hello pretty, new, awesome couch."

"Still think you should've asked me first," I muttered. "It's my house and my couch."

"But think of all the time and aggravation I saved you," J.J. said. "If I'd asked, you'd have said no. Then I'd have asked you again. And you'd have said no. Again. Then I would've nagged and badgered and argued with you... And you would've said no. And round and round we would've gone until you either agreed or I'd have gotten fed up with the whole thing and gone ahead and bought it without your consent anyway. Either way you were going to wind up with a new couch. Your home was begging me for a new coach.

'Please, J.J. It's so drab and boring here. Please, we need your help. Make me prettier and more interesting.' So, I did. And this way, you got it without all the arguing and yelling first." J.J. tilted his head and pointed at his cheek. "Now, give me a kiss and say you're sorry so I can finish making dinner before it winds up overcooked."

"I'm... sorry?"

"Thank you," J.J. said happily. "Now, the kiss."

Bewildered, I found my feet carrying me over to J.J. I leaned in to give him his demanded kiss on the cheek. I couldn't believe a situation in which J.J. had clearly and outrageously crossed a boundary had wound up with me issuing a half-hearted and puzzled apology.

Any lingering prickles of upset left me with a sigh as I watched the wiggle of J.J.'s round, firm ass as he turned around and strode across the living room and back into the kitchen. He was making me a tantalizing smelling dinner. And I supposed it did make sense to try to not get any grime or dirt on the couch since he'd just bought it.

Wait. J.J. had indicated he'd purchased the couch using his money, right? Or should I expect to find an unexpected charge from a furniture store on one of my credit card bills? It wouldn't surprise me at all if J.J. had rifled through my things while I was out and used one of my in-case-of-emergency credit cards that I had stored buried in the back of my sock drawer to buy this couch he felt I needed so badly.

I supposed it didn't matter. What's done is done. And I did feel kind of gross and sweaty. So, I followed J.J.'s suggestion and went into my en suite bathroom to take a shower and get changed.

Emerging from my shower squeaky clean and fresh smelling, I pulled open the drawers of my dresser and discovered that J.J. had apparently been busy with more than visiting the butcher and buying a new couch today. Folded neatly in my dresser, and displacing the majority of my things, were roughly a dozen new shirts, new socks and underwear, and a handful of new shorts and pants. All of them in bright colors and/or large, bold patterns that looked particularly flashy sitting side-by-side with my understated and tasteful clothing.

"J? Where the heck are my clothes?" I called out, hopefully loudly enough that J.J. could hear me. "And why are all your clothes taking up so much room in my dresser?"

I couldn't really begrudge him for moving some of his things into my dresser. J.J. had to be tired of living out of his suitcase; I know I would be. That didn't mean that I didn't feel distinctly leery as to what fate had befallen my clothing that was no longer in its normal place, though. J.J. had probably just dumped it all carelessly into some random box or garbage bag and stuffed them in the back of the closet or under the bed.

"Oh. Those aren't my clothes," J.J. answered. "Those are the new clothes I bought for you. To replace your boring-ass stuff." I turned from my perusal of the contents of my dresser and saw J.J. leaning against the doorframe to my bedroom. "You know I didn't bring enough clothes with me…" J.J. said. "I wasn't planning on staying as long as I have and I was getting sick and tired of looking like a generic preppy dude whenever I borrowed your stuff to wear."

"So you did buy yourself some more clothes?" I asked. I must've misunderstood him.

Practically, I understood why he'd buy himself more clothes. With as little foresight as he'd put into his impromptu visit, J.J. had only brought along enough clothes for four or five days. He'd been doing a lot of laundry and supplementing what he'd brought by borrowing some of my things.

I'd kind of been enjoying the way he looked wearing my clothes, though. Not because he looked particularly good in them. Although, that's not to say that he *didn't*. The man made anything look good. But it wasn't about how he looked in them but more the thrill I got, knowing that J.J. was in *my* clothes.

And I was self-aware enough to realize that it was just a way that I could mark him as mine without leaving semi-permanent marks on his body.

"No. I bought *you* new clothes," J.J. said again. Huh. So, I had heard him correctly. "These are for you. Why would I have bought myself undies? You know I don't wear any. These are all for you. All the socks, and shirts, and shorts. You needed clothes that weren't dull as fuck. And this way, I get to keep wearing your clothes while also not looking fucking boring." I was still processing that—and his thought process—when J.J. walked over to my closet and threw it open. "I couldn't figure out how to find out who your tailor was… without your phone here for me to snoop through…

so, unfortunately, there wasn't much I could do about your suits," he stated.

"You... Wait... What?"

Well, thank goodness for small flippity favors, I supposed. If J.J. had his way, no doubt I'd show up on game days looking as ridiculously loud and flamboyant as he did. I still couldn't believe the bright orange suit he'd worn to one of his games last year. Although, the game had been the day before Halloween. So, I guess, it had been sort of appropriate. Just horrendously eye-assaulting.

"What do you mean what?" J.J. asked. He peered at me eagerly awaiting my... What? My thanks?

"You can't just... How do you not realize..." Was he truly that clueless? Was J.J. so lacking in common sense or societal understanding that he didn't realize that you just can't go around and replace another person's clothing whenever you feel like it? "What the heck, J.J.? There's nothing wrong with my clothes and I fully expect them to make their way back into my dresser from wherever you put them. Feel free to keep the things you bought for yourself. That's fine. But I want my stuff back. Now."

"Yeah... I'm gonna have to go with a... no on that one," J.J. said, nibbling on his lip and a guilty, sheepish expression finally appearing on his face.

"Uh huh. And why is that?" I asked as I crossed my arms across my chest and gave him an unimpressed look.

"Because I already had them picked up by a local charity?" My jaw dropped at the audaciousness of J.J.'s reply.

"Right now your clothes are being given away to homeless dudes. I felt a little bad about subjecting those already in an unfortunate situation with your boring, blah clothes. But I figured beggars… and I mean, literal beggars… can't really be choosers, huh."

"Holy. Frick. Are you… Are you flipping kidding me?"

"I'd take your yelling at me a lot more seriously if you used some fucking swear words," J.J. said.

I didn't have a headache… yet. Much to my surprise. But I closed my eyes and rubbed my fingertips over them and my forehead because it felt like I should have a headache after being confronted with so much of J.J. being… J.J. today.

"Anything else?" I managed to croak out. "Is there… anything else that I'm going to discover missing, or altered, or replaced, or, or… J.J.'ed?"

"Did you just use my name as a verb? That is fucking fantastic. I like it. Do it more often."

"Not. The. Point. J.J. I just… I don't think I can take any more surprises from you today."

"Nah. That's it."

I sighed in relief. I was still annoyed. But at least this was as annoyed as I was going to get with him today. And my aggravation was at a manageable level. So, it would be okay.

"Just the couch. And the clothes. Oh… and the towels."

Dang it. Seems my sigh of relief was premature.

"The towels?" I asked faintly.

Did I even want to know? I hadn't noticed anything different with the towels. And I currently had one wrapped around my waist. It was the same old towel I'd had for years. Wasn't it? It certainly looked the same.

"You can't really go wrong with white towels. So, the ones you had weren't horrible. But these ones are made of bamboo, they're super soft and fluffy, and I got them in the extra-large size. I liked the way the towels you had offered a delicious tease of leg because they didn't want to wrap all the way around your gorgeous ass and thighs. But I know that bugged you. So, I splurged on the over-sized ones."

Oh. Huh. That was actually... kind of thoughtful of him. I hadn't really noticed the change. And while I thought that J.J. was imagining me being bothered over the size of the towels I'd had, it was sort of sweet that he'd thought of something to rectify that situation.

"You did?"

"I did."

I parted my fingers, peeked at J.J. between them, and saw him smiling at me. It wasn't his usual cocky, I'm-better-than-you smile, or his smirking I'm-internally-laughing-at-you smile, or even his sly I'm-sneaking-something-past-you-but-you-don't-know-it-yet smile. This smile just looked like one of simple happiness and contentment. Of nothing but enjoyment of being in my presence.

It was a smile I felt my own lips curling up to match.

Against my own will. Against all my better judgment and knowing that none of what we were doing together made sense. What magic power did this man have to soothe my grumpy moods—ones that he inevitably caused in the first place—and turn me into a big ball of goopy affection?

"Thanks. For the new towels," I told him.

"No problem. Anything for you, babe," J.J. replied. "Now. Get your cute little butt into some of the new clothes I got you. Or not," J.J. said, raking an appreciative gaze over my towel-clad body. "Dinner's ready. I made brownies for dessert, too."

It was a good thing that it was the off-season and J.J. and I both needed to add on some weight. We should probably do it in a healthier way than stuffing ourselves with gooey, calorie-laden, chocolate deliciousness. But I wasn't going to mention that right now. Not when… "Are they like the ones you made last week? With all the extra stuff added to them?" I couldn't remember everything J.J. said he'd mixed into the batter when he'd made brownies last week, but those things had been bonkers delicious. We'd managed to polish off the entire pan of them in two days.

"Duh. Like I'd make them any other way," J.J. replied.

"Nice. Alright. I'll be out in a minute. I'll just throw some clothes on."

"Or not. Clothing optional dinners should be more of a thing than they are. In fact, I might remove my own clothes and we can both dine au natural."

In a blink, J.J. had his shirt off and flung onto the floor. Then he stood gazing at the towel wrapped around my waist, clearly waiting for me to remove it in a similar manner.

"I'm not eating dinner… or any of my other meals… naked," I informed him, crossing my arms across my bare chest. "That would be… weird." Even just contemplating sitting down naked on one of my dinette chairs gave me an itchy wrong feeling. I'm not really sure why the thought of dining while not wearing any clothes gave me a case of the heebie-jeebies. Probably because meal time and nakedness didn't correlate together in my mind. Like soap and peanut butter; to me the two things just didn't go together.

"I'd say it's your loss," J.J. stated. "But it's not. It's my loss. I'd would've been the one who would've gotten to look at you naked while we ate. Get me hungry for something while I'm sating my appetite with another. Too bad."

J.J. ran a hand down the ridges of his pecs and abs, drawing my attention and taking it downward with the movement of his hand. Then both hands grabbed onto the waistband of his loose athletic shorts and pushed them down. The silky nylon fabric easily slithered down and pooled around his feet. And, unsurprisingly, J.J. had not been wearing anything under his shorts. So, now, he was standing there completely naked. And partially erect. My mouth watered.

Maybe he was on to something about the possibilities behind spurring on one hunger while feeding another. Nope. No. The thought of consuming food naked still gave me the weirds.

"I'm clearly a much nicer guy than you are because I'm not depriving you of the joy of getting a naked dinner companion," J.J. said as he turned around and strolled out of my bedroom. His tight ass flexed with each step that took him out of the room.

My lips twitched as a smile tried to break free. I'm not sure what niceness had to do with foisting an unusual situation on somebody. But it looked like I was about to find out if some truly fantastic eye candy was about to make up for the strangeness of eating with a naked man.

Chapter Fourteen
Jaime

How did J.J. get his steak to taste so good? Whenever I made myself steak it tasted like… beef. It was *okay*. But whatever J.J. did to his steak made it taste like juicy, savory, seared meaty heaven.

"Mmm," I moaned around my last mouthful of steak. I was going to be savoring this taste for a while. Or… at least until I replaced it with the equally delicious flavor of J.J. brownies. "How are you so good at cooking?"

J.J. stabbed his fork into the last bit of food on his plate—a spear of broccoli. And why would you end your meal on a vegetable—even one that did taste as good as these ones did—when you could end it with steak juice lingering on your tongue? "I've been cooking for myself for a long time," he replied. Odd. While that seemed like the sort of thing J.J.

would normally boast about, he stated this like it was just a tidbit of information not worth pursuing as he kept his gaze trained on his plate. "I was always pretty independent growing up and it was easier for my parents for me to feed myself around my hockey schedule."

My mom had always treated it as a personal challenge to tackle my demanding hockey schedule while I was growing up. Making sure I was well fed, had the gear I needed, and made it to wherever I needed to be on time while also juggling her part-time job as a school librarian and taking care of my dad and younger sister, Delia. Dad had also done what he could. Manning carpools and helping with fundraisers and booster club concessions on the weekends and when he could cut out early of his job selling insurance. But I supposed not all parents could make the level of commitment to their child's activities as my parents had.

And I realized that I must've subconsciously been paying more attention to J.J. Johnson than I thought I had before we'd started hooking up. Because little snippets of interviews and articles about him flashed through my brain and I was easily able to recall that, while he frequently and fondly talked about his childhood best friend and how he was the one who'd originated J.J.'s hockey nickname, he only occasionally mentioned his hometown in Iowa and almost never his parents.

Looking at him now, sitting naked at my small dining table—and wasn't that still odd? Sitting with a naked man while we ate.

Not that I could see much of him other than his bare chest and arms. A delicious feast for my eyes. But even though I couldn't see the rest of his naked body hidden by the table, I knew it was there. And it was severely messing with my mind that J.J.'s bare butt was resting on one of the two chairs in the small eating area of my apartment. A chair that I had sat on before. A chair that my friends and teammates had sat on before. I'm not sure I'd ever be able to let anyone sit in that chair ever again now that J.J. has had his naked butt sitting on it.

Anyway... looking at him now, as he clearly had no intention of making any follow up statements to his brief comment about his parents, it made me incredibly curious about why he never talked about them.

My curiosity was only further peaked when J.J. aimed a bland, fake smile at me and changed the subject.

"How did your workout go earlier?" he asked. "I don't suppose you can give me any hints about what your trainer is focusing on with you for this season? Not that I'll need it to be better than you again this season, but I'll still take the insider info if you give it to me," J.J. said with a hint of his usual cocky glimmer reappearing in his eyes.

I rolled my eyes at him because, really, except for when I had sessions with my trainer, J.J. and I had been working out together. So, he knew, firsthand, what my exercise regimen was. "Nothing special," I told him. "And you're not better than me on the ice."

"I, the media, the commentators, and the stats beg to differ."

I reminded myself that the man had just fed me a delicious meal and that getting annoyed with him wouldn't serve any purpose. It's what he was after and letting his comment get to me would just let him win. "I think you'll find that you're wrong. And we can go online right now to look up those so-called statistics."

"Nah. We still have brownies to eat," J.J. said. Which... Oooh. Brownies. "My trainer told me I should start laying off the sweets and unnecessary calories, so I'm making sure to get as many into you as I can." Since he was here in Minneapolis with me, J.J. had been having his sessions with his trainer via Skype. I'm not sure J.J. was telling the truth about the advice from his trainer, but that did seem like something he would do.

That should probably also make me angry—the idea that he'd intentionally sabotage my diet—but I was a grown man, a professional athlete, and I knew how to eat in moderation to not mess with my preparedness for the coming season. Besides... brownies. *J.J.'s* brownies. Those were worth some extra crunches or minutes on the treadmill.

Sufficiently distracted by the thought of dense, gooey, chocolaty yumminess, I let the matter drop of which one of us was better. I was pretty confident that we were evenly matched or that I had a slight edge over J.J. but I didn't want to run the chance that an internet search would prove me wrong. I already had the feeling that going up against him on the ice was going to be harder now that we'd been intimate, I didn't need to psych myself out with any concrete data comparing our performances against each other in the past.

"So, you're saying it's time for dessert?" I asked as I stood up and began gathering our dishes to take them over to the kitchen sink.

"Hmm. And… How thorough was your shower earlier?"

"Huh? What do you mean?" I was confused by J.J.'s question that seemed to come out of left field and had no bearing on anything we'd been doing or talking about.

"I mean… How thorough was your shower earlier?" J.J. repeated. "Because I think I've thought of a way to convince you to, at least, eat dessert naked. And then, maybe, once you've eaten naked once, I won't have any trouble getting you to do it again."

I in no way trusted the wicked glint in his eyes or the sly smirk on his face.

"Nuh uh. Not gonna happen," I informed him.

"We'll see about that. Go get your sexy ass on the bed. I'll be in in a moment."

I gave the dishes a quick rinsing blast of water and glanced at the tray of brownies sitting next to the stove. They were just sitting there looking all decadent and tempting. "But… but… the brownies," I protested.

"Oh, we'll get to the brownies, no worries," J.J. assured me. "But first I need you to get all naked and splayed out in bed. So get going," he said, waving his hands in a shooing motion. "You may as well get yourself situated on your stomach right away, as soon as you get your clothes off. For efficiency… so you can get your brownies sooner," he added.

"For efficiency…" I faintly echoed.

"Yep. Go on," J.J. told me. "I'll be right behind you."

Since J.J. had requested that I get on the bed on my stomach, I took that to mean that J.J. intended to top tonight, lending his last comment a naughty connotation that it otherwise might not have had.

I cast my mind back to last night and recalled that the silly quarter J.J. had jokingly insist we utilize—which he'd given its own place of pride, front and center on top of the nightstand on his side of the bed—had landed tails up last night, which had decided that I'd been the one topping last. So, since that made it J.J.'s turn to top—even without a coin flip—I went ahead and did as he requested. Entering my bedroom, I shed the clothes I'd donned after my shower. Which had been, thankfully, plenty thorough. Then I pulled back the comforter on my bed and arranged myself belly-down on the sheets.

I had only a moment to spare to think that the sheet I was laying on didn't look like my usual white cotton sheet, when J.J. followed me onto the bed mere seconds later. He draped his naked body over mine, every inch of the tawny skin covering his chiseled muscles pressing against mine.

This. This. This was a much more appropriate application of nakedness than eating dinner.

"Mmm. This is nice but it's not convincing me of anything. Other than the fact that, in bed really is the best place to be naked," I informed him.

"I'm just getting started," J.J. replied. "By the time I'm done with you, you'll definitely be singing a different tune." Whatever retort I was going to offer up was driven out of my head as I felt J.J. trail his mouth along the sensitive patch of skin on the back of my neck. "God, these freckles," he muttered against my skin. "Can't get enough of them."

He spoke quietly enough that I'm not sure I was supposed to hear him. But, what he said, sent a rush of warmth through me. Like a lot of people with lots of freckles, I'm sure, I've never cared for my freckles. They were just a source of teasing and one more thing to make me stand out from everyone else. But the way J.J. seemed to love kissing, and licking, and running his fingers over them… I was gaining a newfound appreciation for all of my small orangey-bronze splotches.

J.J.'s mouth continued making a path down the length of my spine. Tenderly brushing featherlight kisses to my skin, causing prickles of awareness everywhere his lips touched. And prickles of need everywhere they didn't. I still wasn't sure how J.J. thought this was going to convince me of anything. If all he wanted to show me was that his mouth was good for more than making smart alecky comments and saying things that irritated me, I already knew that. That had become readily apparent the first time J.J. had put his mouth on my dick.

But if the man wanted to waste his time trying to change my mind about nakedness outside of the bedroom by worshipping me with his mouth, I wasn't going to tell him not to. I'd break the news after he was done that, whatever he'd been trying to do, hadn't worked.

Although it did seem as though things were about to get interesting as J.J.'s mouth didn't stop its descent once it reached the swells of my ass. Nope. Those plush lips just kept right on going. Going, going, going... until...

"Holy sweet mother of mercy!"

I'd never thought of myself as being particularly inexperienced, even if my sexual experience had never lived up to all I could've wanted it to be. Being in the closet was like that. But I'd never thought I'd been missing out on anything other than frequency or a deeper connection than fast, anonymous hookups would allow.

But as J.J.'s lips brushed against the puckered opening of my ass, followed up by a lazy swipe of his tongue... it occurred to me that I'd never had a guy's mouth on that particular location on my body before. And I most definitely had been missing out.

Rimming was something I was aware of and had read about, but I'd always scoffed it off as being one of those things that sounded like it would feel good but in all reality was probably weird, awkward, and, frankly, gross. Taste and germ factors alone, who would want to put their mouth... there? And having someone's face up close and personal with that part of your anatomy... Like I said, there was no way that could be as alluring as the articles I'd read made it out to be.

However, now that I was faced with the reality of having J.J.'s tongue licking and probing my opening, I have to say that I couldn't give a flying leap if it was weird or gross for him. All that mattered was that it felt stupendous—A+++, triple gold stars, all the glittery stickers in the world stupendous—to be on the receiving end.

"Fuck! J. Don't stop. Never stop. So good. So good. So, so good," I babbled as tingles of ecstasy raced through my body.

The glide of his tongue was somehow soft and firm at the same time. And the hot, slick wetness made me crave more. More and more and more. While, in the best way, I also wanted it to stop. Because the teasing caresses of his tongue weren't enough. I needed his cock plunging into my ass. Now. As soon as possible. So, he needed to stop what he was doing so he could get that hard cock inside me, filling me up until the tension he'd caused exploded in glorious orgasm.

And if I'd thought the rough scrape of his stubble against my thighs had been exhilarating… that was nothing compared to how good it felt dragging and scratching against the sensitive, tender skin on the inside of my butt cheeks.

"Ungh. This ass. Could lick it all day. All night. Every night. Never get enough." J.J.'s moaned pronouncement rumbled and vibrated against my hole. It tickled and, for some reason, my brain knew that the best relief for that would be for me to jam my ass backward, insistently grinding against J.J.'s face. "I'll lick you so much and so often that I'll lick all your hair away."

That odd statement startled me enough that the dual thoughts "Is my asshole too hairy?" and "Would J.J. like it if I waxed or something down there?" penetrated through my haze of lust and need. However, I didn't have much time to start freaking out or get too paranoid about the relative hirsute status of my anus because J.J.'s tongue driving into me and licking the slick interior walls of my channel pushed any and all coherent thoughts out of my head.

"Aaahhnnngh!"

Who knew that my eyes rolling back in my head had a noise? It was apparently a shriek, that turned into a moan, that morphed into a breathless gasp. And now I was left panting and trembling like I was in the homestretch of running a marathon.

And when J.J. reached his hand underneath me and wrapped his fist around my cock while he kept his tongue firmly lodged in my ass—taking long, slurping licks and jabbing, teasing thrusts—I discovered that my brain short-circuiting also made a noise. It sounded something like "Aahblehpltehmph".

"That's right, babe. Give me that ass. I want it all," J.J. implored me as his firm grip started working over my aching, dripping cock with fast, short strokes.

J.J. was feasting on my ass like it was the steak he'd made us for dinner and he hadn't eaten in weeks. And I was loving every single, solitary moment of it.

My feverish brain couldn't figure out which sensation to focus on. The hot, wet probing of J.J.'s tongue into my hole or the teasing, flickering licks and nips to my rim or the stroking, rubbing, hot friction along my hard cock. All of my synapses were firing. Sparkling, whirring, swirling fireworks of pleasure exploding in my mind.

As good as it all felt, I was still unprepared for the orgasm that ripped through me. "Jaaay. J. Uaagh. Come… coming," I cried as though there would've been any way for J.J. to miss the way my cock twitched and throbbed in his hand before splurting out a geyser of cum. My wet, plentiful load coated his hand as J.J. stroked me through my climax, releasing me only when I slumped down into a boneless, satiated lump on top of my mattress.

"Holy fuck, you're a mess," J.J. commented from somewhere above me. "A sexy, gorgeous mess."

I couldn't disagree with him. I felt like a mess. I also didn't feel like moving anytime in this next century. However, a frantic, squelching, schlepping noise prompted me to rotate my head enough that I could glance over my shoulder. Above and behind me, his legs straddling one of mine, J.J. kneeled and quickly jerked his dick.

His hand glistened with moisture and, somewhere in the blissed-out and dazed recesses of my mind, I understood that J.J. was using my cum to coat his dick as he jerked himself off. Frick, that was hot.

I became even more of a mess when J.J. stroked himself to completion and his cum joined the rest of the bodily fluids decorating my body, streaking in long ribbons across the skin of my ass and lower back.

"Gorgeous. Simply fucking gorgeous," J.J. panted. He kept his body weight off of me but slumped down partially on top of me, his body supported by one elbow and the hand he hadn't been using to jerk himself off with. Much like he'd done before he'd destroyed my ass and my mind with his mouth, J.J. brushed a soft kiss to the back of my neck. "You stay here," he said. As if I had any other option. I wasn't kidding about having absolutely no energy or wherewithal to move for the foreseeable future. "I'm gonna get the brownies."

J.J. climbed off the bed and gave my butt a fond pant while I lay there trying to make sense of his last sentence.

I was bemused that J.J. was able to move around and have full powers of cognition after what we'd just done. My mind was a muddled fluff filled with the whirring repetitive thought of *Holy fuck. Holy fuck. Holy fuck.* Never before in my life had I ever been so disgustingly, gloriously covered in so much cum and spit. I felt thoroughly debauched. A giddy smile stretched my lips and a silly, incredulous, cum-drunk giggle spilled from my mouth.

"I'm back," J.J. announced as he strolled back into my bedroom in all his naked splendor. And he was carrying the pan of brownies. "Oh, good. You haven't moved." He settled himself down next to me on the mattress, scooped up a chunk of brownie with his fingers, and said, "Open wide."

My mind was still fully offline and all my body knew was that J.J. was the bringer of all the wonderful. So, with no hesitation, my body obeyed his directive and my mouth dropped open.

The rich, decadently fudgy flavor of the brownie exploded in my mouth and I let out a moan of pleasure and enjoyment reminiscent of the sounds I'd made while J.J. was gorging himself on my ass. Oh, that was good. So, so good. Sabotage levels of good. Because I knew that if J.J. kept making brownies like this, I'd keep eating them. And there's no way I'd be in peak condition heading into the new season if that happened.

I'd like to think that J.J. wouldn't do anything so underhanded and diabolical, but this was J.J. Johnson we were talking about. He'd do it in a heartbeat. He was probably doing it right now and I didn't even care because that's how darn good those brownies of his were.

"See…" J.J. said in a soft, cajoling voice. "See how much better they taste because you're eating them naked? I told you I'd convince you to eat dessert naked. And now that I've done that, we can move on to eating our other meals together naked."

Yeah. That still wasn't going to happen. Consuming food while naked still seemed weird and wrong to me. If I had any energy or body coordination after coming my brains out, I'd get up and throw some clothes on before eating any more of the brownie J.J. was holding up to my lips. So, no matter what J.J. thought, I, for one, was going to keep eating with my clothes on.

Unless J.J. rimmed me before each and every meal. Then I'd happily agree to do whatever the heck he wanted. And if he told me to do a naked samba across my living room on my way to sitting down at my kitchen table with my bare everything hanging out… I would happily cue up some music and shimmy my parts to his heart's content.

But short of that…

However, telling J.J. any of that would not only reveal to him how much control he could wield over me at any time, if he should so choose, it also wouldn't get me any more tasty morsels of brownie shoved into my mouth in the here and now.

I ignored the smirk on his face that clearly said that he thought he'd won this contest of opinion between the two of us. He hadn't won, he just didn't know it yet. He'd find out soon enough. Grumbling out a nonsense noise, I requested "more please," then opened my mouth so that J.J. could keep feeding me delicious brownies. And if some small part of me felt a tingling thrill that J.J. was hungrily watching me eat dessert naked, like he wanted to devour me much the way I was devouring his brownies… I was going to ignore that too.

Chapter Fifteen
J.J.

"Ow! What the fu-u-udge?" Jaime cried out, barely managing to turn his almost accidental swear into something more PG-wholesome, after my flailing arm smacked him in the face.

It was kind of impressive, really. How committed the man was to keeping his language soap-in-the-mouth clean. Ridiculous and pointless... but impressive.

Fuck knows I'd be swearing up a storm if I'd been rudely awakened in the middle of the night by the forceful application of a limb to the face.

Actually... come to think of it... what had awakened me? And had caused me to be so startled that I'd lost control of the appendage in question and it had wound up colliding with Jaime's face?

It was a mystery. Or at least it was until my phone peeled out with a ring that sounded way too loud and obnoxious for… 3:47 in the morning. Ugh. If it had been my phone making that rude racket, then no wonder my body had reacted the way it had. It's just too bad that Jaime had been in literal arm's reach to get some of the effect of that reaction.

Jaime batted my hand away when I reached toward his face in order to reassure myself that I hadn't hurt him too badly. "For God's sake, I'm fine. I'm fine," he repeated when I made a dubious scoffing sound. "Just answer your danged phone. It's gotta be important if they're calling you at this time of the night."

Shit. I was nowhere near lucid enough to have formed that conclusion. But Jaime was right. Middle of the night, hours before the ass-crack of dawn phone calls pretty much spelled trouble. I'm not sure who in the hell would be calling me. I wasn't exactly on most people's important—disturb-their-sleep important—news contact lists.

I probably should look to see who was calling. And since Jaime wasn't letting me apologize or inspect him for injury through touch, I rolled over and reached for my phone laying on the nightstand on my side of the bed. Huh. I suppose after de facto living with Jaime for over a month now, I could consider this side of the bed to be my side.

When I saw my best friend Greg's name flashing across the screen, I frantically grabbed my phone and answered it.

"Cuuuuube… Duuuude… Aah-ouuuuuuu…"

I pulled the phone away from my face and looked at it in disbelief. What was up with Greg? I hadn't heard him sounding this high since... the last time we'd been high. Which was all the way back in high school when we'd gigglingly accepted a suspect-looking joint off of the constantly stoned kid in our class.

You know the one. Every high school seemed to have one. The guy who was strangely mellow, always falling asleep in class, couldn't string two sentences together, and you could smell his weed funk-cloud aroma from ten feet away? Sheesh, I don't know what strain of weed that kid had rolled in that joint or what the fuck else he might've had mixed in there, but Greg and I had gotten so high off our asses.

And that was how Greg sounded now on the phone. High off his ass. Snorting and laughing and howling like a demented werewolf. At three-something in the morning. What the hell was going on?

"Greg?" I asked after I put the phone back to my ear. "What's going on? Why are you calling me so late? What's wrong?"

I didn't get an immediate answer to my questions, instead there was the sound of Greg giggling, then a scuffle, and a mumbled, feminine, "Oh, for Pete's sake. Greg. Give me that." Then, over the phone, came the sound of Greg's wife, Crystal.

While I would gladly donate a kidney to my lifelong best friend, if he needed one, I'd sacrifice a kidney, both lungs, and any other vital organ she might like for his wife. The woman who made Greg smile like a besotted idiot and had given him three smart, beautiful, wonderful children—while graciously allowing me to be their godfather—was a woman to be treasured, and worshipped, and adored. She'd also put up with being my friend since the days where I'd taste-tested different brands of glue to figure out which one tasted better. I'd do anything for that woman. Which she knew but, thankfully, didn't try to exploit all that often.

"Johnny?" she said and… Ugh. Doing anything for her meant that I had to tolerate her using my real first name. Or, at least, the childhood nickname version of it. God. At least she didn't tack on the 'Little' in front of it, like my parents and, seemingly, every other adult in my hometown of What Cheer, Iowa persisted in doing. "Oh. Johnny. I'm so sorry. I didn't know Greg had gotten ahold of his phone. I was afraid something like this would happen and that's why I'd hidden it from him in the first place. Or, at least, I'd tried to hide it from him."

Crystal didn't sound upset or as if anything was wrong. She sounded tired. But it was the middle of the night and, frankly, she often sounded tired since she juggled a full-time job, three kids, and a Greg.

But I was still concerned as to why my friend sounded so little like his usual self, so I asked her, "Why are you hiding Greg's phone, Crys? What's going on? Why does Greg sound higher than the space shuttle? Is everything okay?"

"Greg broke his leg this afternoon," Crystal replied with an affectionate-sounding sigh.

"Holy crap," I gasped.

"Yeah. We finally got back from the emergency room a little while ago and Greg is stoned off his ass on pain meds," Crystal said. "Apparently when you supply all of the local doctors and the hospital with pharmaceuticals, they give you the good stuff when you get injured. Who knew? The downside of that is that now I get to deal with a high-as-a-kite Greg. Fun times for me. I was worried he'd start prank calling people or dial some country neither one of us has heard of before, which was why I hid his phone from him. I'm not sure how he found it, but at least he only called you."

"Holy crap, Crys. Is he… Is he okay? I mean… obviously he broke his leg, but is he okay?"

Next to me, Jaime let out a sympathetic noise. I doubted he was able to hear much beyond my side of the conversation but he clearly had caught on that someone I knew—someone who would want to bother me in the middle of the night with the news—had hurt themselves. He was such a nice guy. I'd fill him in on what was going on with my friend once I got off the phone with Crystal.

"Yeah. He'll be fine," she answered. "Six to eight weeks and he should be good as new."

Ugh. That was going to suck. I'd broken a couple fingers before and that had been inconvenient and annoying. But I'd had to deal with that for only half that time and, as long as I kept them properly splinted and was careful with them, my hand had still been partially functional. I didn't want to even imagine how much of a pain in the ass a whole broken leg would be.

"Still, that's going to be hard on you having him laid up for that long," I said. "And we both know Greg isn't the best patient in the world, either. Are Barb and Dennis going to be helping you out with the kids?" Greg's parents, who only lived a couple of blocks away from Greg and Crystal, were doting and devoted grandparents and they often played babysitter, chauffer, spectator, and playmate for the kids.

"Oh, I'm sure they will," Crystal answered. "Once they get back to town. They're currently on the cruise we gave them using the bonus Greg earned this year. They're off trying to spot whales off the coast of Alaska."

I made myself a mental note to splurge on some sort of luxury vacation that I could send two of my favorite people in the world on. It was nice of them to spread their good fortune around to Greg's parents, but Greg's hard work should be rewarded. Greg and Crystal deserved all the good things in life. And a little extra bribery, so they continued to put up with me, wouldn't hurt.

"When do they get back?" I asked.

"I think... another six or seven days?"

Crystal's parents had moved to somewhere in New Mexico a couple years ago and I wasn't sure what other sort of support they had in town. Was there someone else they could call to help out until Greg's parents returned? They were going to need it. Especially during these first couple days, where they were all trying to figure out just how limited Greg's mobility would be, what he'd be able to do and what he'd need help with, and how much medication he'd need to take and when. And that was without taking into

196

consideration how the kids would react to their dad being injured. How would this wrench in the well-oiled machinery of their family routine affect them?

"Crys... that's a lot of time for you to be by yourself with the kids and an injured hubby. Why don't... Why don't I fly out and give you a hand for a little while? Until Barb and Dennis are back and can pitch in." I blurted the offer out without really thinking about it first.

But once it was out there, Jaime's warm hand brushing against my bare hip was a soothing reassurance that he probably didn't even realize he was giving. I would probably be of little to no help with the kids—I only saw them in small chunks of time throughout the year and I couldn't recall ever having to be in charge of them before. But even my mediocre help had to be better than nothing.

"You really don't need to do that, Johnny. We'll be fine," Crystal calmly stated.

I'm sure they would be. Crystal was disgustingly competent. But I didn't want them to be just fine. I wanted them to be good. Excellent. Worry-free and relaxed. Well... as much as they could be with Greg having a broken leg and all. And with having to rely on me to step in and play parent so this broken leg bump in the road disturbed their routine as little as possible.

"I'm coming," I told her. "No arguing. So, you might as well accept it and lay out the special 'We Heart Cube' welcome mat."

"I threw that thing out after you gave it to us for Christmas," Crystal dryly informed me.

"No! Say it ain't so."

"It was one of the ugliest things I'd ever seen in my life."

"It was one of a kind!"

Only a couple inches away from me, Jaime quietly murmured, "Good. Then, hopefully, I won't have to worry about one of those showing up unexpectedly in my home."

And, through the magic of technology, Crystal, unknowingly, echoed his sentiments, saying, "Thank fuck for that. Now I can rest easy, knowing there are no more of those visual abominations out there." *Hmpfh. Philistines, the both of them, with no sense of style or whimsy.* Crystal sounded hesitantly hopeful as she asked, "Are you sure you don't mind coming to Iowa to help with the kids?"

"Not at all," I told her. "It's the off season. I'm not doing anything else right now." I felt the loss of Jaime's hand as he removed it from my hip. And I sensed him, more than felt him, shift his weight to put a little bit of space between us. A frown creased my brow, but I didn't have the attention to spare to figure out what was up with him just this second. "I'll even help out with Greg," I told Crystal. "'Cause that's the kind of nice guy I am."

"You're a wonderful guy, Johnny. You always have been and we both know that I know that, so don't even try your usual modest denials."

"I think you might be the only person who's ever used that word in relation to me," I said.

"Wonderful?"

"No. Modest," I said.

"That's because you don't let the rest of the world see the real you," she replied. "Greg and I are the lucky ones in that regard. And the kids, too, of course."

"I hate that it took this for it to happen, but it'll be nice to spend some time with them. I should come visit more often."

Jaime's bedding rustled as he slid out from under the sheets. My eyes idly traced the path he took, over to his dresser, where he pulled out a pair of briefs—in a bright turquoise color that looked stunning against his pale skin—then slipped on a t-shirt and a pair of cotton sleep shorts as well.

Jaime donning clothes indicated to me that he planned on exiting the bedroom. For some reason, the freak didn't like roaming around his own house naked. I'm not sure who he thought would be bothered by his nudity. I sure as fuck wouldn't be and, as far as I knew, he and I were the only ones routinely here who'd be around to see him walking around the place in his birthday suit. Like I said... freak.

"You should," Crystal agreed. "But we all understand your time is limited and we'll take what we can get. It'll be good to see you, Johnny. Let me know your flight info and when we can expect to see you, okay?"

"Okay. Love you."

"Love you, too. See you soon."

After I hung up with Crystal, I lay snuggled between Jaime's soft sheets. I was a little bummed and a little relieved that he hadn't noticed that I'd switched his plain white ones with ones that were a pale seafoam-y green. Little by little, I was making his drab dwelling prettier and nicer.

Jaime didn't even have the excuse that he was too distracted by frantic headboard-banging sex when we turned in for bed tonight. That's not to say we hadn't had sex. We had. And like all the fucking we've been doing, it was awesome. It had just been a little slower and gentler than some of our get-the-anger-and-aggression-out bouts of fucking had been. So, Jaime certainly should have noticed the much better sheets—that I'd accidentally-on-purpose forgotten to mention—that had been under him as I'd plowed his ass.

Oh well. I'm sure he would notice at some point. And then I'd either be rewarded with sex or punished with sex. The whole thing was a win all the way around for me. Make Jaime's—and, temporarily, my—surroundings prettier as I saw fit and get sex.

Fuck, it sucked that Greg had broken his leg. For everyone's sake, I hoped it healed quickly. I also hoped that Crystal did a better job of hiding Greg's phone this time around, or else he was bound to call someone he shouldn't. Like Tuvalu. Or his boss.

At least Greg didn't have any exes to drunk dial while he was stoned off his ass; Crystal was the only girl he'd ever dated. They'd even managed to keep their relationship going during college while she was at the University of Iowa and he and I attended the University of Wisconsin.

I'm not sure how long I laid in Jaime's bed, letting my sympathy and worry for my friend wash through me and trying to work through the logistics of which airport it would be better to fly into before driving to our hometown of What Cheer. But it slowly occurred to me that it had probably been a fair bit longer than just a few minutes. Where had Jaime gone to and why hadn't he come back to bed? It was the middle of the night. He'd been gone for much longer than it would take for a quick pee or getting a drink of water. Heck, he'd been gone much longer than it would've taken to do both of those things.

Had he left under the assumption that I would want some privacy for my phone call? That hadn't been at all necessary, but it wouldn't surprise me. That was the sort of sweet, thoughtful gesture that Jaime would do. I'd have to go find him and tell him that I hadn't needed for him to leave his own bedroom while I was on the phone with my friends. I didn't keep secrets from them.

Well… other than that they didn't know I was currently shacked up with my on-ice nemesis in Minnesota and had been for over a month. But other than that…

And I didn't feel any need to keep anything about them a secret from Jaime. In fact… Maybe… Maybe Jaime would be interested in coming to Iowa with me.

I'd been doing my utmost best to fuck Jaime Johnson out of my system. As often as we physically could. In between all the other stuff we'd found ourselves doing together. Like…

like… a couple. It was… unexpected. But, despite what some people might think, I wasn't an idiot. And six weeks of trying and failing to fuck Jaime enough that I'd be sick of him had demonstrated to me that… I wasn't getting over Jaime Johnson any time soon.

So, maybe it was time for something else. Something more like… a relationship. Some kind of thing.

Huh.

Did I necessarily want to have Jaime in my hometown and meeting the people that had known me since before I'd learned to walk? Known me growing up and seen me in all my gross geeky phases? The people who probably, definitely, had photographic proof that, once upon a time, I'd had a bowl cut, acne, and braces… all at the same time? On top of that, bringing Jaime with me to Greg's house would throw the doors wide open to all the embarrassing and horrifying stories Greg and Crystal had about me.

And my parents. Ugh. My. Parents.

There's no way I'd be able to go home and not see them. It just wasn't that big of a town. Which meant that if Jaime came along… he would meet them. There'd be no way to avoid it. Did I really want Jaime Johnson to be exposed to the strange entities that purported to be the beings that spawned me?

Jaime only knew me as the awesome hockey player, cool guy, and sexual stud that I currently was. What would he think of me if he caught a glimpse of the man behind the curtain of who I was now? I guess the only way to find out was to yank on the curtain cords and show him all of me. Not just the best parts of me that I was currently showing him.

So, there was really only one thing for me to do.

I flung the sheets aside, pulled on a pair of sleep shorts—out of deference for Jaime's clothed state and because this was the sort of question you probably didn't ask a dude while you were only in your birthday suit—and wandered out to track down my errant Jaime.

Chapter Sixteen

Jaime

I knew I'd only regret it and wind up spending way too much time scrubbing it back out, but I was incredibly tempted to drizzle globs of melting ice cream directly onto the plush fabric of the bright blue couch J.J. had purchased. It was the middle of the night, although closer to morning than I'd like to think about, and I was spooning my feelings into my mouth, one frozen scoopful at a time. I was a pathetic cliché.

What in the world had J.J. done to me? Last week it was most of a pan of brownies. Tonight I was shoveling in a large serving of ice cream into my mouth. Granted my mindset while I was gorging myself on sugar was vastly different this time around than it had been the last time. But, either way, the highs and lows of being around J.J. was clearly wrecking my nutritional self-control.

Not that I should be feeling any lows that needed a gigantic application of sugar to fix. There was absolutely no reason my feelings should be hurt that my... J.J. ... had rushed to answer a phone call from... whomever it was that had called him. In the middle of the night. It was clearly someone he was close to. Actually, two someones because I'd heard J.J. call one of them Greg and the other Chris.

And just because it sounded like he was leaving to go visit them, after saying that he wasn't doing anything else important right now, didn't mean that I should be feeling any of these ridiculous twinges of jealousy, or sadness, or upset. Or hurt that I counted as nothing important to him. Not. At. All.

I should be glad that J.J. was leaving. I hadn't invited him to come to my house. I hadn't explicitly asked him to stay. He just had. And then, while he was here, he'd had the gall to start replacing my stuff. First it was my couch, my clothes, and my towels. And now it was my sheets. Although, J.J. seemed unaware that I'd noticed the new sheets. What would it be next time? Would I come home to find an entire wall of my apartment missing because J.J. took some ridiculous offense to it? Really, I should be feeling absolutely nothing other than relief that he was finally taking himself and leaving.

Absolutely nothing other than relief.

I spooned another heaping mound of mint chocolate chip ice cream into my mouth.

"Oooh. I want some. Did you save me some?" J.J. asked as he made his way out of my bedroom, his phone call apparently over.

"No. I didn't save you any," I told him. Which was the truth. I'd scraped and scraped all the last bits of the creamy, green, frozen goodness out of the carton. I tried to contain my smirk as I intentionally neglected to remind him that there was also a carton of moose tracks in the freezer. And that one was still mostly full.

"Oh, well. Guess I'm out of luck then," J.J. said, shrugging. Dang it. Spite wasn't as much fun when the spite-ee didn't care. He settled on the couch next to me, bumping my shoulder with his and causing me to drip a droplet of ice cream onto my leg. "You didn't have to leave. It's your bedroom and I don't mind if you listen in on my phone calls," J.J. stated.

"Well… I wasn't sure…"

There's no way I was going to admit that I left because I'd felt like an unwelcome third wheel. The whole time he's been here, J.J. had either spent his time with me or hanging out in my apartment, waiting for me. Or so it felt. The phone call he'd gotten had been a jolted reminder that I wasn't the only person in J.J.'s universe. What had been an even more unwelcome realization, was that I had enjoyed feeling like the only person in his world.

"Besides it was just Greg. And then his wife Crys… um… Crystal," J.J. corrected himself. "…after she wrested the phone away from him. They're my oldest and closest friends. I've known them both since elementary school," J.J. said.

And now I felt like a giant pile of dog doo for being jealous of J.J.'s childhood friends for pulling his attention away from me. "Apparently, Greg broke his leg yesterday and Crystal won't have anyone to help her with him or their three kids until Greg's parents come back from the Alaskan cruise they're on."

"And you're going there to help," I stated.

That's what I'd overheard him saying and I wasn't going to pretend like I hadn't. I was going to act like the thought of J.J. leaving, like what we'd been doing together for the past six weeks didn't matter, didn't bother me in the least. I didn't want to give him the satisfaction of knowing that I didn't want him to go and that my apartment would probably feel empty and far too quiet and calm with him gone. I liked quiet and calm. I did. I just needed to remind my aching heart of that fact.

"Yeah. I am," J.J. confirmed. He reached over and, using the tip of his index finger, smeared up the drip of mint chocolate chip ice cream off my leg, then licked it off his finger, emitting a pleased sound. "You could... you could come with me. To Iowa." I looked over at J.J. and saw him shooting me quick glances out of the corner of his eye. Nervous and uncertain was a strange and unusual look for J.J. Johnson. "I know... Iowa. Blech," J.J. said, pretending to gag. "Nobody willingly goes there. Especially the tiny nothing speck on the map that is my boring hometown. But it's where my idiotic best friend and his family insist on living, so I'm forced to make the trek back there a couple times a year. It's not... it's not *so* bad."

To make sure J.J. wasn't throwing this offer out there out of some misguided sense of politeness or pity, I asked, "You want me to come with you? To visit your friends?"

J.J. rubbed the back of his neck, where I could've sworn a faint redness was blooming. "Yeah. And… uh… probably my parents as well," J.J. replied with an embarrassed twist of his mouth. "It's a small town. They'll know we're there and we won't be able to avoid them. As much as that'd be nice," he said with a mutter.

"You want me… To meet. Your parents?"

"No," J.J. stated emphatically, turning toward me with wide eyes and taking my hands in his. "I don't want you to meet my parents." I was about to get huffily miffed when J.J. added, "I'd like to not have to meet my parents. It's just something that'll be unavoidable if you come to Iowa with me. So, I wanted to warn you about it." Shy was also a strange look on J.J.'s face. But it was with a shy smile that he said, "I want you to meet my friends, though."

"Yeah?"

The moment seemed ripe for a serious discussion of what we were doing with each other. We'd clearly moved far past the temporary, impetuous fling stage of whatever this was. But J.J. seemed just as hesitant as I was to actually talk about what all of that meant. I was still grappling with the notion that I didn't dislike J.J. Johnson as much as I'd always thought I had. Or rather, the traits that used to drive me around the bend and made me want to smash his face in with my hockey stick were now merely annoying and sometimes amusing quirks of his personality.

But the moment passed, after a charged minute with J.J. and I staring at each other, when J.J. joked, "But at least I'll be around, so it won't be as boring as it usually would be. I really have no idea how Greg and the bunch can stand it there when I'm not around to make it all so much more awesome."

How did I get myself into these situations? And what was it about this man that he had me agreeing to go along with what he wanted even when my brain was shrieking at me that it was a bad idea?

"Alright. Yeah. Sure," I said. "I'll come to Iowa with you. Meet your friends. And your parents."

Obviously J.J. wanted to get to Iowa to help out his friend as soon as feasible. But it still seemed like no time at all had passed between that hours-before-sunrise conversation on my couch to us driving down a stretch of highway in Iowa, bounded on both sides as far as the eye could see with fields upon fields of corn.

There'd been the stages of booking two airline tickets to Des Moines, throwing a week's worth of clothes in a suitcase, driving to the Minneapolis airport, boarding our plane, waiting to get on our plane—so, so much waiting—the relatively short hour-long flight, and getting our rental car in the interim.

And just like that, here I was sitting in the passenger seat of said rental car and fast on my way to J.J.'s hometown and getting an intimate insight into how he'd grown up and the people who were the closest to him.

So far, my first experience with the state of Iowa was… about what I'd expected. I'd grown up in the suburbs of Chicago, so I was used to the flatness of Illinois. Iowa was just as flat, the land expanding out to the horizon with nary a ripple or hilly bump. But, at least, urban Illinois had stuff to look at. Buildings, people, roads, parks, more buildings. Iowa… just had the corn. With only the occasional billboard or pig farm as the extent of visual excitement, I felt like I'd stumbled across another dimension. I'd never felt like such a city boy until now.

After an hour-and-a-half of corn, corn, pigs, and more corn, J.J. flipped the blinker on the rental car for the exit ramp of What Cheer, Iowa. Population of 607 people. Wow. J.J. hadn't been kidding when he'd said his hometown was small. There'd been more kids who attended my high school than the entire population of J.J.'s hometown. Actually, I think there'd been three times more kids in my high school than lived in this tiny little spot of Iowa.

"What Cheer?" I asked. "That's a—"

"Stupidly crappy name? I know," J.J. said. "Not sure what idiot thought that one up. Personally, I think they must've misunderstood what the old dude... we'll assume it was an old dude that named the town... was saying. I always assumed he was asking 'What's here?' and everybody just heard him wrong. And I'll tell you what's here. Nothing. Absolutely jack shit nothing."

"Okaayyy..."

"I don't know why the hell Greg and Crystal are so attached to the place. Sure, Greg got a good job supplying the hospitals and clinics in the surrounding area and they tell me it's a great place to raise kids... But, whatever. How great of a place can it be to raise kids when there's nothing to do other than husking corn every fall and you have to round up all the kids from ten different small towns across three counties to have enough kids to form a school district? When we were wrapping up college, I told them... it's one thing to be so dumb you want to settle in Iowa, of all places. But at least pick one of the so-called cities. But nooo... They had to stubbornly pick the place we grew up in so their kids could live in the same town as Greg's folks."

We drove through a downtown—if you could even call it that—that was about two blocks long and was mostly made up of red brick buildings from around the turn of the last century. Driving over a small creek, we went past the only gas station I'd seen in town, which also seemed to be combined with the only convenience store and restaurant dining option available. Then there were another couple blocks of houses closer together along the tree-lined streets before they started getting further and further apart as we moved away from the center of town.

Driving by the What Cheer Public Library, which was smaller in size than the only gas station, I commented, "Huh. There really isn't a whole lot to do here, is there?"

"What tipped you over to that realization?" J.J. asked. "Was it the complete lack of any stores other than the Dollar General, the lack of any form of entertainment like a movie theater or even a bowling alley, or the fact that we've driven past more cemeteries than bars or places to eat?"

"Uh… All of that?" I replied.

"And, to think, we drove in from the west. There are twice as many cemeteries past the east end of the town." J.J. dryly and morbidly told me. "If the zombie apocalypse started today, the folks living in What Cheer would be tragically far outnumbered by the number of dead rising from their graves."

Okaaay… That was a terrifying, if unlikely, prospect.

"But not to fear. For a town of around six hundred people, What Cheer for some reason has four churches we can choose between to try to claim sanctuary in. Before the zombies conquer us and eat all our brains."

"You seem to have thought about this a lot," I observed faintly.

"Hmm," J.J. hummed. "In middle school mostly. I don't really recall if the zombie apocalypse and brain devouring was something I was afraid of or something I hoped for."

J.J. flipped the blinker on again before making a turn down a narrow, unmarked two-way lane that seemed to be taking us back into the countryside. A minute or two later and he was pulling our rental car into the long driveway of a light blue split-level house with white trim.

It looked like we were here. Time for me to meet J.J.'s friends.

I hoped they liked me.

I hoped that I liked them.

I really hoped I didn't puke all over the rose bushes planted to the left of the front stoop.

Chapter 17
J.J.

Over the past six years that they'd been living in this house, I'd probably spent a total of a month's worth of days staying at Greg and Crystal's house. However, the unremarkable blue house felt like home in a way that my condo in Kansas City—where I'd lived full-time for the past four years—didn't. I guessed the cliché was true—home is where the heart is. And this home contained the people I loved most in the world.

I resisted the urge to glance at the man in the passenger seat of the rental car, whose Minneapolis apartment had also started to feel sort of home-like. My brain was only going to think about what I let it think about and I didn't want to think about what that could mean regarding my feelings for Jaime Johnson.

"Well, we're here," I announced unnecessarily. Jaime's smile looked sort of grimace-like, so I reassured him, "There's nothing to worry about. They're going to love you."

Nope. Still not thinking about... feelings things.

Huh. I wonder if I should have told Greg and Crystal that I was bringing Jaime with me.

Oh, well. Too late now. He was here with me and they'd just have to deal with it. I'm sure it would be fine. Greg and Crystal were friendly, welcoming people. And they put up with me. Compared to the wild amusement park that was me, Jaime was a calm, boring stroll in the park.

After we got out of the car, I nonchalantly told Jaime that I'd bring our suitcases in later. That would make it easier if, just in case, Greg and Crystal weren't okay with Jaime's presence and we had to lug our stuff to a motel in nearby Oskaloosa for the duration of our stay. I didn't say that part out loud. Jaime already looked like he was going to hurl, I didn't want to add to his nerves.

Before I even had to knock on the front door, it was thrown wide open and a grinning Katie Phillipi beamed her happiness to see me through the glass storm door.

"Uncle J.J! You're here!"

"Pipsqueak!" I cried back at her. "You're my favorite thing I've seen all day!"

Katie had always taken after her mother, with the same tangle of dark hair, bright blue eyes, and big contagious smile. But at the age of four, my eldest godchild and honorary niece was the spitting image of her mother at that age. Or near abouts. And I could say that with good authority since I'd first met Crystal in kindergarten. Katie tended to be more laidback and go-with-the-flow like her father, though.

No. The one who'd inherited Crystal's high-octane, nonstop energy was two-year-old Daniel. His sturdy little toddler body, with its mop of blond hair that would probably darken to a light brown the way his father's had as he got older, barreled past his sister and collided with the storm door with a thump. His blue eyes—the same indigo shade as Crystal and Katie's—were partially obscured by a long hank of that hair. And they'd either taken him to an inept hairstylist or they'd cut his hair themselves, because Daniel was sporting a clumpy, messy faux mohawk.

"Unka J! Unka Jay! I's pooed onna potty!" Daniel announced with all the glee and pride his little body could hold.

"That's awesome, D-man," I told him. That was the sort of thing you congratulated a kid about, right?

"Don't get too excited," Crystal said as she appeared behind her two older children, baby Resa propped on her hip. She swung the storm door open but didn't move out of the way so we could actually enter the house. "This morning he also peed all over the floor. Although, that might just be a boy thing and not a potty-training-toddler thing. Pretty sure Greg did too last week."

"You try aiming when you've got a broken leg, woman. We'll see how well you'd do," called a voice from further inside the house.

"It'll still work if you're sitting down," Crystal called back. "Why don't you try that? And your leg wasn't broken last week, you idiot." Crystal swiveled her attention over to Jaime, who was nervously hovering behind me on the front stoop. "And who do we have here?" she asked, shooting me a fast curious look before she smiled a big smile at him.

"Um. Hi. Jaime Johnson," Jaime said as he reached his hand out to shake Crystal's.

"You're adorable," Crystal responded. "Much cuter in person than you are on tv. And it was a rhetorical question. I know who you are. I'm more just curious as to why Johnny didn't mention he was bringing a... *friend?*"

I groaned and dropped my head back at her slip of calling me by my real first name. Well, childhood nickname. I'd known going into this situation that there'd been absolutely no chance of Jaime not learning what it was. Didn't mean I had to like it, though. I hated being called Johnny. Or John. Or any variation of my given name.

"Johnny?" Jaime repeated, with curiosity and a hint of glee in his voice.

"Oops?" Crystal said. Funny, but she didn't look sorry. Mischievous? Yes. Sorry? No.

"Johnny? Really?" Jaime asked again.

I ignored his curiosity. All the while knowing I'd wind up answering all his questions later, anyway. "You gonna let us in, Crys? Or are we just going to stand here on the front step, in front of an open door, letting all the bugs in and the AC out?"

217

Katie started chanting "In, in, in" while Daniel joyously shrieked "Buuuuuggggs!" Resa, being a baby, burbled some spit bubbles. Then added some gas bubbles out of the other end as well. I'm not entirely sure how to interpret that as to which option she was voting for.

"Thanks for that, Johnny. You know I'm going to find Daniel trying to pry open any and all windows and doors to let bugs into the house now, right?"

"You brought it on yourself, Crys."

"Just go ahead and get your cute little butts into the house," she said. "And I'm including your butt in there, Jaime."

I turned around, placed my hand against the small of Jaime's back, and nudged him to proceed me into the house.

Katie immediately asked him, "Will you read me a book? I got bunches you can pick."

Daniel latched himself to Jaime's leg like a little chunky spider monkey. Then, he looked up at him and said, "Hi. I pooped inna potty."

"So, you mentioned," Jaime said as he looked over his shoulder at me with wide, surprised, and uncertain eyes.

"Go on, I'll bring the suitcases inside," I told Jaime. "If you do read Katie a book, just don't pick *No More Monkeys Jumping on the Bed*. That evil book needlessly tries to brainwash all the fun out of kids. There's absolutely nothing wrong with a little mattress trampolining."

"It's a classic," Crystal stated. "And we're not getting rid of it, no matter how many times you ask or try to hide it, Johnny."

I mouthed the words 'evil' and 'brainwash' while hovering my hands around my head in my best pantomime. An action that was cut short by an *oouf* of pain and surprise when Crystal elbowed me in the stomach.

"Oh. Uh. Okay," Jaime replied, seemingly uncertain how to react to this whole exchange.

Jaime let Katie lead him toward their playroom, Daniel clinging to his leg with a death-grip to his shorts the whole time. I might not get to see them or spend as much time with them as I'd like, but my honorary niblets were incredibly important to me and I felt a warm glow over seeing Jaime with them and interacting with them.

"Sooo… Jaime Johnson?" Crystal asked.

"Yeah," I replied, rubbing the back of my neck and offering her a sheepish smile. "It's okay that I brought him along with me, isn't it?"

"That depends," Crystal answered. "Is he here voluntarily or did you kidnap him? Is this a Stockholm Syndrome situation? Does he have selective amnesia and not remember that he doesn't like you?"

"No, you smartass. He's here voluntarily," I told her.

"Just making sure. I mean… I know Greg has said that you've had a major man-crush on the dude for a while…"

"Have not," I muttered half-heartedly. It was probably silly to keep denying that I've been interested in Jaime for a while. Not now, now that we were... whatever we were.

"Yuh huh," she continued, shooting me a dubious look. "But even if I'd known that Jaime Johnson was into guys, you're not who I would've pictured him with. Sorry." Crystal shrugged as if her words didn't feel like she'd just lodged a poison arrow into my chest. "He's just so... And you're so..." She paused as she mentally fumbled around for something to say that probably wouldn't sound horribly insulting. To me. Finally, she shrugged again and finished with, "I just would never have expected it, is all."

It stung. But only because there was a fair amount of accuracy to what she'd said and alluded to. I wasn't the kind of guy I would've expected Jaime to go for either. But surely, I had some redeeming qualities that would make a guy like Jaime want to keep me around. And the fact that he'd chosen me—when even my closest friends couldn't understand why he'd done so—just meant that I had to appreciate that he had and make sure I treated Jaime the way he deserved so that he wouldn't regret or question his decision.

"Yeah," I sighed. "But here we are. Try not to scare him off, m'kay?"

"I won't if you won't."

Chapter Eighteen
Jaime

The kids kept me busy and occupied for the rest of the afternoon. So, it wasn't until we were all sitting down to dinner that I brought the topic of what Crystal had called him back up.

"So. Johnny?" I inquired, as I speared a cherry tomato out of my salad with a fork then popped it into my mouth.

"Ugh. Yes," J.J. groaned. "The first J in my name is for John. That's what's on my birth certificate."

"And you don't go by that because...?" I asked. The name John Johnson wasn't the... best. But it wasn't *horrible*.

"'Cause that's also his dad's name," Greg answered around a mouthful of grilled pork chop. "And since everyone in What Cheer knows everyone else, everybody already knew his dad as John. So, our J.J. grew up being called Little Johnson or Johnny Junior."

J.J. made a puke-face at his opinion of both those names. I suppose, for obvious reasons. What self-respecting guy wanted to be called 'Little Johnson'?

"That's what the second J is for?" I asked. "Junior? You're John Johnson Jr.? Huh. Three Js."

"That's why I started calling him Cube," Greg said. "J cubed." Greg followed that statement up with a defensively muttered, "What? It made sense to me."

"Actually the second J is just for Johnson," J.J. explained. "I'm not actually a Junior. My dad and I don't have the same middle name. But when we were about to move on to middle school, I decided that I wanted to just be called J.J. for John Johnson."

"But... J.J. Johnson? Wouldn't that make you John Johnson Johnson? That doesn't really make sense," I commented.

"Eh. I was ten," he replied. "I just knew I didn't want to be called John Junior or Little Johnson anymore."

"And you couldn't have gone by your middle name?" I paused for a moment as I thought. "Actually, what is your middle name?"

"Yeah, Johnny, tell him what your middle name is," Crystal said.

"And why you didn't want to use that name either," Greg added with a giant grin.

"It's Harrison," J.J. stated, rolling his eyes.

I blinked. Wait. Wasn't the name Harrison usually shortened to... "So..."

"Yeah. I would've been Harry Johnson." J.J. grunted a laugh. "That for fu-uuumble wasn't going to happen." J.J. glanced at the little cuties messily shoveling their food into their mouths at the table with us. *Yeah. Not so easy to hold back on the swearing, was it?* "Especially, not in middle school. Do you seriously think I wouldn't have punched each and every person who called me Harry Johnson?"

"True story," Greg said. "He let me say it once. Second time... Pow. Fist to the nose. I mean... we were... what? Five? Six at the time? So, it wasn't like he could hit as hard then as he'd be able to now. But there was still blood and I still cried."

J.J. rolled his eyes at the outrage on his best friend's face over an incident that had occurred more than twenty years ago.

"I don't know what your parents were thinking, giving you that middle name," Crystal commented, as both she and J.J. ignored Greg's complaining. It probably wasn't the first time she'd heard that story. "I mean... I know your parents, so I know... Anyway. I know I'm not the only one who still calls him Johnny," Crystal said. "At least, not around here. But I'm probably the only one he lets get away with it."

The smile J.J. sent Crystal's direction looked strained but grateful. I wonder what he was grateful for? That she hadn't continued with whatever it was that she was going to say about his parents? Was whatever it was related to why J.J. didn't mention them very often and had admitted that he didn't want to see them even though he knew we would on this trip to his hometown?

I found myself eager to meet his parents. Not because I thought we were ready for the Meet the Parents step of a relationship—it seemed pretty obvious to me that we were in a relationship of some sort—but because it might finally answer my curiosity about them.

"Daddy, I'm done," Katie said, pointing at her empty plate.

"Me, too," Daniel piped in, even though his plate still had scattered bits of food all over it.

Crystal started to push her chair back from the table, but Greg said, "Nah. I'll go take them to wash up. I've got to use the little boys' room, anyway."

"That means Daddy's gotta pee!" Daniel happily exclaimed.

"Sure does, little man. And Daddy will even sit this time so Mommy doesn't get mad at him again," Greg commented.

Katie and Daniel dashed out of the dining room. Greg slowly and gingerly stood up and trundled after them on his crutches.

"I could always go back to calling you 'boogerface' like I did in kindergarten," Crystal stated, as if the interruption by her children, and them and Greg leaving the table, hadn't happened. "And first grade. And second grade. I think I switched over to 'buttbreath' sometime around—"

224

"Oh my God. Why are you like this?" J.J. asked as an uncharacteristic blush stained his cheeks and he mouthed the words 'ignore her' at me.

"Hey. That one kind of came true. At least, if you're into rimming. I assume you are," Crystal stated with a smug smile. "Since you like to use your mouth so much."

J.J.'s face was now a bright pink raspberry color. He sent pointed looks at Resa, who was still in her high chair next to the dining table. Crystal merely, literally, waved his concern away. She, clearly, wasn't concerned about her infant daughter comprehending what she'd said.

Interesting. I'd discovered the person—perhaps, the only person—who could make J.J. Johnson embarrassed. I needed to make this woman my new best friend.

"How do you know about... rimming?" J.J. asked, uttering the last word on a whisper and frantically looking around the room. Presumably, to make sure Katie or Daniel hadn't re-entered the room.

"Once upon a time... in a wild, crazy land called the 1980s..." Crystal said. "There came about this thing called the internet. And people being people, quickly filled up this remarkable technology with cat videos and porn." Crystal cocked an eyebrow and slyly stated, "Gay and bi dudes aren't the only ones who know what rimming is, Johnny. Us straight folks can explore the wonders that is the human butthole, too."

"I have never... I repeat... *never* met this woman before in my life," J.J. stated as he covered his red face with both hands. "Any evidence you may have seen to the contrary or anything I may have told you has all been lies. I don't know her. Really, I don't."

"Uh huh." I was so very, very glad I'd decided to come with J.J. to meet his friends. This moment was priceless. And fodder for all sorts of future blackmail.

"What did you expect, Cube?" Greg asked, leaning against the doorway to the dining room and keeping his weight off of his injured leg. In answer to Crystal's inquiring look and glance behind him, Greg said, "We got to the bathroom and Daniel decided he needed to poop. He's been doing a good job with that, but he likes to sit there and sing every song he can think of to himself while he's doing it. And, of course, Katie also decided she needed to go potty as well. So, I sent her off to their bathroom upstairs. Once they're done, I'll get my turn." Then, returning to the topic that was embarrassing their friend so much, he said, "After listening to you being damn near poetic telling me how great butt stuff was when we were in college, did you really think I wasn't going to try that out for myself? Please. It's like you've never even met me."

Dragging his hands down his face, J.J. turned to me with wide, horrified eyes and said, "I've never met him before, either. I have no best friend. I've never had a best friend. Greg Phillipi who? Never heard of the guy."

"Pffftht. You love me and we all know it," Greg responded.

J.J. heaved a large sigh then stated, "Anyway. In my parents' defense, Harrison is a little better than my dad's middle name. Which is Richard." Greg, Crystal, and I looked at J.J. in disbelief and shock. "Yeah. Neither one of us won in the middle name department," he said. "What with having a last name that's a euphemism for cock."

"Dick Johnson," Greg quietly mouthed with an appalled grimace. "Some surnames… you've got to be careful what names you pair them with."

A thoughtful expression crossed J.J.'s face followed by the return of his usual brash humor. "Hmm. Hey, Jaime?" J.J. asked.

"Um. Yes?"

"What does your first name mean in French, again, babe?" he asked me.

Greg flicked a quick, surprised look at me at J.J.'s use of that endearment. Perhaps because it made it blatantly clear that J.J. and I were more than casually involved. At least, to the level where he had no qualms about throwing out his pet name for me in front of others.

I didn't have a problem with J.J.'s friends knowing about us. Sure, it had made me nervous to let others in on what we were doing. I'd known that agreeing to travel to his hometown with J.J. would lead his friends to make the correct assumptions about us. But I'd had plenty of time on the plane to work through those nerves and accept that it was going to be what it was going to be.

Answering J.J.'s question, I resignedly stated, "It translates to 'I like' or 'I love'.

J.J. wasn't the only person not entirely thrilled with the name they'd been saddled with. Once I'd reached the age where some of my peers started taking French as a foreign language, I'd been inundated with people asking me if I knew what my name meant in that language. Especially every year leading to Valentine's Day because I'd, somehow, gotten stuck with the number fourteen on my hockey jersey.

With my name translating as it did, my jersey number, and growing up in a town called Romeoville... was it really much of a surprise that I'd wound up saddled with the hockey nickname I had?

"Uh huh. That's what I thought," J.J. said with a giant smug grin. "So, when... if?... you ever come out... The headlines are going to write themselves, aren't they?"

"Oh, God." I could feel myself blanch, while Greg started snort-laughing and Crystal reached across the table and gently patted my arm in sympathy.

I'd had the last name of Johnson for the last eighteen of my twenty-five years—since my parents had been able to adopt me and change my last name—and, as stated above, I'd been aware of the translation of my name for at least the last twelve or so years. How had I never before made the connection that J.J. had just made? If I ever came out, the media, the fans, and the internet were going to have a field day with me. Ugh.

"I'm sure it'll be fine," Crystal stated. J.J. started to open his mouth, probably to contradict her. But Crystal flashed him a mom-glare and slowly and deliberately repeated, "It. Will. Be. Fine."

Proving that mom-glares work even on people in their twenties who actually aren't even your children, J.J. nodded and unconvincingly echoed, "Yeah. It'll be fine. Course it will be. The internet's not completely full of assholes."

Her edict apparently put forth into the universe, Crystal stood up from the table and said, "Well. I think Katie and Daniel have had sufficient time to thoroughly destroy both our bathrooms. J.J. and Jaime, one of you rectify that. And the other one can round up the kiddos, wrangle them into their jammies, get them eight million glasses of water, then tuck them into bed." Crystal efficiently unbuckled the baby from her highchair and handed her off to J.J. "Greg and I are going to bed. It's been a long day. We'll see you in the morning."

J.J., looking surprised to be holding a baby and summarily pressed into service and dismissed, turned to me as we both declared, "Not it."

Chapter Nineteen

J.J.

What Cheer, Iowa was never going to be my favorite place. Growing up, I couldn't wait to be able to leave this tiny speck of nothingness and go somewhere, anywhere, else. But I had to admit, Greg and Crystal did have a pretty sweet setup here.

Their house was a sprawling split-level style house that was probably built sometime in the 1980s and it sat on a giant corner lot with a huge yard next to houses with equally huge yards. And while the house had all of its original quirky character, it was thoroughly updated and stylishly decorated with a minimalist modern farmhouse feel. At least, what décor you could see under the general clutter and stuff that accumulated whenever multiple people—the majority of whom were under the age of five—all lived together in one house.

There was also plenty of space for their three kids to be kids. Besides all the space inside the house for all their toys and the large yard, back behind their backyard neighbor, there was a large open field that I know the kids could romp in to their heart's delight.

And the guest bedroom Jaime and I were in—the one I usually stayed in when I visited—while technically in the lower level, didn't feel like it was stuck in some neglected, dingy basement. Because the property had been contoured to create a slope away from the house, the lower level was exposed on the back of the house and the guest room had full-sized windows that overlooked the large expanse of their lawn and let in plenty of light during the day. Not that there was much of a view of anything through those windows, other than some fireflies winking in the darkening night, when I directed Jaime there and deposited our luggage next to the room's dresser.

After Crystal had given us our marching orders and retired to her own comfortable bed for the evening, Jaime and I had had a brief silent argument—him squinting his eyes at me, me raising my brows and widening my eyes at him, Jaime scrunching up his freckled nose and curling his upper lip, me narrowing my eyes and giving him an unimpressed look and frown—before I had sighed and reluctantly agreed to tackle the bathroom messes and leaving the wrangling of Katie and Daniel for bedtime to Jaime.

Jaime had definitely gotten the better end of that deal. Sure, he looked exhausted. And I felt bad thrusting him directly into childminding mode only a couple hours after he'd met the little darlings. But at least he didn't end up looking like he'd gone a couple rounds with some angry defensemen the way I did.

I'd caught a glimpse of myself in the mirror as I'd exited the bathroom the kids shared on the second floor, and my dark, chin-length hair was poofed out on one side and damp and stringy on the other. I had a smudge of something blue—I'm hoping it was toothpaste—smeared on one cheek and both my shirt and shorts were crumpled, wrinkled, and soaked with random wet splotches.

"Oh my God," I groaned as I stripped my wrecked shirt off and threw it into a corner of the room. "Remind me to ask Greg why he wanted kids. And what the fuck they're feeding those little monsters to turn them into destructive, bathroom-destroying hooligans."

"You thought cleaning up after them was bad? I'm the one that was stuck getting them ready for bed," Jaime reminded me. "Have you ever tried to get a pair of pajamas on a four-year-old? They wriggle and squirm and try to 'help' you. I didn't really have the heart to tell her, but jumping on the bed, running around the room naked, and bending her arms in ways that should be anatomically impossible are in no way helpful."

"I am so ready for bed," I stated. "But there's no way I can climb into bed without a shower first. I don't even want to think about what I might've gotten on me when I was cleaning up that mess."

"Oh. A shower sounds really good," Jaime commented with a filthy moan that normally only I could get him to make. I suppose I had, indirectly, prompted him to make it this time, as well.

"Yeah? It should be big enough for two." I looked at Jaime and while, normally, a statement like that from me would be accompanied by a leer or suggestive eyebrow wiggle, tonight it just came with a tired smile. "No funny business," I promised. "I'm too tired and I'm sure you are too."

Jaime hummed an agreement.

And I had meant what I'd said. Truly I had. I'd had no intention of trying for any sexy stuff at all. Until I was reminded that the sight of water streaming over the naked, freckled, leanly muscled body of Jaime Johnson was enough to get my dick hard and eager for attention. It probably would even if I was dead, so a little exhaustion was nothing.

But I wasn't a complete dick, even if it felt like that portion of my anatomy was telling me that we didn't need sleep that badly. So, even as I stepped up behind him and snugged my partially erect dick against Jaime's glorious ass, I made a new promise to myself that I would back off if I sensed even an iota of noninterest from him. If Jaime really wanted to head straight to bed to sleep after our shower, I'd graciously back off and go with that plan. I just wanted to throw out that there was another avenue of action we could take instead.

Thankfully, Jaime emitted a soft, pleased noise when my dick rubbed against his ass and his "I'm not sure how much I'm up to doing" wasn't a no.

"That's okay," I told him. "You just brace yourself against the wall and get comfy. I'll do all the work."

"What do you…" Jaime started to ask.

Clearly his mind wasn't still stuck on rimming like mine was. I might've been embarrassed and horrified by Crystal bringing the topic up,but it had reminded me of how much I'd loved doing that to Jaime. And how much he'd seemed to love me doing it to him.

Jaime quickly caught on when I slid my body down the length of his, settling on my knees behind him. The tiles on the shower floor were only marginally warmed from the hot water of the shower and their hard surface wasn't terribly forgiving to my poor knees. But it was all going to be worth it once I got my mouth on his delicious pink hole.

"Oh. Ooooh. Jay," Jaime moaned as I nuzzled my nose into the gentle valley at the top of the crease of his ass. I cupped my palms around the swells of his ass and gently parted his two firm, round cheeks. I finally got the first of the naughty words I liked prying out of him, when I licked a long swipe from that sweet valley I'd just smelled and down to his hole. "Frick. Fu-fuck. Fuck. Oh, fuck. You're gonna… you're gonna… I don't want anyone to hear this. Hear me. Aah. Fuck, Jay."

"Shh." I licked another sweeping taste up and down his crease. "No one's going to hear anything," I told him.

Not that I had any idea about what sounds could or couldn't be heard traveling from this downstairs guest bathroom and up through the rest of the house. Jaime was the first person I'd brought with me to Greg and Crystal's house, ergo he'd be the first and only person I drove sex noises from. But my concern with any awkwardness over possibly being overheard was far outweighed by my desire to drive Jaime wild and get him to release any and all sex noises and profanity that I could.

Because he deserved to be rewarded for being dragged to the middle of nowhere and having to put up with my friends, of course. I was a giver that way.

I focused my attention on that tight little hole and flickered the tip of my tongue over and against it, trying to tempt it to soften and loosen for me enough that I could start working my tongue inside him.

"Let me in, babe," I told Jaime. "You taste so fucking good but I want more. Give me more, love."

I have no idea where that word came from or why it felt so good tumbling from my lips, but I had more important things to focus on. Like the way Jaime shifted his legs further apart to give me more access to feast and the way his whole body shivered with delight as he wrapped his hand around his hard dick and started jacking himself as I dove back between his cheeks.

"Jay, Jay, Jay. Sh-shit. Shit. So good at that. Not gonna last, you're so good."

I released a happy-sounding hum at that. Because I was so good. Good at rimming. And good at being good for Jaime.

My ministrations to Jaime's hole were rewarded when his rim softened and allowed my tongue to slide right on in. His salty, musky taste was even more intense inside his smooth, hot channel. It was seriously addicting and, if I didn't need it for other things and it wouldn't be incredibly awkward, I'd love to keep my tongue buried in his ass all day, every day.

I groaned with pleasure as I plunged my tongue in and out of him, tongue fucking him at a fast pace, while also periodically pausing to lick and slurp and tease his rim.

Jaime's hand on his cock worked at the same frantic rhythm. Up and down and up and down his shaft. Then, each time I'd pull my tongue out to play with his rim, Jaime's hand would stay on his cockhead, giving it special attention, twisting and rubbing and squeezing.

"That's it. Get yourself off for me, love," I said. "I wanna feel you come with my tongue as your hole clamps down on it and refuses to let go."

I recognized the desperate and pleading tone of Jaime's voice as he cried out my name again. "Jaaay!"

Knowing he was on the brink of coming, I buried my tongue back into his tight hole as far as I could. The rippling, pulsing, quivering of his channel as Jaime's cock erupted and cum shot all over the shower wall was everything I could've dreamt it'd be. I felt so connected to him, so close, his orgasm caused a corresponding echo of pleasure within me.

My eyes rolling back in my head, I quickly wrapped a hand around my own cock. It only took a couple of strokes and I was coming as well. My cum splattering onto the tile floor of the shower even as Jaime was still panting, quaking, and recovering from his own orgasm.

"Fuck," I panted out. "Now... Now... Now I think I'm more than ready for bed."

"Yeah," Jaime agreed, his own voice still faint as he struggled to catch his breath. "Don't... uh... don't mind me if I just fall asleep here."

"Nah. C'mon, babe." I gave his rump an affectionate pat, the water still cascading over us from the showerhead making his skin wet and making the soft tap sound sharper and harder than it was. "Into bed with your sexy ass. It'll be much more comfortable than here. Especially because the hot water is bound to run out sooner rather than later."

For a man who'd just been pleasured out of his mind, Jaime sounded remarkably grumpy as he muttered, "Fine."

As I stood up on slightly trembling legs, Jaime rotated around to face me. His blue eyes looked sleepy but serious as his gaze ran over my face. It looked like he wanted to say... something. I don't know what. And it seemed like Jaime didn't either as his mouth parted but nothing came out right away. His hand came up and cupped my cheek, the pad of his thumb softly brushing over the crest of my cheekbone. Jaime's eyes kept surveying my face and I patiently waited, letting him look his fill until he was able to get out whatever it was that was on his mind.

I'm not sure how long we stood there like that. Long enough that the water temperature was edging toward room temperature and, probably, fast on its way to freezing. Whether Jaime couldn't figure out what it was he wanted to say or decided not to share it with me, I watched as the intent look in his eyes faded away to be replaced by his normal calm expression.

"Thank you," was what finally came out of Jaime's mouth.

I was positive that that wasn't what he'd been thinking or intending to say, but I let it go for now. If there was something Jaime wanted to tell me, I was confident enough in us that I figured he'd tell me when the time was right or he'd figured out how he wanted to say whatever it was.

"You're welcome," I replied. "I'd like to say the pleasure was all mine, but that would be a flagrant lie. The pleasure was most definitely mutual. Maybe even tipped a little bit more toward you."

"You're ridiculous," Jaime said. "Doesn't it ever get old, being so full of yourself?"

"It hasn't yet. And you like me that way."

"God help me," Jaime mumbled as I leaned in and brushed a kiss to his soft lips.

"Pfffth," I scoffed. "C'mon, love. Let's get to bed. We've got a busy day tomorrow, babysitting three kids and a Greg."

Chapter Twenty

Jaime

I'd been determined to spend the day ignoring the new endearment J.J. had used last night. And how that one little word had caused my heart to start racing alarmingly and my world to tilt itself on its axis. And how much I'd actually enjoyed both of those sensations. It had to have been a simple slip of the tongue, right? Something said in the heat of the moment?

Just because J.J. had used the word love didn't mean that he'd meant...

Despite my best intentions, it was all I'd been able to think about all day. Around and around my mind went. Did I want him to mean that he loved me? Did I not want him to mean that? And did I... Was there any possibility that I could return those feelings that I wasn't sure if I was hopeful existed or not?

I spent the day in a state of J.J.-brain. So, it was a good thing I wound up spending the day with Greg, who, unknowingly, allowed my mind to wallow in all things J.J.

After Crystal had left for work this morning, with a warm hug for me and a cheerful "Bye-bye, buttbreath" to J.J., he had gathered up the three kids and taken them to their playroom and suggested that I spend the day relaxing or keeping Greg company.

Greg was still somewhat loopy from his painkillers and, in between fitful bouts of napping and trying to rearrange his body on the couch so he was as comfortable as he could get, the man spent his time telling me anecdotes from his and J.J.'s childhood and listing off all the good things he could come up with about his friend.

"As soon as… as soon as we knew we were having Katie," Greg related. "Cube was the first person we thought of to be our baby's godparent. We actually had a hard time figuring out who to name as a godmother, but Cube was a shoe-in for godfather right from the start. Same thing with the other two kids. He's godfather for all three of 'em." Greg released a pained grunt as he adjusted the cushion wedged under the cast on his leg. "We woulda done that even if he hadn't bought us this house."

"He… J.J. bought your house?" I asked incredulously.

"Oh, yeah," Greg replied. "Biggest fucking wedding present we never asked for. And he didn't make a big deal about it, either. The deed was just slid into a picture frame, wrapped up, and placed on the gift table with all the toasters, wine glasses, towels, and other stuff from our registry, as pretty as you please." At my open-mouthed shock, Greg defensively protested, "We tried to give it back. We did. Between the house and the five acres it's sitting on, we figure J.J. probably plonked down almost a full year's salary on this thing, since this was... hmm... I think Crystal and I got married just after he'd gotten his first two-way contract to play for the Stealth."

If J.J. had been paid about what I had been when I'd been signed by the Loons, Greg probably wasn't too far off with his estimate.

"See... that's the thing about J.J. He's not always... the best with his words. He can come off as abrasive or aggressive or—"

"Arrogant?" I threw out.

"Hm. Yeah, that too," Greg agreed. "But his love language has always been giving. Of his time, his money, his attention. If you're one of the people he cares about, he'll give you anything he thinks you need. Even if you never ask for it."

"Like a couch?" I asked as some of J.J.'s past actions started taking on a different meaning than I'd initially given them.

"A couch, a car, a homemade five-course anniversary dinner, a two-week vacation, a fucking house... Oh, yeah. If J.J. loves you, he's giving you stuff."

I very badly wanted to tell Greg about all of the things J.J. had replaced for me without asking. All the dinners he made while he was staying with me. All the activities we've done together. And ask him if he thought those things were signs of J.J. feelings for me.

But before I was able to do so, Greg made one last mumbled comment on the subject, "It's why his parents have gotten jack shit from him" and then he was off and relaying another anecdote from their youth. This one concerning something about switching people's mail so that nobody in a three-block radius had received their own mail for a week before the boys had been caught and reprimanded. Greg seemed to find the whole incident hilarious, although in his mildly stoned state, everything seemed hilarious to him. But all I could think was that the boys had been lucky they'd been let off with a warning; tampering with mail was a federal crime.

I let Greg ramble on about whatever crossed his mind. A lot of it was about J.J. or the kids. But not all of it was and I just sort of tuned those stories out. I didn't know who he was talking about and I didn't want to devote the mental energy to figuring it out.

Instead, when he launched into one of those stories, my mind turned itself back to J.J.

I mentally replayed the couple of times he'd called me 'love' last night and tried to recall the exact tone of his voice when he'd said it. I re-ran through all the things J.J. had been happy to do for me and give me while he'd been staying with me in Minneapolis. And I tried to weed through the quagmire of what all those things made me feel.

I was already well aware that my attitude toward J.J. from the past seasons playing against him and even at the start of the summer—when I could barely tolerate him and idly wished for him to vanish off the face of the Earth—had changed. Through lust, intimacy, and spending more time with him off-the-ice my antipathy toward him had evolved into a sort-of friendship. With plenty of affectionate tolerance and sex. Lots and lots of sex.

But was that all that I was feeling for him?

I figured that if it was, then I'd be a little sad when this whatever-we-were-doing came to its natural end at the start of the upcoming season. And I'd be able to look back at this summer spent with J.J. with nostalgia and fondness.

However, I had the sense that when—if—J.J. and I ended our relationship, I would be devastated. Cry-my-eyes-out-and-gorge-on-Haagen-Dazs-and-sappy-movies level of devastation. And I wouldn't look back at this summer with fondness, but regret. And anger. And sadness. Not that it had happened, but that it ended.

I didn't want things with J.J. to end when the summer ended.

I had no idea how we'd be able to pull it off. We played for rival teams. We lived hundreds of miles apart in different states. Our schedules would only rarely sync up for us to be able to spend in-person time together.

When you're a pro hockey player, relationships are already hard. I've seen it work for some of my teammates and not work for others.

Add in all the obstacles that were in the way of J.J. and I making a successful go of it and it was depressingly daunting.

But I think I wanted to try anyway.

I hadn't gotten to where I was in life by not setting goals and working as hard as I could toward achieving them. What was a long-term relationship but one more giant, rewarding goal?

I'd just finished deciding that I really needed to sit down with J.J. and establish if he wanted the same thing, when I heard him calling my name.

"Jaime? Hey, babe, could you help me put the munchkins down for their naps?"

J.J. appeared in the doorway to the living room, his head of dark hair messily tousled from playing with his nieces and nephew and his t-shirt and shorts no longer as pristinely clean as they'd been when he'd donned them this morning. They were now decorated with drying streaks of Play-Doh, stray crumbs from lunch and/or an afternoon snack, a sprinkling of glitter, and bits of stuffed animal fur.

"Sure," I responded. I glanced over at Greg and saw that, while I'd been zoned out and thinking, he'd drifted back off into another nap. "I've got my charge down for his afternoon nap, I suppose I can help you with yours."

"Great. Thanks." J.J. ducked out of the doorway, then ducked back into it just as quickly. The smile on his face

looked nervous and sort of apologetic as he said, "Um. So…
Just like I thought would happen, my folks know I'm in
town. They've demanded a dinner appearance from me…
er… from us tonight. That's… uh… You don't mind…
Would you like… Um. I could go by myself, if you'd rather
stay here with Greg, Crystal, and the kids."

While J.J. hadn't quite managed to get the words out, I
calmly accepted his invitation to join him for dinner with his
parents. "Just let me know when and where and what time
we need to leave and I'll be glad to join you for dinner with
your parents." After all, I'd just now made the decision that I
wanted to continue being with J.J. One of the next logical
steps was meeting each other's families. I'd already met his
best friends and his honorary niblets—the family he'd
chosen—so it only made sense to take the opportunity that
had presented itself to meet his parents as well.

"Hmmpf. You say that now," J.J. muttered. "Once you
meet them, you won't be feeling so glad."

Dinner with J.J.'s parents had seemed to start fine. J.J. and I had made it to the diner on time. Five minutes early, actually, since I'd Googlemapped the directions and practically shoved J.J. out the door so we could make it to the nearby town of Oskaloosa, where the diner was located, in plenty of time.

We sat down at the table the waitress showed us to; J.J. across from me and his father to my left while his mother was on my right. When we first arrived, his parents and I had done the polite smiling and exchanging of names thing. John Johnson—the elder one, not my J.J.—asked about our flight and our drive from the airport to town. Linda Johnson commented that we were lucky we'd arrived just after the weeklong heat wave had broken. We'd all glanced through the laminated diner menu and given the waitress our selections when she'd come back around to our table.

It was after we'd ordered that I noticed something odd. Something that… Frankly I have no idea what I was witnessing. But it was creeping me the heck out.

J.J.'s parents looked normal. Like a generic midwestern couple, in their early to mid-sixties, with the passage of time adding some extra padding around their midsections and gray hairs to their dark brown hair and wrinkles to their lightly tanned faces. Seriously, they looked normal. The kind of people a director would cast in an AARP commercial about staying active and fit in our retirement years.

However.

They sure as frick didn't act normal.

Both Linda and John sat completely still in their chairs, not moving—not a twitch, not a fidget, not a twiddle of a thumb—and, seemingly, barely even breathing as they stared blankly into space. In complete. And. Total. Silence.

Except, every few minutes, one of them would seem to boot back up and comment on something or other. But not to J.J. or I. To each other only. And it was usually something to do with farm machinery or some inconsequential anecdote about running into a client of theirs– from their farm machinery sales company– at the grocery store or the gas station or in line at the post office.

Meanwhile, J.J. had also seemed to shut down. He'd also stopped talking and, intentionally or not, was also ignoring everyone else at the table. He was keeping himself happily occupied by waging a war between the various paraphernalia on the table. The sugar packets and half-and-half cups were barricaded behind a wall of the jelly single-serve packets. And the Sweet 'n Low and the artificial creamers were tucked behind a fortress of salt and pepper shakers. It was real vs. artificial coffee additives, with balled up straw wrappers serving as the weapon of attack. And, so far, it appeared as though 'real' was winning. I think.

Meanwhile, I was having an out-of-body experience wondering if I was even there. Nobody was talking to me. Nobody was looking at me. Nobody seemed to remember I was occupying the fourth chair at the table. Had I disappeared? Turned invisible?

For all that they'd supposedly demanded his presence for dinner, John and Linda Johnson paid no more attention to

J.J. than they did the waitress, the people in the booth next to us, or the actual danged booths we were sitting on. I could understand if they weren't terribly interested in me. They didn't know me and probably hadn't been expecting me to join them for dinner this evening. Not that they'd outwardly shown any surprise—or anything else other than politeness—when J.J. had introduced me to them.

But J.J. was their son. Their only child. And I had no earthly idea how long it had been since they'd last seen him, but I had a feeling it'd been a long while. And they were ignoring him. While he was less than three feet away from them. Why had they even wanted to see him if they weren't even going to look at him or talk to him? What kind of parents acted like this toward their only child?

One of those rebooting moments by J.J.'s parents came just at the same moment that J.J. flicked over one of the salt shakers while emitting a whispered "kerrrrboooom!" A small explosion of salt spilled out of it and onto the table. Not that the reboot seemed to have anything to do with J.J.'s actions or noises. Neither of his parents seemed to notice or care about what J.J. was doing.

Linda sat up straight in her chair, her eyes refocused back on her husband, and an actual expression—excitement— settled on her face.

"The new John Deere catalogue came in the mail today," she told John Johnson, a big smile on her face. From the few details J.J. had passed along about his parents on the way to dinner, I'd found out that his father sold farm machinery and his mother managed the office; making John's appointments, fielding phone calls, following up with clients, making sure the bills got paid. That sort of thing. So, for them, maybe getting a John Deere catalogue was a big deal? "You'll never guess what's in there."

I wasn't sure about John, but I for sure would never be able to guess. I could recognize a John Deere—the green and yellow color scheme was pretty recognizable—but it never would have occurred to me that they made enough products to need a catalogue nor what special thing might be in there to cause anyone—even someone who had a business dependent on their products—to be so excited about it.

"They're finally rolling out the new G5 Universal display," Linda said, answering her own statement. "You'll want to make sure you're familiar with its features so you can offer it to our clients. The JDLink M modem and the StarFire 7000 Universal receiver are also out, but those don't seem like they'll be as much interest for our clients as the new G5."

I have no idea what in the heck any of what she'd just said meant. And J.J. didn't seem to care. He was still engrossed in his table clutter battle. After the weakening of the salt and pepper shaker battlement with the loss of one of the salt shakers, the Sweet n Lows seemed to be trying to swing the tide of war by sneaking around the far side of the jelly packet wall so they could flank the sugars and creamers.

At her voice, John Johnson also perked back up from whatever sleeping-with-their-eyes-open condition he and Linda seemed to have.

"Really?" he asked, enthusiasm and interest in his voice. "That is exciting. I'll be sure to brush up on that info first thing in the morning. You're right, our clients are going to want this product."

And then… Linda and John just… powered back off. After John's pronouncement, their eyes lost focus, the expression left their faces, and silence once more descended.

None of the three people in the booth was acting like tonight's behaviors were at all out of the ordinary. Was this how J.J. and his parents usually were with each other? Them in their own little world where only they and farm machinery existed? And J.J. off in his own little bubble, left to his own devices and to find his own entertainment to keep himself occupied?

What in the holy bejeebers was going on here?

The rest of dinner continued in the same fashion. J.J. did sweep his mock battle to the side when the waitress brought him his cheeseburger. And John and Linda, obviously, moved around as they ate their own meals. But there was still no interaction between them and their son. And vice versa.

Like, I said. It was creepy.

A couple of times, I tried to throw out some conversational gambits.

"Do either of you watch baseball?" I asked. When that got me no response, I threw out, "Football? Golf? Soccer? Tennis? Any sports at all?" Surely, they would at least admit to watching J.J.'s games during hockey season. My parents and sister weren't big hockey fans, but they tried to catch as many of my games on tv as they could.

"No. We don't care for sports," was the extent of the response I got, spoken in a lackluster tone of voice by John Johnson the elder.

"What do you two like to do in your spare time?" I asked. They couldn't sell farm equipment all day, every day. Right?

Not even a cricket made a peep. Forks scraping across ceramic plates were particularly grating when there was no. Other. Sound.

"What kind of hobbies do you have? Mr. Johnson? Mrs. Johnson?" Maybe using their names would be the key. You can't ignore someone who addresses you by name. Right?

Apparently, you could.

I was bewildered by Linda and John Johnson. And getting irritated at their son. Why was J.J. allowing me to flounder like this? This was the first time I was meeting his parents and it was going *horribly*. If he didn't have a darned good reason for his inattentiveness, I was going to be p.o.'ed.

"Do you... have hobbies?" I feebly asked.

A one word "yes" from Linda had my right eye twitching.

After that, I gave in and gave up. Clearly nobody besides me wanted to converse like normal, polite, civilized people did when they were out for dinner.

We finished eating in silence—the only table in the diner where chit-chatting wasn't adding to the murmur in the air— and John reached for the check with a polite smile for our waitress. Even though J.J. had to make considerably more money than his parents, I noticed that his fingers made not a twitch toward the check. Which was odd, because he routinely tried to pay any time we went out to eat together and for all the groceries he bought to stock in my apartment.

Once the bill was paid, there didn't seem to be any incentive for any of us to linger and draw this uncomfortable and strange evening out any further. Out of politeness, I let John and Linda proceed, then I stomped my way out of the diner.

I hadn't even been aware that I knew how to stomp. But stomp I did, with J.J. trailing behind me.

When we'd both climbed into the rental car and buckled our seatbelts, J.J. placed his hands on the steering wheel and quietly said, "I'm sorry."

I wasn't in the mood for his apology. At least, not without a flipping explanation first.

"What in the heck was all that?" I angrily demanded as I pointed back at the diner. "That... that... What was that?"

J.J. sighed. "I wish I knew. I'd love to give you some sort of answer. But... That's what my parents have been like for as long as I can remember. I don't know if they didn't want kids. Or just didn't want me. Or... Or if they just don't know how to act any other way. I really don't." He turned to face me. And in the dim light of the car interior, his eyes looked so... sad. "You sort of get used to the not-looking-at-you thing. And the stillness," J.J. said. "It's the no talking... That's what was the worst." He sighed and then quietly admitted, "I used to keep a journal. When I was a kid. Of how many days passed between them talking to me. And how many words they said when they did."

I was horrified. And sad on behalf of a younger J.J. Johnson.

"How many…" I paused to clear my throat, which felt constricted with sympathy for how lonely growing up like that must have been. "How long was the longest time you recorded?" I asked.

"Four days," J.J. replied. He said it factually, as though having one's own parents not talk to them, while you were living in the same house, for the majority of a week was no big deal. Something that he'd just accepted, growing up as their child.

I cringed when I recalled how J.J. had once mentioned that he'd been very independent as a child. No wonder. He'd practically lived as a ghost in his own childhood home.

"For a while, I kind of had the notion that my parents were alien pod people. Sent to Earth to observe the human race. And I was a prop for them to help them blend in. Appear more human themselves. Silly, right?"

I wasn't going to knock whatever coping mechanism tales J.J. had spun for himself as a child. "No. I don't think that's silly at all," I told him. "Although, I don't think aliens really exist."

J.J. dismissed that with a "Pfft" and a flick of his hand. "Whether they do or not," he said. "The real issue is that those two make such unconvincing humans that surely their alien bosses would've recalled them back to their home planet by now if they were aliens."

"How old were you when you stopped thinking they were aliens?"

"I dunno. 26? Yeah, it was probably sometime last year," J.J. said. "Although sometimes I still find myself wondering… Maybe their people didn't want them back and now they're stuck here. I know if I was a member of their alien race, I wouldn't want them back."

My annoyance with him had quickly evaporated like a wisp of fog on a hot day and now I just felt the urge to reassure him that there were people in the world that cared about him. Even if the parents he'd been stuck with had all the warmth and emotional depth of an android, there were other people—me, in particular—ready and willing to shower him with affection and… well… love.

I'm not sure I was quite there yet, but I was already on a sled racing down an icy hill, careening wildly out-of-control, headed toward a thump into a snowbank of love.

I unbuckled my seatbelt and wrapped my arms around J.J., as best as I could with the center console between us, and told him, "Well, we got it out of the way and now you can go back to not seeing or thinking about them." J.J.'s huff of agreement still sounded sad, so I suggested, "Why don't we head back to Greg and Crystal's? I bet they've got some ice cream tucked away in the freezer that we can pilfer."

"Ice cream does sound good."

"And because you've had a long day helping out with the kids, I'll let you lick it off of me. How's that sound?"

"What's this?" J.J. asked, pretending to be shocked. "Jaime Johnson is going to voluntarily eat something while he's not wearing any clothes?"

"No. You'll be eating something while I'm not wearing clothes," I corrected. "What can I say? You made a really strong argument with that brownie. If the ice cream is just as enjoyable, I might just have to change my opinion on dining naked."

"Oh, it'll be enjoyable all right."

J.J.'s cocky smirk wasn't nearly as big or effortless as usual, but it was close. And that was all I'd been aiming for. Getting J.J. back to the aggravating, conceited, charming, sweet, loveable, self-assured ass that he was. The one that I was finding far too loveable than was probably wise.

Chapter Twenty-One
J.J.

I'd offered for Jaime and I to stay longer to keep helping out with Greg and the kids. But Crystal had reassured me that her parents were now back in town from their cruise and were more than ready to get their turn with the little gremlins for a while.

Greg had also mentioned that "I'm kind of over hearing you and Jaime fucking at all hours of the day. The house isn't as soundproofed as you seem to think it is."

I was… not going to pass that bit of information along to Jaime.

I did make a mental note that the Phillipis could use some soundproofing as one of their Christmas gifts this year. Just in case I managed to convince Jaime to come back with me for another visit.

So, now that Jaime and I were repacking our stuff, getting ready to drive our rental car back to the airport in Des Moines, it was probably time for us to start discussing... stuff. Relationship-y type stuff. We'd flipped the calendar page over to August while we were in Iowa and, in theory, we had a month and three quarters left before Jaime and I had to be in separate locations for our teams' separate training camps.

In reality, it was probably closer to a month and a half. Even though the first week of training camp was just for the rookies and those the team were trying out—to see if they wanted to add them to the regular roster for the year—the team usually wanted the veteran players around for that week as well. So that we could do PR interviews and photo ops at various events, get all our team paperwork squared away for the year, get checked out by the team doctors and trainers, catch up with returning teammates and meet and welcome prospective new teammates, etc. All the fun stuff that makes the start of each season a frenetic whirlwind after a couple months of off-season downtime.

But I wasn't sure what Jaime wanted that month and a half to look like.

Was I heading back to Minneapolis with him? That's what the return ticket I'd purchased had planned for. Or was Jaime anticipating that when we got to the Des Moines International Airport—shit, that made it sound larger and grander than it was—he'd go his way and I'd go mine? Back to Kansas City. This would be a good time to bring things between us to a natural end, if that's what he wanted to do.

I was trying to figure out how dickish it would be to start up a relationship discussion while we were still at Greg and Crystal's house—where he was reliant on me for transport to get him out of this nothing town in the middle of nowhere, instead of, say, at the airport where he'd have convenient jet-fuel-filled conveyances of escape if things got awkward or strained—when Jaime casually stated, "Remind me to look up our team schedules. I'm pretty sure you're back in Minneapolis playing against us in January and I want to see if it's during the dates where the U.S. Pond Hockey Championships are being held at Lake Nokomis." Jaime neatly placed the last of his freshly laundered and folded clothes in his suitcase and zipped it closed. "I stumbled across it last year and spent a free hour watching one of the games and I think you'd get a kick out of it, too."

I wasn't entirely sure, but it kind of sounded like... "That's... that's five months from now. Are you... are you making plans for us to do something together five months from now?" I hesitantly asked.

I could tell that my question had discombobulated Jaime. "I... am." Jaime paused for a second and then stated, "I didn't even think about it. I just... I just assumed we'd still be together. But January... that's... that's five months away, isn't it?"

"I knew it! I knew it!" I cried. "I knew if you got to know me more, you'd realize that I'm awesome. And now you can't get enough of me."

Offhand, with a distracted look on his face and a small wave of his hand, Jaime muttered, "Don't be an idiot." Jaime went back to nibbling on his bottom lip as he thought. With a baffled tone of voice he admitted, "When I think about us not being together in the future... I feel all... empty." He fluttered his hand in front of his abdomen. "Inside. Empty and sad and... lonely. But when I think about being with you... planning for and stealing away moments where we can be together... I feel... warm and happy and... squishy. It's gross."

I could've done without the disgruntled and surprised expression on Jaime's face as he confessed that I made him happy, but I'd take it.

"Awww, babe. You make me feel all gross and squishy, too," I said, grabbing his hand and lacing our fingers together. I could feel the giant, sappy, goofy grin on my face and was vaguely annoyed by it, but I opted to ignore that feeling, for now, while I reveled in the joy I felt that Jaime seemed to be feeling the same thing I was. That, despite the fact that it was still probably an unwise and foolish idea, we both wanted to be with each other.

Jaime crinkled his nose—his freckles bunching and blurring together—as he asked, "So, we're gonna... we're gonna keep this going? Even after the season starts?"

Using our interlaced fingers, I tugged Jaime closer to me, until our bodies were lightly brushing together. "I know it'll take a lot of planning on both of our parts, but... yeah. That's what I want," I told him.

"So, we're... boyfriends now?" You'd think he'd just swallowed a mouthful of fish—I still found it funny the guy had been subjecting himself to eating a food he so strongly disliked all these years—the level of disgust that pursed his mouth after he uttered that word.

"Yep," I agreed, giving the last 'p' sound an extra pop just to watch the way it caused Jaime to flinch. "Jaime and J.J. sitting in a tree…" I started to sing. Poorly. I've never claimed being able to carry a tune was one of my many talents. "K-I-S-S-I-N-G." I suited actions to words by claiming his lips with mine for a brief, but steamy, kiss.

"Ugh. You're an idiot," Jaime muttered against my mouth.

"An idiot that makes you all squishy inside," I muttered back before kissing him again. I pulled back far enough to ask him a very important question. "Why do you suppose it's 'sitting in a tree'? I can think of so many better places for kissing to take place. In fact, we've got one right here. A *bed*." I tipped my head in the direction of the bed in the guest room. Sure, we'd already taken off the bedding so it could get laundered, but we could still take advantage of the soft, horizontal surface and consummate our newly established and acknowledged boyfriends status.

Jaime was tempted. I could see he was. He even glanced at the digital clock sitting on the nightstand next to the bed and his brow scrunched as he clearly went through the mental calculations of when we'd need to be at the airport and how long we had before we absolutely, positively had to be on the road to make it there in time.

A sigh of disappointment gusted out of him as he stated, "We can't. We don't have time. To make sure we get there in time to get through luggage check-in, security, and getting to our gate… We just don't have the time."

Fuck, Jaime always had a hard-on for getting to places on time. Trying to convince him that we'd have time for some fast sex would take up more time than I figured we could allot for said sex and it would just piss off Jaime. My shot at getting some would be completely screwed.

But nobody had ever accused me of not being persistent or single-minded when there was something I wanted. And I really, really, really fucking wanted to get down and dirty—really, really dirty—with my newly minted, hot as fuck boyfriend.

Which was why I said, "Fine. We'll just have to wait until we're on the plane, then. The tiny bathrooms aren't the greatest for that sort of thing. But we're both pretty agile and flexible. I'm sure we can make it work."

Jaime looked at me in horror, then flatly stated, "We're not having sex on the plane."

I could practically hear the "you idiot" he had refrained from saying. Which I appreciated. As I think I've established, I wanted our first act as boyfriends to be sex, not an argument. And if he'd said out loud what his voice implied… I wouldn't have had any other choice but to argue with him. Fucking on an airplane might be awkward and uncomfortable, but it wasn't a stupid idea. Much.

"Can you just imagine what would happen if we got caught?" he asked. "That is not the way I want the public to find out that I'm gay," Jaime said. "Let's not have the highlight of our coming out be some flight attendant or other passenger catching us in flagrante delicto on a danged plane!"

Okay. Jaime might have a point with that one. I could almost visualize the focused rage on the face of my agent, Sylvie—after she'd tracked me down so that she could rip my testicles from my body with her bare hands—if I outed myself through an embarrassing public sex scandal.

Jaime had also raised an interesting topic.

"Are… we coming out?" I asked him. I knew that Jaime was out to his team and some people around the league knew I was gay. But we'd never really discussed if we'd ever planned on coming out to the general public.

"Oh," Jaime said. "Um… I guess that's something we'll need to talk about, yeah?"

"Yeah, we probably should," I agreed. "Why don't we get our stuff loaded into the rental car and we can talk about it on the way to the airport. No chance of any nosy kids, Gregs, or Crystals interrupting us."

"Alright."

We loaded up the rest of our things into the car, said our goodbyes—with plenty of hugs, kisses, and tears. By Greg. We also waved a brief hello and goodbye to Greg's parents– who'd already shown up to shower heaps of love and attention on the kiddos–and then loaded ourselves into the rental car and hit the road.

Once I navigated through the traffic of What Cheer, Iowa—AKA the random pedestrians who insisted on walking in the road even though there was a perfectly good sidewalk, kids on bikes, scooters, and skateboards, assorted roaming dogs, and the ten or so cars clustered around the Casey's going for fuel or food—and we were headed back toward the freeway, I brought the topic of us coming out back up.

"So… did you want to come out? To more than just your team?" I asked Jaime.

Because coming out was something that could impact our careers—although, Sawyer Brzycki has seemed to weather it okay so far. Other than the expected rude comments and questions from fans and the media—I treated it with the seriousness it demanded. And, since it would impact both of us, I knew it was something we'd have to both agree to and be happy with. Whatever we decided to do.

"I think… Hmm… I think…"

I wanted to rush Jaime to just spit it out. But I waited, giving him the time he needed to compose his thoughts, and kept my mouth tightly clamped shut even though everything in me wanted to shout at him, "What? What? What do you think?"

Finally, with a helpless sounding sigh, Jaime said, "I think if we're going to be together during the season… which… We both want to do that, right?"

"We do," I patiently answered. *Seriously, just spit it out!*

"Because our opportunities to see each other in person will be so limited during the season, we're going to have to take whatever chances pop up and run with them. And those chances might not always be easy to keep private," Jaime commented. "I mean… if one or the other of us is always rushing off to meet up with the other… at a hotel… at one of our apartments… a restaurant or whatever… whenever we're in the same city or close enough to each other to make the effort to meet up…"

"So, what you're saying is that people are going to see us being together," I summarized for him, when it seemed like Jaime was going to keep rambling on. "There's no way we'll be able to get away with meeting up without being caught."

"Yeah. At least, that's how I see it. Somebody, be it a fan, or reporter, someone with either of our teams, some random somebody… We'll be noticed and, before we know it, it'll be out all over the internet, anyway. Whether we like it or not."

"You're suggesting that we'll have to come out, no matter what," I stated.

"If we want to be together."

"Yeah, if we want to be together. Which, we do," I said again. I know it's what we'd both already said that was what we wanted. But I couldn't help the slight question in my voice, because it was one thing to decide you wanted to be with someone and a whole other thing when that decision precipitated a much larger decision to publicly come out and for the whole world to know about your sexuality. Opening yourself up to whatever comments, judgments, and opinions they'll have about such a basic part of who you are as a person.

"We do. I do," Jaime stated.

I risked a glance away from the highway and toward my boyfriend, to find Jaime looking at me with a settled expression. That lack of doubt or hesitation on his face had a stupid, sappy grin forming on my own face. I could feel it. I was defenseless against it. Fuck it, I figured as I kept my eyes on Jaime long enough to see his own soft, affectionate smile answering my dopey one.

I'd already flicked my glance back to watching where I was driving, when Jaime admonished, "Eyes back on the road, Jay. I'd like to get to the airport in one piece and without having to activate the insurance on the rental car." His words were grumpy and annoyed, but his tone of voice wasn't. And the hand he laid on my knee—giving it a gentle squeeze—felt as fond and loving as his voice had sounded.

"You won't mind... coming out to the public?" Jaime asked. "If that's what we're doing?"

"Nah," I replied. "I never really tried to hide my sexuality all that much," I told him. "I just went about my life and didn't advertise it much. A dozen or so guys around the league already know. My agent knows. Obviously, Greg and Crystal know. My parents... well. They wouldn't know or care if I made it a regular practice to go around schtupping sheep. The fact that I'm gay won't faze them in the least, if the news even registers in their consciousness." We were finally approaching the series of ramps that would take us to the Des Moines International Airport, so I wove my way over to the lane of the freeway that I needed to be in. "It's not that I never wanted to come out," I said. "I just didn't have a reason to really make it an issue."

"But now you have a reason?" Jaime asked.

"Yep. A gorgeous, redheaded, 6'1 ½" tall reason," I said, winking the eye closest to him.

"Hey. I'm 6'2"," Jaime indignantly insisted.

"Are you? Are you really?" I asked teasingly. "Because I'm 6'2" and you're clearly shorter than me. Everyone knows it." I took my right hand off the wheel, raised it up to where I knew he'd see it, and held my thumb and index finger apart a smidge.

"You suck," Jaime said with a huff.

Since he was such a No-swearing-ton, I decided to take his comment literally. "I *know*," I said. "And I'll demonstrate it to you again, once we're in the air and we can make a break for the plane's bathroom."

"We're not having sex on the plane," Jaime immediately stated. Again. It was like a reflex with him. J.J. says something outrageous and… boom! Shoot it down automatically. He moved on, as if I hadn't even made the naughty proposition. "Are you at all worried about how your teammates will react? The ones who don't already know, that is."

I maneuvered the rental car around a couple idiots who didn't seem to know which lane around the Des Moines airport they needed to be in, garnering only a couple angry honks and rude finger gestures, as I cut them off. I didn't really have to think very hard about how to answer Jaime's question. "Nah," I replied, over the insistent and loud horn beep from yet another lost, befuddled, and shitty driver that I zipped us around. "Like I've mentioned before, Sasha

Yuralaev's sexuality is a pretty open secret in our locker room and nobody has given him shit for not being straight. Maybe because he *does* also sleep with women? I don't know. But I don't think we have any overt homophobes on the Snappers. I could always be wrong. But if there are, those guys can go fuck themselves. I'm not going to concern myself with their dumbass opinions."

"Everyone on the Loons has been pretty accepting and supportive of Sawyer and myself since we came out at the end of last season," Jaime stated. "Well... other than Caleb Murphy's initial knee-jerk reaction where he freaked out about having to share a locker room with gay guys."

This bit of info surprised and upset me. I didn't know Caleb "Murph" Murphy personally, but he'd always seemed like a nice enough guy in our brief encounters on the ice. He was a giant behemoth who could smash you into the boards hard enough to make you regret ever choosing to play hockey... but, still, he'd always seemed nice enough other than that.

"What the fuck?" I asked. "It might've taken a couple guys and come torches and pitchforks, but I hope the rest of your teammates shut him the fuck up."

"It was a tense couple of moments," Jaime said. "But it was just a few moments. Some of the other guys stuck up for Sawyer when he told us all that he was gay, which was also when I blurted out that I was gay too. And after they basically told Murph to stop being stupid, he seemed to snap out of it. And before we all scattered for the off-season, after we lost to the Firebirds, Murph apologized multiple times to me and Sawyer and explained that his reaction was based on him stupidly parroting some cruddy ideas and stereotypes his childhood hockey coach… who was also his uncle… had spoon fed him and the other kids on his team. He also told us that he grew up in some tiny town in the middle of nowhere South Dakota and that he'd only ever met one gay person before Sawyer and I."

"Uh huh. Sure," I scoffed. "And I grew up in bumfuck Iowa. Being raised in some tiny fucking backwards, backwoods town is no excuse to grow up to be a narrow-minded dumb fuck."

I pulled the car into the designated lot for the rental company we'd used and pulled into the first open spot I could find.

"At any rate…" Jaime said. "Those couple of weeks after Sawyer and I came out, Murph apologized multiple times, he joined PFLAG… although he was disappointed to find out that their Minneapolis chapter had closed a couple years ago… and he's tried to be a supportive friend. Sometimes, overly so. He kept pointing out guys to me that he thought could be gay or bi and telling me to ask them out. And he promised that once the season started up again, he was going to work on finding me a boyfriend."

"Well, make sure you tell Caleb Murphy that that won't be necessary," I told Jaime. "I already found you a boyfriend. Me."

"Unh uh," Jaime said as he shot me a wink, unbuckled his seatbelt, and opened the passenger's side door. "Pretty sure *I* found me a boyfriend. After all, I'm the one who offered to share a hotel room with you. That's where this whole thing started, so I get the credit for starting our relationship."

"Uh. No," I corrected as I also got out of the car. "I think that this thing between us started with us fighting with each other on the ice. Every time I accused you of high sticking and you denied it... Every time you whined when I sniped the puck away from you... Each push, shove, and punch was us flirting with each other in the language we're most fluent in. Hockey. We just didn't realize it at the time."

"Don't be ridiculous," Jaime stated as he opened the trunk and pulled our suitcases out of it. "That wasn't us flirting, it was just hockey."

"Thanks, babe," I said as Jaime handed me my suitcase.

"You're welcome."

"That was totally flirting," I insisted as we started walking toward the entrance for the rental car company so I could turn our keys back in.

"Was not," Jaime countered.

"Was too."

"Was not."

"Was too."

"Thanks, Jay," Jaime said as I waved for him to go ahead of me into the building.

"No problem, love."

"Our on-ice fighting was not the start of our... relationship," Jaime finished with a whisper, glancing around to see if anyone was paying any attention to us. "That didn't start until we ran into each other in Nevada and I graciously offered to let you share my hotel room."

"I call bullshit." I did my own glancing around, but everyone seemed to be paying attention to their own business and seemed to have no interest in two random dudes walking through the Des Moines airport in the middle of a random weekday. "But… fine. I'll grant you that you did offer to share a room with me and that may have… may have cracked the door for something to happen between us. But. Don't forget that I'm the one who suggested that we start fucking each other. So, if you follow the evidence back to its logical conclusion… I totally get the credit for starting our relationship."

"Do not."

"Do too."

"Not."

"Too."

We continued happily squabbling—at least, I was happy to snip and snipe at Jaime—all through checking in our baggage, going through security, walking to our gate, getting our tickets scanned, and boarding the plane. Obviously, we had to do so at a whisper and using as vague of words as we could. Mostly, the argument consisted of "Me" and "No, me" back and forth.

It wasn't until the flight attendant started circulating around, checking that all carry-ons were stowed away and that all seatbelts were properly fastened, that Jaime and I mutually and tacitly agreed to let the subject drop. Me, so that I could enjoy my indulging in a couple of in-flight cocktails. And Jaime so he could occupy himself with perusing a magazine somebody had left in the compartment on the back of the seat in front of him and then taking a short half-hour nap.

But I still maintain that I was right. I totally deserved the credit for starting Jaime and I down this boyfriend path we'd found ourselves on. And one of these days, I know I'll get him to admit it.

It might take an awful lot of brownies and sexual acts to convince him, but I was willing to do whatever it took.

Chapter Twenty-Two

Jaime

Okay. I can do this. I can *do* this.

It shouldn't be a big deal. Sawyer already knew I was gay. In fact, it was his coming out to the team that spurred me to also come out to the team at the end of last year's regular season and before the Loons started their, ultimately unsuccessful, playoff run. So, calling up Sawyer and telling him that I was dating J.J. Johnson really shouldn't be a big deal.

So what if he and all my other teammates have been listening to me complain about and criticize J.J. for the past several years? So what if I'm now going to have to listen to his gentle ribbing on how I'll have to backtrack on all the nasty things I've said about J.J.?

I still maintained that the things I said are true. J.J. Johnson was egotistical, and arrogant, and cocky, and loudmouthed, and rude. Those things just didn't seem quite so glaring or important now that I've also gotten to see what a kind, caring, giving man he can also be. After meeting his parents I could also understand a bit more why he'd turned out the way he was.

His ability to turn me inside out in the bedroom with his mouth and his dick really shouldn't be understated either.

Since Sawyer had already been through the process of publicly coming out, I figured he might have some good advice for me that I could then be armed with prior to my discussion with the Loon's management on how I wanted to handle my own public coming out. Sawyer was also the only other gay guy on our team—as far as I was aware—and he was somehow managing to have a successful same-sex relationship. I'd take any and all advice on how to handle that, that he might have as well.

I'd probably be feeling more confident about what Sawyer's reaction was going to be to my telling him about my new boyfriend, if I didn't still have my agent's disbelief, followed by his laughter, ringing in my ears.

Kevin has been my agent since my last year of college and I'd confided my sexuality to him when he signed me, so he wasn't surprised about that or that the day had arrived where I'd found myself in a relationship. No… like I'm sure everyone else was going to be, Kevin had been tickled pink over the man I'd chosen to be in a relationship with.

"Oh my. Oh…" After several moments of snorting laughter, Kevin had finally choked out, "We'll have to see if we can get you two some endorsements with Johnson & Johnson. One of their sub-companies has gotta make lube. Or… or Doc Johnson. The… the…" It was getting hard to understand him through his laughter. "Online sex toy company. It's just… it's just…" Some more laughter and then he'd concluded, "too obvious of a tie-in not to tap into."

My attention was snagged by J.J. casually strolling through my apartment in nothing but a pair of skimpy nylon athletic shorts. The hem ended just above the half-way point of his lightly furred and muscular thighs and the silky material lovingly draped over the sexy curve of his butt and the enticing bulge of his groin. The naked expanse of his chiseled abs, pecs, back, and arms was also a visual delight for my eyes.

Kevin's amusement was no competition for all of that. So, I let his chortles wash over me then, once he regained his composure long enough to get me to agree to call him once I had more definitive information regarding going forward with the Loons, I faintly bid my agent farewell and hung up the phone.

After he grabbed a bottle of water from the fridge, J.J. walked over to where I was sitting on the bright blue couch he'd bought—to my annoyance, it was more comfortable than the one he'd replaced and I'd found myself liking the pop of color against the other neutral colors in my apartment. He brushed a kiss to my hair and my forehead before he sat next to me and nuzzled his mouth against the side of my neck.

His words tickled against my skin as he asked, "Have you called Sawyer, yet?"

"No," I sighed. "I was just about to. The call with my agent took a little longer than I expected."

"Why? Was he giving you any trouble?" J.J. asked.

"No. I just had to outwait all of his laughing."

J.J.'s snicker puffed another burst of breath against my skin.

"Okay, well, I'm going to go call my agent. You get your call to Sawyer over with. Then we both need to get a hold of our team's management and work out the timeline of how they want to handle our coming out and announcement of our relationship."

Ungh. Why was a responsible, grown-up J.J. so sexy to me?

"Yeah," I agreed. Then I said, "I should probably also come out to my family."

J.J. let out a choked gasp of shock and disbelief. "What the fuck? Your family doesn't know you're gay?" He grabbed my shoulders and held me in place as his eyes examined my face.

I shrugged and replied, "I don't know. Maybe? They might've guessed, but I haven't actually come out to them." It was sort of embarrassing to admit this at the age of twenty-five, but I explained, "I already always felt like I didn't belong… being the white kid adopted by a black couple. Even my adopted sister is black. So, I always did my best to try to fit in with them the best I could. And it felt like being gay would just be one more way in which I didn't fit in with the rest of my family."

"Huh. I knew you were adopted…" J.J. commented.

Yeah, it's not like it was something I could've hidden, even if I'd wanted to. The first time anyone had ever published a photo of my black parents standing next to a clearly-not-black me and… Denying that I was adopted would've been stupid and pointless. And it was nothing I was ashamed of, anyway.

"Do you think… How do you think they'll take it?" J.J. asked.

I shrugged again. "I don't know. They're pretty liberal, so I don't think they'll have a problem with it," I said. "And, like I said, they may already have an inkling. It's not like I've ever brought any girlfriends around or even pretended to have any interest in girls. I did try once, in… middle school, I think," I admitted. Then I had to shudder when I recalled going on a group date with this girl I was friends with and a half-dozen of our other friends. "It made me feel gross and dishonest. So, that was the only time I tried to fake being straight."

J.J. rubbed my shoulders and leaned in to give me a soft kiss. "Well, if you want me with you when you tell them, you let me know. Hopefully, you're right and it goes well. If it doesn't…" This time it was J.J.'s turn to shrug. "I'll yell at them for you, using all the swear words in my arsenal. And that's a lot."

"Thanks, Jay. I'm sure that won't be necessary but I appreciate the offer."

"M'kay. Just wanted to throw it out there. Now... We both have more phone calls to make so we'd better hop to it." J.J. punctuated his statement with a tweak to my nipple underneath my t-shirt.

"Hey!" I exclaimed in surprise at the brief and unexpected sting of pain.

Then J.J. hopped off the couch and scampered away, laughing, before I was able to retaliate on his own bare nipples.

"Jerk," I muttered under my breath as I ran my hand over the tingling nubbin.

But I let J.J. escape to the privacy of my bedroom so he could make his phone calls while I picked my own phone up off my coffee table so that I could call my friend and teammate, Sawyer Brzycki.

"Noooo!" came the unhappy and loud voice of Sawyer's live-in boyfriend, TJ Reilly. "You can't be dating another hockey player!"

Like me, Sawyer must've also had his phone set to speaker, enabling his boyfriend to listen in on our conversation and contribute his opinion. I'm not sure why TJ was horning in on my phone call with Sawyer, although, since I was sort of friends with TJ, I didn't mind all that much. And perhaps he would also have some supportive and helpful advice for me.

If he could refrain from the uproarious laughter that had been Sawyer's initial reaction, all the better.

"Uh. Teej," came Sawyer's voice. "I'm not really sure it's your place to say who Jaime should or shouldn't be dating."

I'm glad Sawyer said it, because I was definitely thinking the same thing.

"No. You don't understand," TJ said. "If Jaime's dating another hockey player that means his boyfriend can't be in the Puck Bucks."

What the… Okay, I had to ask. "Um. What're the Puck Bucks?"

Over the sound of Sawyer groaning, TJ replied, "It's the group I founded for the male boyfriends and partners of pro hockey players. Since we won't have the needed anatomical features to be Puck Bunnies… even if I'm sure we're all fucking our hockey players like rabbits… I gave us the name of Puck Bucks. Bucks are what male rabbits are called," TJ further explained. "I had custom shirts made up and everything."

"Oookay." I couldn't think of any other hockey players, other than myself and Sawyer, who were in a same-sex relationship. That's not to say that there weren't. I just didn't—and presumably the general public didn't—know about them. "And who else is in the group? Am I allowed to ask?" I asked.

"So far, it's just me," TJ replied. "That's the problem. I want someone else in the group so I have someone else to complain to about the hockey schedule. The stupid diet regimen Sawyer's on and why I can't keep chocolate donuts lying around the house."

"I told you I'd stop sneaking those," I heard Sawyer mutter.

Not that TJ seemed to pay any attention to Sawyer's comment as he continued, "I need someone else in the group that I can trade tips with on how to successfully have video sex with your partner for good luck while they're on the road so that you don't get interrupted by their roommate walking in at an inopportune moment."

"I said I was sorry about that," Sawyer emphatically declared. "And I'm pretty sure Timo saw a *lot* more of me than he did of you on my tiny tablet screen."

"It was still fucking embarrassing," TJ said and I could hear the pouting in his voice.

Frankly, as embarrassed as TJ had apparently been about... whatever it was that had happened between him,

Sawyer, and Timo Sneetsen, apparently... it couldn't possibly be as awkward as I felt now, knowing more than I ever wanted or needed to know about how he and Sawyer kept the spice in their relationship going while we were on the road. Although the tip about sexting was a good one.

"And now you're telling me, I'll still be the only one," TJ stated.

TJ really did sound put out by my choosing to date a fellow hockey player, so I offered, "Once the season starts up again, J.J. and I will be separated again. I'm sure you'd be able to commiserate with him over some of those things. If you want... I can give him your number."

It was sort of a scary offer. TJ had always struck me as being slightly mischievous and irreverent; I could only imagine how well he and J.J. would get along and what sort of trouble the two of them could cook up together. Although, J.J. couldn't get into too much trouble during the season and being hundreds of miles away from TJ, right?

"Oh. That's right," TJ said. "I suppose you two will have it even worse than Sawyer and I. At least I get him here, at home with me, during home game stretches. You and J.J. won't even have that."

The reminder was not a particularly happy one. J.J. and I would be in a long-distance relationship for the majority of the year. And, I'm sure I could count on focusing on hockey only so much to keep my mind off of missing him as much as I was bound to.

"Jeez. Not that helpful, Teej," Sawyer commented.

"Sorry. Sorry," TJ apologized. "I'll... uh... let you two get back to talking. Good luck Jaime."

I assumed TJ was walking away, but after Sawyer gave his own apology and said, "Sorry about that. TJ was having one of his dramatic moments, there" I heard TJ call out, "I heard that, Sawyer Alistair Brzycki!" *Alistair? Sawyer's middle name was Alistair?* "Just you wait. Once I think of some way to punish you, you're in trouble mister!"

"Pretty sure you already punished me by trying to give me the middle name of Alistair," Sawyer replied. "You know very well that's not my middle name."

"No, but your actual middle name is so blech. I'm trying out others until I find one I like," TJ stated.

"Keep trying," Sawyer suggested. This time, I heard TJ's footsteps walking away along with some soft yipping from their pit bull puppy, Huck. "But anyway..." Sawyer said, turning the conversation back to its original topic. "Seriously? J.J. Johnson? That's who you're dating? I thought you hated that guy."

Habit compelled me to say, "I do." Then I corrected myself. "I mean... I did. But then... I got to know him. And he's..."

"Not a cocky, arrogant asshat?" Sawyer asked.

My adopted mother appreciated lying about as much as she did swearing, so I was compelled to admit, "Well... I wouldn't go that far."

"This is the guy who once, during a live tv interview, told everyone that the reason his team had won the game was because he was just a better player than everyone on the other team," Sawyer reminded me. As if I could've forgotten that incident. "That guy?"

At the time J.J. had done the interview, all I could feel was disbelief that anyone could possibly be that full of themselves. Now, though… it sort of made me laugh. Because that incident was just so J.J. and because… "That's not all that there is to him," I told Sawyer. "He's also sweet, and kind, and thoughtful to those he thinks are worth his time and effort."

"And he's treating you like you're worth that effort?" Sawyer asked.

"He is."

"Well. Alright. If you say so, I'll take your word for it. It's your life, Jaime, and if he makes you happy… So. What's the plan?" Sawyer asked. "How are you guys working this? And… are you planning on telling anyone? Other than me?"

"Yeah," I replied with a sigh. "I already spoke with my agent, J.J.'s talking to his right now, and we both have meetings scheduled with management in the next couple of days. Me, in person and J.J. via Zoom. We figure the best thing to do is to get ahead of it and out ourselves before we're caught and somebody does it for us. That way we can, hopefully, control what's being said and how our relationship is presented to the fans before it's a bigger mess than it needs to be."

"Hmm," Sawyer hummed. "I agree. Dating another player would probably be hard to keep under wraps. You might as well be up front and honest about it. Hope that scores you some bonus points with the fans before they freak out and start wondering about how your relationship will impact your playing. Especially when the two of you are on the ice facing off against each other."

J.J. must've finished his phone call with his agent, Sylvie, because I felt his arms wrap around my shoulders from behind and his nose nuzzling into my hair.

"That was our opinion, too," J.J. commented, jumping in on my conversation with Sawyer.

"I'm not familiar with the Snappers' PR people," Sawyer said. "But the Loons people know what they're doing. You might not always like their suggestions, but try to jump through whatever hoops they want you to jump through," Sawyer advised. "Keep the team PR people on your side and they'll do their best to annihilate all the negative publicity that they can. And they'll happily exile the shittier, homophobic reporters from your interviews and press conferences."

I tipped my head up so that J.J. and I could share matching grimaces. The PR gauntlet was not my favorite aspect of my job and all the stuff they'd make us do was the thing I was least looking forward to with publicly coming out. I could ignore and block the horrible haters on the internet, but I'd have to listen to the people who were ostensibly on my side and ordering me around for my best interests.

"Alright," I said, agreeing to go along with Sawyer's recommendation. J.J. murmured his own acknowledgement and agreement.

At least I'd achieved the goals I'd wanted to achieve by talking to Sawyer when TJ came back from wherever he'd gone to and rejoined the conversation.

"Hey. Before J.J. heads back to Missouri, make sure you guys check out a product line called Clone-A-Willy," TJ said eagerly. "They have a wide variety of products for reproducing your partner's dick."

"TJ!" Sawyer yelled.

"That way, before you guys are separated again for however long, you can have one made up of J.J.'s dick. Or your dick, Jaime. Or both. However you guys like to do that. I'm not making any assumptions or judgments." I could hear Sawyer groan as TJ continued. I'm going to assume out of embarrassment about what TJ was talking about and revealing about their private business. "Just make sure whoever's doing it washes all of the molding plaster off," TJ said. "When I had Sawyer do his—"

"Okay. Okay," Sawyer cut him off. "That's... Jaime and J.J. don't want to hear about that."

"No. No. I think we *do* want to hear about that," J.J. said. I looked up at him again and his smile was huge and gleeful. "As a cautionary tale, of course," J.J. stated before he started laughing.

Even though Sawyer wouldn't be able to see me, I rolled my eyes. Naturally, J.J. would be interested in some product that let you make a replica of your partner's private parts. And the fact that someone we knew apparently used such a product.

"Alright, so…" TJ started. But Sawyer must've hit the button to turn off the speaker function on his phone, because TJ's voice cut off before he could share more information with us.

He hadn't hung up, though, because a giant sigh full of frustration tinged with affection came through the phone. "Anyway," Sawyer stated. "I think that's enough about that topic. Although… I've been instructed by an incredibly irate… and sexy!" Sawyer added, obviously in an attempt to mollify his boyfriend, "…TJ that I need to get J.J.'s number for him so that they can get to know each other and commiserate about dating hockey players. Er. Sorry, J.J. I'm not sure why… maybe 'cause he already knows Jaime… but I think you've been demoted from player to boyfriend."

I glanced over at J.J. and saw him shrug, unconcerned with Sawyer's bit of news.

"Meh. That's okay," J.J. said. "I can be Jaime's boyfriend to your boyfriend. The rest of the world will still know I'm the better hockey-playing Johnson on the ice."

"Really, Jaime? This guy?" Sawyer asked again before he said his goodbyes and disconnected our call.

"Yeah? That guy?" J.J. asked in a teasing voice as he came around to the front of the couch, pushed the coffee table back, and knelt down in front of me.

"Yeah. That guy," I said back to him.

I widened my knees, slid my hands along the breadth of his bare shoulders—J.J. was still only wearing a pair of athletic shorts—and pulled him in closer, between my legs.

My hands swept along J.J.'s warm skin, against his shoulders, and down to squeeze the firmness of his biceps, with the fingers on my right hand tracing along the lines of his interlocking cubes tattoo. Then I reversed their course, drawing my hands back upward until I swept them up both sides of his neck and settling them to cup his face in my hands.

I tilted J.J.'s face up to mine so I could show him how I felt about him with a sweet kiss that quickly turned hot and dirty.

"Mmhmm. That guy," I repeated.

Chapter Twenty-Three

J.J.

I knew they weren't really sure what to make of me, but I was all set to suck up as much as I needed to and throw all my best manners at Jaime's parents even before discovering that his mom made the best, orgasmic French toast I've ever fucking had in my life.

"Mmmmm. Mmm mmm mmm." The moans coming out of my mouth were positively pornographic.

Based on the horrified expression on Jaime's face, from where he was sitting across the table from me, mixed with a dark blush of interest and arousal, I'd have to say that Jaime found the sounds I was making to be slightly inappropriate, as well. Especially considering that the other people crammed around the small dining table in his apartment consisted of his mother, father, and twenty-two-year-old adopted sister.

Jaime's sister, Delia, was looking at me with amusement, his mother with bewildered approval, and his father... Well, his father obviously would've understood my vocalized appreciation if he hadn't had his face buried in his own plate of French toast with quieter, but similar, sounds coming out of him.

"This'a so fuckin' good," I mumbled around my mouthful of deliciousness.

"Er. Thank you, J.J.," Suzanne Johnson said. Her pleased smile was replaced with a chiding expression, though, as she admonished, "But you really shouldn't talk with your mouth full. And with all the plentiful and descriptive words in the English language, surely you could find ones that were more appropriate to use at the breakfast table than the f-word."

"Er. Yes, ma'am," I responded meekly.

I cast a furtive glance over at Jaime, but he merely raised his eyebrows at me as if to say "See?"

"I'm still doing my best to convince Jaime to get his teammates to stop using foul language so often," Suzanne said. "But all he says is 'Mama, everybody who plays hockey swears. I can ask until I'm blue in the face, but that's not going to change.'" Her Jaime impersonation was pretty spot-on. She'd really gotten down his favorite I'm-exasperated-with-you-but-remaining-calm tone of voice. "But I have faith in him. If Jaime continues to be a model of decent language for his teammates, then sooner or later they're bound to follow his example."

"Not frickin' likely," Jaime muttered under his breath.

"Maybe if you give them all dictionaries for Christmas, Mama," Delia Johnson said with a laugh. "When Jaime and I were little," Delia said to me. "Mom used to track down the nearest dictionary and make Jaime and I look up non-swear words we could switch out for whatever forbidden naughty words we'd slipped up and used. There's nothing quite like an irritated school librarian shoving a dictionary in your face whenever you swore and making you write down an actual physical list of ten different words that you could've used instead to train you into not swearing."

"Proper and decent language is nothing to laugh at, young lady," Jaime's mom said to Delia, shaking a finger at her.

"Oh, of course, Mama," Delia replied. But as soon as Suzanne switched her attention back to Jaime, Delia aimed an irreverent look in my direction, crossing her eyes and sticking her tongue out.

I stifled my laughter as Suzanne asked Jaime, "Are you ready for the press conference this afternoon? You've got your suit all picked out and ironed? You're going with the dark gray, right? That one always makes you look so grown-up, thoughtful, and intelligent."

"Errrr…" Jaime hemmed, shooting a panicked look at me.

Yeah. Surprising both of us, when I'd asked him about it, Jaime had agreed to allow me to pick out the suits we'd both be wearing to today's press conference that was being held before today's pre-season game between the Minnesota Loons and my Kansas City Snappers. So, he had no idea what he was going to be wearing this afternoon.

Spoilers… it wasn't going to be that boring as fuck, deadly dull, dark gray suit his mom seemed to be jonesing on so hard.

Nah. Once I'd finally pried the name of Jaime's tailor out of him, I decided to have him make new suits for Jaime and I. And, in a fit of whimsy, I decided that we'd be wearing ones that reflected our respective team colors. So, Jaime was going to be in a sexy AF icy blue suit, with a black dress shirt and white tie. And I was going to be wearing an outrageously daring, but also sexy AF, lime green suit that I was going to pair with a white t-shirt.

If we were going to be drowning in the spotlight during our mutual coming out, then we might as well be sexy mofos while we did it.

The Loons management and PR folks had graciously allotted us the time before the game and had turned over their largest press room for us to hold the press conference in. My team's PR people had told me that they were ready and willing to throw their full support behind me after our coming out, but they'd also seemed more than happy that the initial media circus was going to take place at the Loons' facility.

After Jaime had surprised his family with a visit to see them the week before we had to report for our teams' training camps and "surprised" them by coming out to them—they hadn't been surprised. Jaime was right, they'd already kind of guessed/assumed he was gay—they'd thrown their support behind him 110% and declared that they were going to come up to Minneapolis so they could be there in person for our press conference. All three of them had been staying in a hotel just a couple miles away from Jaime's apartment for a couple of days now and Jaime had been spending the time showing them around the city he lived in.

The Snappers hadn't played me in our previous pre-season game and had given me permission to fly in early for this one. I'd arrived yesterday and had only been able to spend a few short hours trying to impress and win over Jaime's fam. The rest of my team was due to arrive in Minneapolis sometime within the next half-hour or so. They were then going to make their way over to the Maverick Arena and were supposed to attend the press conference as a physical show of support for me and the bombshell Jaime and I were about to unleash on the hockey world.

"Don't worry, Mrs. J," I said to Suzanne. "Jaime and I are both ready and, in front of the press, we'll look like nice boys who happened to accidentally fall in love with each other."

She didn't look overly reassured by my pronouncement, however, she stated, "Hmmpf. Well, if you say so."

Popping the last bit of his breakfast in his mouth, Jaime's dad, Arnold Johnson, neatly placed his fork on his plate and stated, "We're so proud of you, son. I hope you know that."

Dabbing a tear from the corner of her eye, Suzanne looked at Jaime—who also was looking a little teary-eyed at his father's comment—then concurred, "We are. We're so proud of you and the fine young man you've grown up to be." Then she turned to me and said, "When we first met Jaime, he was only this little five-year-old. And the whitest little boy you ever could've seen, with this burst of orange-y hair jumbled on top of his head and freckles as far as the eye could see." Suzanne wasn't deterred by Jaime's groan of discomfort at being discussed like this. She simply continued, "You see… When Arnold and I were trying to adopt, we'd already met Delia and were pretty set on taking her home. But while we were in the playroom at the adoption agency and talking with our assigned adoption specialist, Delia walked over and started playing with this other little boy."

"Jaime?" I asked, as if the answer wasn't obvious.

"Yes," Suzanne confirmed.

"Nobody was paying any attention to him and he looked lonely," Delia stated with a small shrug.

"Mmm," Suzanne hummed. "Now, this little white boy, he wasn't saying a single word. And he didn't look like he knew what in the world to do with this little black girl trying to play with him…"

"I was only two at the time," Delia supplied, playing her part and supplying extra details to this story that the two of them had obviously told before. "But Jaime let me boss him around and played whatever dumb game I wanted to play. For hours."

"More like a half-hour to forty-five minutes," Suzanne fondly corrected. "But he was being such a sweet and darling little boy to that little girl Arnold and I had already set our hearts on taking home…"

"So, we decided to take them both," Arnold summarized, fulfilling his portion of the re-telling.

"Awww…" I cooed at the sweet picture of a young and adorable Jaime that they'd just painted. "How come you weren't adopted before then?" I asked Jaime. It was probably a pretty rude question, but I was curious and I wanted to know.

"It took a while before the courts declared me eligible to be adopted," Jaime explained.

"We actually fostered him for a year before we were able to adopt him," Suzanne added.

"I was found abandoned in the dressing room of a Target when I was four… Or, at least, that's how old they estimated I was. No one ever reported me missing and the only thing they had to go on was the name 'Jaime' written in Sharpie on the tag of the jacket I was wearing. That, and some grainy footage of a young woman entering the store with me and then leaving twenty minutes later… without me. I… uh… didn't talk to anyone… um… *anyone* until I was six," Jaime hesitantly admitted with a pained, embarrassed expression on his face. "That didn't help in swaying anyone into wanting to adopt me either. At least, not until Mom and Dad. It didn't matter to them that I didn't talk."

"The therapist at the adoption agency said it wasn't that uncommon in the cases of young children who've been abandoned like that," Suzanne stated, laying a comforting hand on her son's hand on top of the table.

Jaime gave her a thankful smile and patted her hand with his free one. "It's possible Jaime isn't even my real first name," he said. "For all anyone knows, whoever I was with bought the jacket second-hand somewhere or got it from charity and the name was already written on there and wasn't my name at all. And, until the Johnsons adopted me and gave me their last name, my case worker had chosen to give me the last name of 'Lemont' because that's the town the Target was in where I was found."

"Holy fuck!" I exclaimed. "Are you telling me Johnson isn't even your last name?"

"Er. No," Jaime replied. "You knew I was adopted. It didn't occur to you that my adopted parents gave me their last name?"

"*No*. Duh. Obviously not," I said. "Huh. How weird would it be if we didn't have the same last name?" I asked.

I pondered how different things might've turned out if Jaime and I didn't share the same last name. Who knew... without being compared to each other all the time, due to our shared name, the animosity between us might not have flared so hot. We definitely wouldn't have fortuitously wound up sharing a hotel room together at the start of summer. And then there would've been no opportunity for the animosity between us to combust the way it did, into something physical. And then everything that came after that wouldn't have happened. And so on and so on. Our whole relationship might've been destined to never happen.

It was a mindfuck for sure.

"I still think it's weird that you have the same last name and you're now dating," Delia commented with a cheeky smile.

"An opinion you will keep to yourself, young lady," Suzanne told her.

"Yes, Mama."

"Now… Arnold will clean up from breakfast…" Suzanne stated.

"I will?" Jaime's father questioned in surprise.

"You will," Suzanne confirmed. "Delia and I will go take a stroll so we can enjoy this lovely weather and pop into some cute shops I saw around the corner. And J.J. and Jaime will get ready for their media thing this afternoon and the game they'll be playing afterwards."

"Yes, ma'am," we all promptly responded to her commands.

Since Suzanne had declared it so, Jaime and I left his father to clean up the dishes we'd used for breakfast. We both made our way to Jaime's bedroom, Jaime trailing after me.

After he shut the door behind him, Jaime proved that he knew me very well and had known exactly where my mind had gone. "Don't worry, J. Even if I'd grown up with a last name that wasn't Johnson, I still would've disliked you just as much as I used to and we would've been rivals. And I'm sure, at some point, all that animosity would've boiled over and resulted in a blaze of hate sex."

"It wasn't hate sex," I protested. "It was never hate sex. Animosity and annoyance-fueled fucking, sure. But never hate sex."

"Uh huh. Whatever you say, J."

Jaime started pulling off the old University of Michigan t-shirt—a holdover from his college days—that he'd worn to breakfast. And, ugh. Yeah. As a kid who grew up in Iowa and then became a Wisconsin Badger during college… Jaime was right, we were always bound to be rivals. It had been inevitable.

I was pulled out of my drooling appreciation over the acres of creamy, freckled skin he'd just put on display when he said, "And don't think I didn't notice you slip and say that we were in love with each other to my mother."

Oh, fuck.

"Errr… I did?" I asked, feeling flutters of panic and nervousness explode in my chest. I was certainly aware that at some point I'd fallen—and fallen hard—for Jaime. But I'd certainly never meant for the first time I'd ever said the words to him to be in an accidental blurted slip of the tongue over breakfast in front of his parents and younger sister.

"Oh, you definitely did," Jaime replied.

"Fuck."

Jaime crossed his arms across his bare chest, causing his biceps to bulge enticingly, and nibbled on the corner of his bottom lip the way he did when he was nervous. "Did you… Did you not mean it?" he quietly asked.

I hadn't been sure if I'd been ready to say the words out loud to him, but, fuck, I didn't want Jaime to think that I wasn't head over heels in love with him.

"Oh, babe, no. No. I mean… yes," I said. "Yes, I meant it." I went over and wrapped my arms around him. He still felt all tense and stiff within my embrace, but I was determined to have him melting for me again. I ran my right hand up and down Jaime's back, trying to soothe him. "I do love you. I know… it was a surprise to me, too."

"Oh, God. Really, J? That's how you follow up telling me that you're in love with me?" Jaime asked with an incredulous huff of laughter.

When I shrugged—'cause, really, what could I say to that—the tension in Jaime's body let go as he started laughing.

"I love you, too, you idiot," Jaime said.

See? He wasn't any better at his I-love-yous than I was. So, I'm not sure why he felt the need to laugh.

"Nice, love. Nice," I said.

"Meh. You love me." Jaime's smile was the biggest I've ever seen as he made that statement, which also still had a note of incredulity in it.

Pausing to feather kisses across Jaime's face between each of my words, I told him. "I do. I. Love. You."

"Love you, too, J."

Even though we needed to be getting ready for our press conference, the moment absolutely called out for multiple long, deep, *loving* kisses.

And if those kisses between the two of us, who were both only wearing easily removed shorts, led to certain activities that necessitated us to later hurriedly dress in the suits I'd ordered for us... Well. The moment had called for that, too.

Chapter Twenty-Four
Jaime

The light blue suit J.J. had made for me was pulled tight across my butt. Like, really tight. In fact, it was pretty much snug around all the parts of my body.

"You went to Marcel, right?" I asked J.J., futilely and surreptitiously tugging at the fabric over my rear end like I could will it to suddenly become looser.

"Yep. He's a peach. The suits are just how I wanted them," J.J. replied.

"Huh." I was stumped. "He doesn't normally make mistakes, but I think he got my measurements wrong for this one. It's too tight."

"Nah," J.J. said. "I told him to subtract an inch or two here and there. You just always had your suits made too loose. You have a banging bod, everyone else should get to see what I get to take home with me tonight."

"Oh, dear Lord," I muttered.

I was doomed. Doomed to sit through a press conference that was bound to go viral in a suit that blatantly displayed every curve, dip, and bulge on my body. And doomed to be hopelessly in love, probably forever, with the guy who'd caused that situation.

"Relax, love," J.J. told me, which, naturally, did not cause me to relax. "You look totally fuckable. Now, what about me? I mean… I know I look fuckable, but it wouldn't hurt for you to tell me so."

I ran my eyes over the atrociously bright green monstrosity that was J.J.'s suit. I did have to give him credit, it actually did look really good on him. Ridiculously good. And hot. I was eagerly anticipating stripping that suit off of him after the game. And not just because it was hideously ugly.

"Oh, dear—" I spluttered when I saw the t-shirt J.J. had paired with his suit. "What sort of shirt is that?" I asked him, pointing a finger at the white shirt he wore, which had a drawing of a rabbit, sitting up on its hind legs, and with antlers growing out of its head.

"It's my Puck Buck shirt," J.J. stated. "TJ sent it to me. Along with a note congratulating me on becoming the second member of the Puck Bucks and giving me our secret password."

"Secret password?" I whispered.

"Yep. But shhhh… It's a secret. I can't tell anyone what it is. Even you."

"That… that…" I poked a finger at the rabbit printed on his shirt. "It looks like that rabbit has an erection," I commented. I'm not sure why I was so shocked. This was a shirt given and, presumably, designed by TJ Reilly. Of course, the male rabbit would have a noticeable erection.

"I know, isn't it awesome?" J.J. said.

"Awesome… is not the word I would've used," I replied. And… "Holy frick! You can't go in front of reporters wearing a shirt like that! You need to go change. Now!"

"Don't worry about it," J.J. told me. Naturally, his saying so did not cause me to not worry. "If I do this…" J.J. proceeded to do up the buttons on his green suit coat. "All anyone can tell is that I'm wearing a white t-shirt. They can't see what's on the shirt."

Thankfully, he was correct about that. Still, that prompted me to ask, "Why even wear that shirt then? If nobody's going to see what's on it, why wear it?"

"'Cause I'll know what's on it," J.J. responded. "You'll know what's on it. More importantly, *TJ* will know what's on it. Consider it part of my induction process to be part of his club."

"Uh huh." Why was I not surprised by any of this? I knew those two were going to be trouble once they befriended each other.

A guy wearing tan chinos, a Loons polo shirt, and holding a clipboard walked up to J.J. and I. "Five minutes until we get started," he told us.

"Okay. Let's do this, love," J.J. said as he ran a finger down the white tie he'd picked out for me. We'd agreed to keep our PDA as minimal as possible at the arena, otherwise, the look in his eye told me that I'd currently be being kissed to within an inch of my life.

"Yep. Let's do this."

Was it too late to make a beeline to the nearest bathroom to throw up? Probably.

We made our way out to the table the PR department had set up at the front of the press room. Our agents were already seated at the table waiting for us.

J.J.'s agent was wearing a sharply tailored darker than black, black suit with a crisp pale yellow blouse underneath it, to go with his lime green from the Snappers' team colors. And, other than questioning how tight it fit, I was thankful that J.J. had swapped out my suit. Because if he had't, and I'd worn the dark gray one my mom had wanted me to, I would've been dressed identically to my agent, Kevin.

Once we took our seats behind the dead-center of the table, our teammates and coaches started trickling into the press room as well. Ogden Haskins, my head coach, and Jean-Alain Foucher, the Snappers head coach took the seats on either side of our agents while our teammates shuffled into the seats in the first couple rows of chairs that had been set up.

They all, of course, were already aware of what J.J. and I would be announcing during today's press conference.

After we'd approached our respective teams' management, J.J. and I had had meetings with all of our various coaches, letting them know about our relationship and informing them of our decision to make our relationship public. J.J. had also come out to his teammates.

My teammates, of course, had already known that I was gay, so I had just had to update them all on the fact that during the off-season I seemed to have acquired a boyfriend. Who was also a hockey player. On a rival team. And who was also, sort of, my rival.

Once the assorted media personnel had been allowed into the room and they took their seats, with much muttered and whispered speculation as to what the heck was going on, Coach Haskins tapped his mic and addressed them.

I'm not entirely sure why my coach was the one appointed to be the one to speak for himself and Coach Foucher. Perhaps it was because we were in our home arena. Or perhaps Coach Foucher didn't want to have to rely on his, admittedly pretty good, English instead of his native French. Or maybe it was because Coach Haskins already had some experience with dealing with one of his players publicly coming out and knew how to handle the media.

Either way, it was Coach Haskins who cleared his throat and said, "Thank you, members of the press, for being here today. I know you're all wondering what this is all about. Especially, because we didn't give you any sort of pre-conference information. We just told you to show up before today's pre-season match-up between us and the visiting Kansas City Snappers. And here you are." Coach Haskins ran a hand over his shaved-bald head and offered the members of the press a wry smile. "You're probably especially curious because I've got the Snapper's head coach and one of their players up here with me, along with one of the Loons' own, Jaime Johnson." Haskins then motioned with his hand toward Coach Foucher and the assembled hockey players in the audience. "As you can see, before we get to fighting it out on the ice, the Loons and the Snappers are all here to show their support of their teammates. Jaime Johnson and J.J. Johnson are the ones who called for this press conference. They're going to make their statements. And then they'll be taking a few… but only a few… questions from you. And, as I'm sure you've learned about me over the past few months, those questions had better be respectful or else I'll have no problem with throwing you out on your asses."

J.J. and I had had some discussions about who was going to say what during this press conference we'd requested. They'd often turned into heated arguments that had then turned into heated make-up sex, but we'd finally compromised on J.J. reading out our short pre-prepared statement, which he, unfortunately, wouldn't let me see beforehand and letting me field the majority of whatever questions from the media. Naturally, I was nervous about what he was going to say, but I thought—hoped—that giving him some time to think about what he was going to say would cut down on some of J.J.'s naturally outlandish tendencies.

While there was no spot-light in the room, I couldn't help but feel as though the focused attention of our teammates and the gathered reporters was a harsh, blinding glare.

"Thank you all for being here today," J.J. started out, politely enough, after he made a minute adjustment to his microphone, raising it up more directly in front of his face. "As I'm sure everyone knows, I don't believe in bullshitting anyone or spouting off the usual PR line of crap. So, I'm not going to bother to dress it up all pretty or beat around the bush about this. I'm gay." The hush of expectation was deafening as J.J. took a breath before he continued, "Jaime Johnson is also gay. And today, we're announcing that we're dating each other."

The upswell of noise from the media spectators had begun even before J.J. had finished speaking.

"How long have you two been together?"

"How is your relationship going to affect how you play against each other?"

"Has it already affected how you play against each other?"

"What do your teams, your teammates think about this?"

"What's the league's position on this?"

"Are you both staying on your teams or are you going to try to be on the same team?"

"There's got to be some sort of league rule against this."

"How are the fans going to trust that you two aren't rigging the games you play against each other?"

"Is somebody looking at the games they've played to see if this... this... relationship affected the outcome of those games?"

"There's no way two players being involved won't impact their teams. And their games. Sure, the league can't allow this."

It should've been hard to distinguish all of the questions and comments thrown at J.J. and I from each other, they were being yelled one on top of the other. But each one felt like a clear, singular barb being shot into my heart.

J.J. had done his part and told them what we'd needed to tell them. Now, it was my turn. I tried to tease out some of the easier, simpler questions to answer from amongst those being bombarded at us.

I tapped my microphone to make sure it was turned on and to try to garner the reporters' attention so I didn't have to shout over them to be heard. "J.J. and I started dating during the off-season. After last year's playoffs. So, so far, we haven't had the opportunity to play against each other as boyfriends. This afternoon's game will be the first."

"And your teams are seriously going to let you two play against each other?"

I couldn't tell which incredulous voice lobbed that question at me, but I went ahead and answered it. "Yes. They are."

Coach Haskins immediately backed me up, saying, "The Loons and Snappers have every confidence that Jaime and

J.J.'s relationship won't impact this afternoon's game. Or any other future games our teams play against each other."

Apparently also wanting to voice his support for his player, Coach Fouchet spoke up for the first time and stated, "Oui. Ze Snappers will play Johnson and, as we did in ze playoffs last season, we will beat ze Loons and ze other Johnson."

"What a load of shit," commented a male voice from the reporters' section of the audience. Judging from the way Erica Norquist—a reporter I recognized from her frequent interviews with us for a Minneapolis-based sports magazine—was shaking a finger and whisper-yelling at the man next to her, he was the one who'd made that rude comment. A fact that was confirmed when I saw his mouth moving as he then said, "Players shouldn't date other players. Whether they're playing on the same team or on different teams, there's no way that's not going to fuck with the game. Their personal shit will be all over the ice."

Whoever he was—I could see the bright red lanyard with the word "Press" repeatedly printed on it in white around his neck, but wasn't able to see his name badge identifying which media outlet he was with—I had a feeling today was probably going to be the last time he was ever allowed inside the Maverick Arena as a member of the media. Multiple Loons PR people were frantically scribbling all over their clipboards and Coach Haskins looked about two seconds away from blowing his top and either yelling at the idiot or climbing over the table and hunting him down and introducing him to his fist.

However, it wasn't Coach Haskins who lost his temper with the reporter. No. It was my team Captain, Carsen "Apple" Appleson.

"You know what's a load of shit?" Carsen asked, as he stood up and swiveled around to face the irritating reporter. The motion had been so quick and sudden, that the chair he'd been sitting on wobbled and fell over. "You are. You're a complete load of shit."

The outburst was surprising and unexpected from my team Captain. Carsen—who'd gotten his hockey nickname due to his All-American, blond hair, blue-eyed, square-jawed good looks, along with it just being a shortening of his last name—was normally a personable and charming favorite with the press. In his interviews, he always had a smile, a joke, and an intelligent and thoughtful sound-clip for them. Even after some of our worst losses and our cruddiest games, Carsen kept his good humor and never let the press' pointed and, often, insulting questions get to him.

Leland "Griff" Griffin, the Loons starting goalie and Carsen's best friend since college—and roommate, when they happened to play for the same team—righted Carsen's toppled over chair. He then pulled on Carsen's shirt, clearly trying to get his attention and/or get him to sit back down.

But Apple was having none of that. He continued to rant, "When we play hockey, we play hockey. Sure, it matters which players we're up against. That's how you strategize and determine how you're going to have the best chances of winning your games. But if you play in this league, at any level, for any amount of time, you're going to wind up playing with guys you like, guys that are like brothers, guys that you hate, guys whose weddings and birthday parties and children's baptisms you've gone to. And then you're going to also wind up playing against some of those very same guys. Sometimes all within the same fucking season even. We play when we're mad with these guys, happy with these guys, sad with these guys. So, no. No. It doesn't matter if players are dating someone on an opposing team. It wouldn't and shouldn't even matter if they played on the same team. In fact… In fact…"

Griff was now verbally shushing Carsen and also pulling so hard on his shirt, it looked like it was going to rip.

Carsen ignored his friend. With an I-don't-give-a-flying-fig smile that I've never before seen on his face, Carsen stated, "In fact… Griff and I have been together since college. Romantically." When that bombshell ripped through everyone in the room, he continued, yelling to be heard over the furious upswell in talking,   "That's twelve years. And we've actually been married for the past ten years."

Holy fuck. And, yeah. If ever there was a time where a substitute word wouldn't cut it, this was it. Fuck.

Obviously, I'd had no idea that was going to happen. The wide-eyed, gaped-open mouth expression on Griff's face indicated that he hadn't either.

"Fuck. Apple just outed the both of them," J.J. said. I could barely hear him over the continued comments and questions, now being lobbed at Carsen and Griff instead of J.J. and I. "What the fuck was he thinking?"

I didn't have a fricking clue. I'd known our press conference was bound to wind up being a media circus. How could it not be? And, on the one hand, I was grateful to Carsen for yanking the spotlight off of myself and J.J. But good gravy, he'd just multiplied the chaos by a gajillion.

And we still had a hockey game to play in a couple hours!

At least, I assumed we did. I doubted the NHL would give our two teams an exception and let us move our game to a more convenient day. As in, when the members of the teams hadn't brought down upon themselves a metric boatload of confusion and distraction and flaring emotions.

Possibly some assault, or at least harassment, accusations from members of the media, as well, I thought when I saw Loons defenseman Caleb Murphy rip the rude reporter's press pass from around his neck and fling it to the ground. He then grabbed the reporter's phone—which he'd been using to record the press conference and the ongoing chaos from the double-whammy revelations—from his hand, flung it to the ground, and then stomped on it with his gigantic foot.

Meanwhile, the two head coaches and assorted PR personnel were trying to wrangle and herd the other reporters toward the exit doors and out of the press room. The reporters were not making it easy on them, wiggling and trying to dart around them, continuing to hurl questions at… everyone. J.J. and I. Carsen and Griff. The very coaches they were trying to dodge. Any of the other players they thought might have an opinion and might be willing to share it with them. *Everyone.*

Somehow, possibly with some mystical goalie magic, Griff managed to cut through the swarming mass of two team's worth of hockey players and had made his escape out of the conference room. Carsen wasn't fairing as well and was surrounded by a ring of reporters two deep who were practically shouting their questions in his face. He looked rumpled and flustered. But a pleased smile was curling the corner of his mouth.

J.J. and I remained seated in our chairs behind the conference table. There really was nowhere else for us to go with the rest of the room teeming with talking, yelling, moving bodies. And it seemed sort of irresponsible to me to duck out of our own press conference.

"So, that went well I think," J.J. commented as he reached over and grabbed my hand, which had been resting on top of the table, threading our fingers together.

"Oh, yeah. Perfectly," I sarcastically agreed. "Just like we'd planned."

Sylvie, J.J.'s agent, leaned forward and looked at the two of us. "You know," she said. "I've been trying to think of ways to get more billable hours out of this guy. So, thanks for that. Wish I'd thought to bring some fuckin' popcorn, though. This show's been entertaining as fuck."

Kevin, my agent, had propped his elbows on the table and buried his face in his hands sometime around the time that Carsen had outed himself and Griff. At Sylvie's words, he raised his head, looked at her, then at us, then glanced back at Sylvie. "Y'all are nuts," he said. "I thought we were trying to manage this situation and avert a viral shitshow. That's obviously out the window now. On the plus side, my wife has been eyeing a European river cruise and I now have some good leverage to get a bonus and possibly some sort of hazard pay from my bosses."

"Everybody out!" Ogden Haskins roared, finally having reached the end of his frayed patience. "This press conference is over! You wanna keep yelling at us, come back later and yell at us to score some fucking goals in the fucking game we're still playing this afternoon!" He punctuated his next hollered "Out!" by shoving three reporters out one of the doors.

"You want me to pull the fire alarm, Coach?" Murph yelled over the squawking reporters, who seemed to be catching on that they were actually being physically, forcibly removed from the room. "That ought to clear them all out."

"No!" yelled multiple people at once in response to Caleb Murphy's question.

"Son, the last thing today needs is a visit from the local fire and police department," Coach Haskins told him. "You wanna be helpful, grab a reporter and politely show them the way out. Okay?"

"Sure thing, Coach," Murph answered as he proceeded to wrap a long arm around two terrified looking reporters and sweep them toward the nearest open doorway.

"I figure you two are probably out," Kevin said. "But, Sylvie, whaddaya say we go find the nearest liquor and go drink ourselves a snootful?"

"Kev, you darling man, that sounds like a marvelous idea," Sylvie replied. She rose gracefully from her chair, smoothed a hand down her suit, then laid a hand on J.J.'s shoulder. "I am so proud of you, you know," she told him. "You did good today, honey." Then with a wave of her hand, she indicated for Kevin to join her and they both ducked out the back door to the press room that we'd come through earlier.

Slowly, but surely, the press room was emptying of people. It was left looking like a tornado had swept through. Multiple chairs were toppled over. Water bottles, pens, and notepads lay abandoned and strewn all over the floor. And... was that somebody's shoe in the corner? Who the heck had managed to lose a shoe? And how?

Soon, J.J. and I were some of the only people still in the press room.

Caleb was standing guard by one of the doors, huffing and puffing and looking like he was more than prepared to wreak more havoc on anyone who dared to re-enter it. Sasha Yuralaev of the Snappers was talking to my teammate, George Nickleby, and showing him something on his phone. Coach Fouchet was rapidly speaking to somebody on his phone, presumably in French, and complete with agitated gestures of his free arm. And Timo Sneetsen, who played center on the Loons first offensive line with me, was sitting in a corner of the room... serenely reading a book? What the... I didn't even have the words.

"You know… if we really wanted to fuck with everybody… I'd let you win this afternoon," J.J. said with a smirk.

"Let me… Let me?" I asked, outraged. "There will be no… I don't need you to let me *anything!*" I protested angrily, shoving up out of my chair. It didn't even occur to me that we were probably, once again, going to be the center of attention of the other people still in the room. I was too irate for that to even seep into my awareness. "I'll beat you this afternoon fair and square. Just like I always do."

"Yeah. Not last year, you didn't," J.J. silkily replied as he also, much more gently, pushed back his chair and rose to his feet.

"I… I… We won last year!" I loudly reminded him. "We knocked you out of the playoffs."

"Yeah… But that wasn't you," J.J. said. "If I'm recalling correctly, your goal numbers during that playoff series were abysmally low. It was the rest of your teammates who won that series. Not you. And, even though the Snappers lost, I scored more goals than you. And that's what matters."

"You just watch," I told him. "I'm going to kick your butt today." I poked J.J. in the chest in emphasis. "And then the next time we play each other I'll kick your butt again." Poke. "And the time after that!"

J.J. flicked my hand away from his chest. "Yuh huh. Sure you will."

Oooh. That cocky, arrogant, conceited, egotistical…

"What do you say we make this interesting?" J.J. asked. "If you do somehow manage to kick my *ass*... I'll do something similar to your ass. Except swap out lick for kick. And if I win... which I will..."

"I'll what?" I asked indignantly. "What will I have to do if *you* win?"

"Hmm." J.J. pursed his lips as he thought. "Actually... I kinda want the same prize. For me to get to lick your ass."

"You..." Huh. That was... "Okay," I agreed after a moment. It really wasn't a fair wager. After all, regardless of the outcome of today's game, it seemed like I was going to be the winner.

"Fantastic, it's a bet," J.J. said. Instead of holding his hand out for us to shake on our wager, J.J. leaned forward and kissed me. "Good luck today, love."

"You too, J."

"Eh. You're the one who's going to need it."

From the weekly online edition of Minnesota Match-ups

All's Fair in Love and... Hockey?

By Erica Norquist

It's taken a little longer than anticipated, but hockey fans are finally going to get to see their very own Romeo and Julien take to the ice when the Minnesota Loons host the Kansas City Snappers this coming weekend.

Not counting the pre-season match-up between these two teams, which was held only hours after players Jaime Johnson and J.J. Johnson came out as homosexual and announced that they were in a relationship with each other, today will be the first time these two players will be on ice together. Unlike the pre-season game, which the Loons won 5-3, this game will count toward both teams' efforts to once again make the Stanley Cup Playoffs.

Initially this on-ice reunion of star-crossed hockey lovers was slated to take place in October. However, due to J.J. Johnson being on the IRL and recovering from a tear in his coracoclavicular ligament when the Loons suffered their defeat at the hands of the Snappers earlier in the season, we have had to wait almost two months—when these two divisional rival teams were scheduled face off against each other again—to see the awaited lover's quarrel for the puck.

The level of rivalry between the Minnesota Loons and the Kansas City Snappers might not be quite at Shakespearean levels—both teams only being founded during the NHL's expansion in the early 1990s. But with the only current instance of two players dating each other while being on opposing teams, this weekend's match-up promises to finally deliver a glimpse into how they, and the hockey world, will handle the conflict between love and hockey.

Note: While Carsen Appleson also revealed, at the above-mentioned press conference, that he and current teammate Leland Griffin—both of the Minnesota Loons—were married to each other while they played on opposing teams earlier in their professional hockey careers, that relationship had not been known to the general public at the time. Thus depriving all hockey fans any prior experience with getting to witness an icy lover vs lover showdown.

Chapter Twenty-Five

Jaime

"J, which one of these suits is mine?" I yelled to my boyfriend, who was still futzing with his hair in the bathroom. He'd recently had it cut a little shorter—curling just below his ears—than he tended to wear it and was still not completely happy with how it looked.

It was a sincere question. J.J. and I had been officially boyfriends for roughly three-and-a-half months, had spent two thirds of that living in different cities, and he'd still somehow managed to swap out all of the suits hanging in my closet. The entirety of my wardrobe had undergone a metamorphosis and looked nearly identical—to me, at least—to J.J.'s wardrobe.

He claimed it was to make it easier on him so that he didn't have to pack any clothes to come visit me—when he was able to visit me—since he could just borrow my clothes now. He also said it was so—and I quote—"everyone would be jealous of how fuckable my boyfriend is."

So, before I started getting dressed for tonight's game between the Loons and the Snappers, I needed to know if mine was the emerald green suit or the pale mint green suit. They were hanging side by side on the garment hooks J.J. had also, somehow and some time, installed in my closet.

"Obviously, the emerald green," J.J. answered as he leisurely strolled out of the bathroom, a cloud of steam puffing out with him.

"Oh. *Obviously.*"

"Babe, the darker green would wash out my skin tone," J.J. said. "But on you... on you..." He trailed a series of featherlight kisses across my bare shoulder. "On you... divine."

I'd have to take his word for it. Green was green, right?

But we really didn't have the time for the ideas his mouth—having detoured and trailing down my left arm—was giving me. I wish we did. But we didn't. I wanted to make sure that J.J. and I were both at the rink well before we technically needed to be there.

Both of our teams had given us the opportunity to opt out of staying in a hotel with the rest of our teammates when we were playing in each other's home cities and I didn't want to do anything to make them regret their generosity or make them rescind the offer.

Being in the same division, in addition to the one preseason game, J.J. and I were scheduled to play four regular season games against each other—two in Minneapolis and two in Kansas City. That wasn't a whole lot of time together, especially considering the regular season lasted for just over half of the year.

While J.J. had had to miss one of those games because of the injury he'd sustained after an unfortunate and unlucky bounce against the boards, we'd still had that time together while the Loons had been playing the Snappers in their home arena.

We would get some additional days around the holidays— my parents were getting Thanksgiving this year and Greg and Crystal had claimed Christmas—but even some of that time would get eaten up by time spent in airports and in the air. And, for once, J.J. and I were both fervently praying that we wouldn't be selected for the All Star Game. A whole week we could spend together? It would be heaven.

And the couple of times throughout the season where the teams we were playing just happened to be in cities not too far apart... Well, J.J. and I had sympathetic road roommates and what the team didn't find out about...

So, with the additional assistance of regular and frequent Skype calls—I really should get TJ a fruit basket for that particularly useful tip—J.J. and I had been making our relationship work.

It wasn't always easy. And both of us felt the strain of the distance, but we were committed to making our relationship work. Not being together was simply unthinkable.

"J. You need to… Mmm. You need to…" I really didn't want to stop him. His mouth was doing wickedly enjoyable things to the skin of my back. "We have to get dressed and head to the arena," I told him.

"But do we have to? Really? Really, really?"

"Yes, we have to," I replied. "Really, really."

"Fine." J.J. nipped at a bit of skin just above the waistband of my briefs. "I'll be back later," he whispered to my… butt, I was guessing.

That was a promise I was going to hold him to.

"Kiss my ass!" I yelled at my boyfriend as he gleefully laughed and raised his arms in celebration of the goal horn going off. That goal should never have happened. J.J. had illegally stolen the puck from me because… "You fucking tripped me!"

"Oh, I did not," J.J. replied with his usual irritating, cocky smirk. "You fell over all on your own because you skate as well as a four-year-old."

"You did too. You tripped me!"

"Did not."

"Did too."

"No. I didn't. If I'd tripped you, the ref would've called a penalty on me. But he didn't. Because I didn't trip you."

"You did so trip me, you ass," I accused again. When J.J. shook his head at me and started to skate away, I'd had enough. "You tripped me and you know it," I said, giving him just the tiniest of shoves to make sure he knew I was serious.

"Did you... Did you just push me?" he asked incredulously. "Seriously. You pushed me."

"I did. Just like you tripped me."

"I didn't trip you." J.J. swung his stick and thwacked it against my skates, knocking me off balance. I fell over onto the ice. Again. "*Now* I tripped you."

"Oh, it is on, you... you..." I struggled to get my gloves off. The dang things were adhered to my hands from all my sweat.

"For the love of fuck, would you figure out how to fucking swear, babe?" J.J. shrugged his own gloves off. Much more easily than I had, the jerk.

"F-fuck off!"

323

"Better. Better. You know. Mostly."

At that comment, I balled up my hand and punched J.J. in the nose.

Even though this was hockey and we were fighting, I had plans for his mouth later. I was trying to be careful of where I aimed. There was also no way I was going to direct any of my hits anywhere near his shoulder. J.J. had only been back off the IRL for a couple of weeks, I didn't want to reinjure him. It was bad enough worrying over it with him the first time.

"Son of a bitch!" he exclaimed. "You fucking hit me!"

I took advantage of his disbelief to land a punch to his stomach. It's okay. It was mostly padded.

"Holy shit," he panted out. "Okay. We're doing this."

How had I forgotten how much it hurt to get hit?

J.J. had definitely not hit me with his full strength. I've watched enough footage of the man fighting before and that blow to my hip—also incredibly well-protected with pads— had not been his best effort.

"Guys? Really?" Mitchell, one of the referees for today's game, skated up to J.J. and I as we were fighting. "I figured you two would be past this shit."

I glanced up and saw that, beyond Mitchell, we had a loose circle of players from both teams positioned around us, watching us. None of them looked as though they wanted to break up or join our fight, although the fans beyond the glass were yelling at them to fight—as hockey fans were wont to do.

"I'm going to have to call you both for fighting," Mitchell said. "You were both probably the fucking instigator in this so I won't even bother tacking on the minor. Johnson, Johnson... both of you five minutes in the box."

I wasn't normally one to argue with the refs—mostly because I didn't incur a lot of penalties where I'd need to—but this was... "Bullshit!" I yelled. "J.J. tripped me. Intentionally. So, he started it. Where's the penalty for that, huh?"

Mitchell turned to look at J.J. with a raised brow.

"He's right. I did trip him," J.J. said. "After he accused me of tripping him and shoved me. Loverboy was already upset. I figure, why not go ahead and do the thing he was mad at me for?"

"For fuck's sake," Mitchell muttered.

"And then he hit me. On the nose," J.J. happily informed the ref, pointing at his nose. Which was only looking a little pink and irritated from the barely-there graze of my fist.

"Jesus fuck." Mitchell raised his eyes to the arena ceiling. Not that I thought any deities were watching this evening's game or would respond favorably to his profanity.

One of the linesmen skated up to confer with Mitchell. "What's the hold-up?" he asked. "This might just be a pre-season game, but I'm pretty sure all these guys are supposed to be playing hockey. Not just standing around. Throw whoever needs to be thrown into the penalty box into the penalty box and let's get this game back on the clock."

"You heard the man," Michell said. "Johnson. Johnson. Off to the box, the pair of you. Five minutes."

J.J. and I both started skating toward the penalty box, Mitchell keeping pace behind us to make sure we followed through with his ruling without any further incidents.

"This is such bullshit," I couldn't help but complain again. "You hit me," I loudly reminded J.J.

"You hit me first," J.J. reminded me back, just as loudly. "And you even got more hits in than I did. I only hit you the one time before this guy broke it up." He jabbed a thumb over his shoulder at Mitchell, who still looked fed up with the both of us.

Climbing through the door into my side of the box, which the attendant was patiently holding open for me, I turned to look through the plexiglass partition separating me from my boyfriend. "I didn't hurt you, did I?" I asked him.

"Nah," he replied. "Those little love taps? You've hurt me worse than that before." J.J. gave me a wink big enough and obvious enough that even the spectators in the top nosebleed seats could've seen it. I felt myself blush bright pink as I realized he was alluding to when things got a little heated between us in bed and I found myself paddling his tight, round, spankable butt. "But if it'll make you feel better," J.J. said. "You can kiss all my owies and boo-boos tonight when we get home."

The Penalty Bench Attendant in J.J.'s side of the box was clearly trying to stifle his snickers at our exchange. But, for him, J.J.'s comment had been pretty tame. It was less than the kinds of things I'd been prepared to hear come out of his mouth.

So, I ignored both attendants listening in on our conversation, settled myself on the penalty bench to wait out the rest of my five minutes, and said, "We'll take turns. You kiss mine; I'll kiss yours."

"It's what we usually do," J.J. agreed. "That's why I always keep my lucky quarter on me." J.J. patted his chest, over the area where I knew the quarter was resting, warmly and securely.

The sentimental idiot had had a hole drilled into his "lucky" quarter and then strung onto a chain that he wore around his neck. Even underneath his hockey jersey. Even when we weren't in the same city where using the coin would be needed to determine which of us would be bottoming and who would be topping.

Frick, I loved that idiot.

Epilogue
--The First One--

Jaime

"Baaaaabbbe... Jaime. Jaime. Jaime. Loverboy. My love,"
J.J. slurred through the phone. At the unholy hour of... three
in the morning?

"J? Did you drink all of the champagne yourself?" I asked
him. "You're supposed to pass the bottle around and share it
with your teammates."

The second I'd seen the second hand tick to zero and the
lights had gone wild, while confetti rained down from the
ceiling of Heller Arena, I'd known my boyfriend would end
the night blitzed out of his mind on celebratory champagne
and alcohol. But J.J. sounded beyond drunk on the phone.

The level of drunk that was possibly—almost definitely—going to land him on some vlog feed and go viral all across the internet.

His team had just won the Stanley Cup, though. So, I supposed some allowances had to be made.

"I won the Stanley Cup!" J.J. shouted.

I winced and held my phone further away from my ear. "I know, J. I was there," I reminded him.

And hadn't that been a treat.

Naturally, I was thrilled that J.J. had done well throughout the playoffs and made it all the way to the Finals. And I was so ecstatic that it felt like I would burst when he and the Snappers pulled off the win during Game Six.

But sitting in the family box with the girlfriends and wives and parents of the Snappers players instead of being out on the ice, having my own shot at the Cup... had been a bit awkward and disappointing.

The Loons had finished off our season strong and we'd easily made the playoffs. We faced only a minimal challenge in sending the Griffins back home to Phoenix in the first round. Jason Teague, my partner from the charity golf tournament over summer, hadn't been too thrilled about the outcome of that series. And the Snappers had also handily skated past Nashville in their first round series.

Then it was the Loons facing down the Snappers in the second round of the playoffs—a rematch of last year's first round. But unlike last year, the Snappers had bested the Loons and had advanced on to the Stanley Cup Finals. While the Loons had the joy of cleaning out our lockers and beginning our off-season.

So, I was proud and happy for J.J. that he'd made the Finals and, now, won the Cup. But I was also sad and frustrated and disappointed and jealous that it wasn't me that had been drinking copious amounts of champagne out of the greatest trophy in the world tonight.

It hadn't prevented me from attending his games and cheering him on. But that didn't mean that I wanted his wild celebration shoved in my face. I wasn't over my post-playoff funk just quite yet.

"Tell him! Tell him!" male voices loudly chanted wherever J.J. was calling me from.

Oh, goodie. At least J.J. wasn't alone for his foolish, ill-advised, drunken festivities. But what in the heck did they want somebody to tell some other him? And was I the "him" that needed to be told something?

"I won the Stanley Cup!" J.J. repeated, still at eardrum shredding levels of shouting. "And I got you something."

"You... What? You got me something because you won the Cup?" Why did my mind immediately flash to the image of some cheap, you-tried-your-best consolation trophy that he would insist on prominently displaying in my apartment? Possibly supergluing it somewhere I wouldn't be able to miss seeing it on a daily basis. "What did you get me?" I hesitantly, and against my better judgment, asked.

"A tattoo!"

"You... what?"

I was pretty sure I didn't have any chunks of time missing from my memories and I didn't see how it would've been feasible for J.J. to drag me to a tattoo parlor and have something permanently embedded in my skin without my knowledge. But J.J.'s tone of voice had sounded so pleased with itself that I actually gave the length of my body a quick look-over. Just to reassure myself that I didn't see or feel any hint of a non-consented-to tattoo on my person.

But nope. I felt perfectly as intact and unmarked as I had been when I'd returned to J.J.'s apartment in Kansas City after watching the last game of the finals at the arena with Greg and Crystal. And I was pretty sure I hadn't been sleeping that deeply—I'd known J.J. was going to be out pretty late celebrating his win with his teammates, so I wasn't going to bother waiting up for him—that I wouldn't have noticed somebody attacking me with a tattoo gun.

"A tattoo," J.J. said again. "The boys and I went to a tattoo parlor to get tattoos to celebrate winning the Cup," he explained. "But instead of a Cup tattoo, I got a tattoo for you. It's on my ass, so you're the only one who'll see it."

"I can see it right now," a voice called out from someone who must've been standing near J.J. "Put some fucking pants on, man."

"Can't believe I'm gonna have to see that every time Cube's in the locker room with us," another voice complained. "Some things just can't be unseen."

Yeah. As professional athletes, we were routinely completely naked around numerous people on a regular basis. So whatever J.J. had gotten tattooed on his butt... it

331

wasn't going to stay for-my-eyes-only as much as his drunken brain had convinced him it would be.

"Lemme see, lemme see." How many drunken idiotic hockey players were crammed into that tattoo parlor in the middle of the night? Oh, those poor tattoo artists having to deal with that mess. I hoped all the players remembered to tip well. "Oh. Tha's not right," this additional voice slurred as he must've gotten a glimpse of whatever J.J.'s tattoo was. "Funny. But wrong. So, so wrong."

I pinched the bridge of my nose and scrounged around for my most patient and loving—*I loved this man. I really did love this idiot. For some reason*—tone of voice that I could manage at three in the morning and asked, "What did you get tattooed on your butt, J?"

"Wouldn' you like to know?" he slyly slurred back.

"I would. That's why I asked."

"I'mma be home soon. I'll show it to you... I'll show it to you..." J.J. had to pause what he was saying to let out a drunken belch. *Why* was this the guy I'd fallen in love with again? "You'll see it then," he said when his blurry brain remembered he was talking to me on the phone. "And you're gonna love it. I know it. You're gonna wanna put your hands all over it and your mouth and—"

"Okay, I think that's enough of that." A voice cut J.J. off, then came on the line. When he continued talking, I recognized the amused voice of Sasha Yuralaev. "It wouldn't bother me to hear more details of what you're gonna do to Cube's newly tattooed ass once we get him back to his place, but I don't think that's the kinda thing you want anyone else to know. And the rest of the guys are looking a little grossed out. Although, that could just be from the booze. So, I'm takin' Cube's phone and hanging up now, okay, Loverboy?" Sasha said.

"Oh. Uh... Okay. When you—"

It seemed like Sasha wasn't really waiting for my acknowledgement of what he'd said. As I was telling him that J.J. should have his keys on him, Sasha's attention had already turned back toward the teammates he was with. "Torby... if you're gonna puke, for the love of fuck, there's a garbage can right there." Then the line disconnected.

Oh well. If I cracked open a window, I'm sure I'd be able to hear a herd of drunken hockey players when they got here to drop off my inebriated boyfriend. If J.J. had forgotten his keys at the arena, misplaced them since then, or couldn't remember how to use them to let himself in, I'd press the button to buzz him into his building.

I wondered how far away the tattoo shop was that they'd gone to. And how long it would take the slightly-more-sober members of their group to wrangle them up and get them organized enough to start heading for their homes.

I really doubted I was going to want to get my hands or my mouth on whatever J.J. had gotten tattooed on his butt. The thing was bound to be all inky, and oozy, and covered in whatever tattoo artists put on tattoos once they were done doing them. But I was awfully curious—and leery—of what new image he'd gotten permanently embedded into his skin. And for me, according to him.

I just hoped it wasn't something embarrassing or obviously about me. Please let it not be a giant I heart Loverboy or something with my name. Tattoo artists were supposed to discourage people from getting a tattoo of their partner's name, right? I think I've heard that before.

What sort of foolishness had that sappy idiot had put on his butt?

Epilogue
--The Second One--

J.J.

Holy fuck. Looking at the nearly three-foot-tall gleaming metal trophy that I had currently laying across my bed, I was still having trouble believing that I'd actually won the Stanley fucking Cup. You'd think that the month between the last game of the finals and when my day with the Cup had come around would've been enough time for it all to sink in. But it still really hadn't.

Some part of me expected that when I woke up each morning, I'd find out it had all been a dream. Or I'd get a phone call telling me the whole thing had been a mistake and the Snappers hadn't actually won the Cup. That *I* hadn't won the Cup.

How the hell was this my life? Sure, I'd always told everyone that I knew I'd win it one day. And that was the predominant thought in my own mind—it had to be. If a player didn't think they stood a chance of winning the Stanley Cup, then why the hell were they even playing the game? But it was still one thing to *think* you'd win it. It was a whole other world to actually *do* it.

It was all I could do not to whoop and holler and dance around my apartment in sheer glee. Because a) it's the ever-fucking-loving STANLEY CUP and b) I could now pretty much control where I'm going. I hadn't really told anyone other than my agent and the head coach and some of the management, but with my contract up for renewal this year, I wasn't planning on staying with the Snappers.

It felt kind of shitty to cut and run on the team that I just went to the Stanley Cup finals—and won—with, especially with how supportive they've been this season with my whole coming out as gay and being in a relationship with another player on a rival team thing. But this whole long-distance relationship with Jaime thing was getting pretty exhausting. It seemed like a huge chunk of our time when we had the time to see each other—when our playing schedules synced up and allowed—was spent in airports and on a plane instead of actually with each other.

The sneaking around to hotels when our games were in cities near each other was kind of hot. I kind of kept expecting Jaime to balk at having to do that. I know it made him uncomfortable to have his road roommate cover for him while he blatantly broke his team's curfew rules. But he hadn't so far.

Still, it only made sense to make some changes to minimize the distance between us. And, ultimately, try to wind up on the same team or, if we could swing it, land in one of the cities with two teams—like New York—or an area where they were so close together, we could easily live in between the two and commute. There were a couple different options for that in New England and the southeastern portion of Canada.

But if anyone was going to hop teams, it made more sense for me to be the to do it, since Jaime was pretty happy with the Loons. Especially as he had the support and friendship of his teammates, Sawyer Brzycki, Carsen Appleson, and Leland Griffin, some of the only other out queer players in the league. Jaime also had several years left on his contract, so unless the Loons took leave of their minds and traded him, he was going to be with them for a while yet and didn't have the flexibility I had in trying to relocate to a team closer to his boyfriend. But since I did… I had put some feelers out with the new expansion team that was starting up in Des Moines and it looked like I was only days away from signing a deal with them.

While that wouldn't put me on the same team as Jaime— something that probably wouldn't be a great idea anyway, both personality-wise, leaving-the-game-out-of-our-relationship-wise, and fan-discomfort-and-grumbling-over-how-our-relationship-would-impact-the-team-wise—it was closer than Kansas City. As I already knew from when we'd gone to visit Greg and Crystal, a nonstop flight from Des Moines to Minneapolis takes less than one-and-a-half hours.

Driving it would take just over three-and-a-half hours, if I wanted to skip the airport hassle.

There were a couple other teams close to Minneapolis—the Chicago Suns and the Pontiac Firebirds—but I knew a new expansion team would jump on a player willing to sign onto their team for whatever they wanted to offer him. With the Cyclones I also wouldn't have to deal with an already established roster or long, drawn out salary negotiations that would have to work around an established team's more limited available funds under their salary caps.

Additionally, the Cyclones were getting assigned to the Eastern Conference, while the Loons were in the Western Conference. Which meant that if—when—I joined them, I would only be up against Jaime possibly three times a year. And those games wouldn't have quite so much weight to them, unlike our previous divisional match-ups had had.

Despite my claims in the past, I was well-aware that hockey was a team sport and that there were no 'I's on a team, but people being people… Fans and commentators had spent the past season obsessed with speculating how much our personal relationship impacted our playing. And then blaming the one of us on the losing team for that loss. As if either one of us would intentionally let the other one win. People were dumb.

So it just made sense to me that we should probably try to limit how often Jaime and I shared ice together on opposing teams. Unless of course that ice time came about during the Stanley Cup Finals. Then all bets were off. But, at that point, hopefully Jaime and I would've well-established that we deserved to be there due to our playing and not because of some perceived advantage gained by playing against your boyfriend.

And while I'd done all I could to get the fuck out of Iowa after high school, I had to admit that part of me wouldn't mind that moving to Des Moines would leave me only an hour-and-a-half away from Greg and his family. That was a pretty doable driving distance so I could be a more active presence in my honorary nephew's and niece's lives. And it would make it so much easier to pester and annoy Greg whenever the whim struck me. In person, not just over the phone.

"Why is the Stanley Cup in your bed?" my hot AF boyfriend asked as he came out of the bathroom, rubbing a towel over his wet and rumpled ginger hair, a second towel needlessly wrapped around his slim hips and blocking my view of all the yummy cock goodness underneath it.

"You're a smart guy, I'm sure you can figure it out," I told him. "And stop drying yourself off. I want to do that. With my tongue." I loved licking droplets of water off of the cinnamony-colored freckles on Jaime's shoulders and upper arms. It was one of the best parts of taking a shower with him. One of them. Other than the whole naked, wet, and down for showertime bjs, handjobs, and hands braced against the tile wall and fucking thing.

"Pretty sure your tongue doesn't do much to dry me off," Jaime drolly replied. "It being coated in saliva and wet and all. But fine." He stopped drying his hair and tossed that towel into the corner of my bedroom, where a laundry basket in theory was located under the giant mound of dirty clothes, towels, and sheets waiting for their turn through my washing machine. "So. The Stanley Cup?" he asked again as he came to stand next to me at the foot of the bed. I turned back around so that we were now both looking at the engraved, highly-coveted, priceless, and irreplaceable monument to hockey's history and greatness. "Actually, first tell me… how. How did you manage to get the Cup Keeper to leave you alone… in your bedroom… with the Stanley Cup?"

"Would you believe me if I told you I bribed him?"

"No."

"Asked him pretty, pretty please?"

"Also no," Jaime replied.

"Knocked him unconscious and tied him up so I could do whatever I wanted with it?"

"Now that… *that* I'd believe."

"Well, that's not what happened," I said. "It took a little bit but… I really did just ask him if I could. I told him that, ever since I was a little kid… like so many other little kids… I dreamt of winning the Stanley Cup. And now that I had, I wanted the Stanley Cup in my room watching me over me in my sleep. And so that, when I woke up from dreaming about winning the Cup, I'd see it there… sitting in my room… and know that my dream had come true."

"And… he bought that bullbaloney?" Jaime asked.

"He did," I replied, sounding as obviously surprised and bewildered as Jaime did. "Maybe because my request sounded a lot tamer than some of the other requests he gets from Cup winners." I paused for a minute before confessing, "Or maybe it's because I had to promise that he could stay in the living room, only twenty or so feet and one door away from it." Jaime grunted a non-committal agreement, allowing that that concession might've helped. "At any rate… here it is. Isn't it gorgeous?"

"Okay. So… why?" Jaime asked again. "Why is the Stanley Cup in your bed?"

"I figured this would be the best place for it," I told him. "So you'd could be the most comfortable when I bend you over and fuck you on top of it."

"Fuck… fuck me… on top of… Are you out of your flipping mind?" Jaime hollered in disbelief. "You can't… we can't…" He pointed from me to the Cup. At me. At the Cup. Then, flailing his arms around in the air, he insisted, "We're not having sex on top of the danged Stanley Cup!"

"Shhhh…" I shushed him, casting a worried look at my closed bedroom door. Which I had locked and barricaded with a chair under the doorknob. Just in case. I motioned with my hands that Jaime should keep his voice down. "The Keeper's just in the other room. We're going to need to be quiet so he doesn't hear us."

"Quiet? But… but… but… We can't… We can't…" Jaime spluttered before he managed to quietly, thankfully, hiss out, "We're not going to be doing anything… in a room with the *Stanley Cup*… that's going to need us to be quiet."

"It's my day with it," I said with a shrug. "I get to do whatever I want with it, yeah? That's the rule, right? Some guys take it golfing. Some take it out on their boats or to Disneyland with their kids. Me? I want to have a threesome with it and my sexy boyfriend."

Jaime tore his gaze away from the trophy—it was really hard not to stare at it. It was so silver and shiny and... the STANLEY CUP—and looked at me, his eyes wide and his mouth hanging open as he attempted to splutter out... something. Some other protest or rebuttal or goody-goody reason why having sex with, and on top of, the Stanley Cup was a bad idea. Meh. I didn't really care one way or another. I know what I wanted and fuck if I wasn't going to get it. I was a fucking Stanley Cup winner goddammit.

"C'mon, babe." I turned cajoling eyes on him, trying to make my dark brown eyes look as irresistible and begging-puppy-dog-like as I could. "Pleeeease? It's my day. And this is what I want to do with it. Please, love?"

My begging eyes must have been more effective than I thought, because, after huffing out a sigh of annoyance and resignation, Jaime capitulated. "Fine," he grumbled as he moved his hands to the twist of fabric where the towel around his waist was secured. Just as the knot was letting go, he paused. "Wait. Why am I the one getting fucked over the Cup? I'm pretty sure it's your turn to bottom. So shouldn't I be the one fucking you?"

"Phfftht. *I'm* the one who won the thing. That automatically bumps it back to being my turn to top."

"Yeah. Fair enough." Finally, Jaime dropped the dark blue towel from around his waist and climbed onto the bed on his hands and knees. "I can't believe I'm doing this," he muttered as he cautiously scootched closer to the Cup, then hesitantly put his hands on the far side of it and hovered over it.

Huh. It was a nice view. A mouthwatering view. I'd never argue that. A naked Jaime Johnson, his creamy, freckle-adorned skin just begging for me to run my hands and mouth all over it and his delectable ass facing toward me, waiting for me to come and claim it. The Stanley Cup. Two things that cropped up in pretty much all of my fantasies. Buuuut… it wasn't quite right.

"You're not even touching it," I complained. "You need to be *on* it. All the way. Belly and bits and balls in actual contact with the Cup please."

Jaime grumbled some more, complaining, "Of all the stuff you get me into." But. He did it. He actually did it.

Hesitantly, Jaime lowered his body down, letting out a gasp when his lower abdomen and all his fun bits came into contact with the trophy. Whether from shock and disbelief over having his parts of his intimate anatomy pressed up against hockey's Holy Grail or because the metal it was plated in was probably kind of cool against his bare skin.

"Oh, yeah. That's more like it. Now. Stay there. Don't move. At. All," I told him. "I'll get the lube. And then we're doing this."

I quickly grabbed my bottle of lube off of the top of my nightstand—before Jaime had too long to reconsider what we were about to do and change his mind out of some sort of sense of propriety or good taste or something—and flipped it down onto the mattress near Jaime's hip so it'd be within convenient reach. Then I pushed the soft cotton sleep shorts I had on off my hips and let them fall to the floor.

Now that I was as naked as he was, I climbed onto the bed behind Jaime, my knees on either side of his. I grabbed hold of his hips and pressed him against the trophy as I ground my hard cock against the curve of his ass.

"Oh. You weren't kidding," Jaime commented. "We're... just going right to it then. No foreplay?"

"I won you the fucking Stanley Cup. And I'm naked. You need more foreplay than that?"

Jaime looked over his shoulder at me and raised a brow as he gave me a skeptical expression. "Oh, please. You didn't win the Cup for me. You won it for you. Maybe the other guys on your team. A little. But, mostly for yourself. Just like every other player who's ever played for the Cup."

"Eh." That was about as much as I was willing to concede to his argument. "Not really the point."

"Yeah? What is the point?"

"You're in the presence of the Stanley Cup and your boyfriend is naked. You still want to tell me you need more foreplay than that? That's more than enough to get me ready to go. As you can tell," I said as I rubbed my stiff cock harder against Jaime's ass.

I moved one of my hands off of his hip and grabbed onto one of his ass cheeks and spread them apart so that I could rub the length of my cock in the sensitive crease and tease at his hole.

"Hrngh," Jaime whimpered. "Fuck."

God, I loved how much Jaime loved having his hole played with. Driving him crazy—crazed enough to start swearing—was one of my favorite pastimes. I couldn't imagine it would ever get old.

"I'm still going to need to be prepped," he reminded me.

"Yeah, yeah, yeah." As if I'd ever forget that. I wasn't a sex idiot.

I rubbed the head of my cock against his puckered hole one more time—because I felt like it—then I reached down to grab the bottle of lube. After glooping a decent amount onto my fingers, I smeared it around his hole. But when I tried to get some of it inside of him, I could barely get just the tip of one finger in. I was pretty surprised. Jaime was awesome at bottoming when he took his turn doing it and usually his ass gobbled my fingers up as soon as I got them anywhere near him.

"Babe. You need to relax. Or this isn't going to work."

"Agh. I can't," he groaned. "All I can think about is the fact that I'm getting dick particles all over the Stanley fricking Cup."

"Dick particles?"

"And if we keep going, I'm going to wind up getting my bodily fluids all over it. And I'm pretty sure I have the imprint of Patrick Kane's name permanently embedded in my stomach. That'll be fun to explain to everyone when they see it in the locker room when the season starts up again."

"Nah. His name is closer to the bottom. I think you're on top of the names from the 70s or 80s," I told him. When Jaime didn't huff out even a tiny laugh at my feeble attempt at a joke, I reassessed my plans for fucking around on the Cup. I wanted this to be a fun and memorable moment for the two of us. But if it wasn't going to happen, then it wasn't going to happen. "Alright. I guess if you just aren't feeling it and can't get comfortable enough to do this, we don't have to."

I didn't think I was pouting, but I must've looked sufficiently disappointed because when Jaime turned his head to look at me over his shoulder again, he rolled his eyes and said, "Fine. You big baby. If it means that much to you... We could... prop it against the headboard? And it would still be in the bed with us while we're fucking. Would that be good enough for your plans for a horribly inappropriate victory celebration?"

I sat back on my heels and envisioned what that would look like. It would be further away than I'd imagined. But the Cup would still be within touching distance—my bed might be big, but it wasn't that big. And two big hockey players and one large trophy would still take up most of the room. Huh. Actually, with the Cup not underneath Jaime, it would be able to catch all of the light beaming down from the gaudy and tacky chandelier my decorator had strongly and vehemently protested against installing and all of its many engraved plates could gleam and sparkle to their full potential. I could appreciate the visual stimulation that would provide. Plus, no matter where the Cup was, there would still be hot, sticky, sweaty fucking with my boyfriend that I was deliriously head-over-heels in love with.

So. Yep. That would still work for me.

"Okay," I told him. "We can do it that way instead." I patted Jaime on the hip and said, "Up you go. I'll get it moved. And you… flip over and lay there looking sexy. I'll be with you in a minute."

After Jaime removed himself from the Cup, I wrestled the not very heavy, but pretty bulky trophy, until it was upright and nestled into the crease of where my mattress butted up against the padded headboard of my bed. I gave it a small pat in apology. I felt bad. I'd promised it a threesome with Jaime and myself and now here I was, relegating it to being just a bystander and spectator instead of an active participant in our sexventure. Ehn. Threesomes were always a crapshoot of everyone being able to get equal time and attention.

The Cup dealt with, I turned my attention back to Jaime and found that he had followed my instruction and was laying on his back in the middle of the bed. And he definitely looked sexy. Not very turned on though, judging from the flaccid state of his cock. My own cock had gotten distracted during the Cup relocation and was down to only a semi-chub. Well, that wouldn't do.

I rotated my body away from the Cup and leaned over to trail a line of kisses across Jaime's shoulder next to my knees.

He hummed a happy noise as I continued the path of my mouth over to the side of his neck. I snuck a peek and saw that Jaime's cock had perked back up from its scandalized and propriety-induced limpness. With my lips sampling a bounty of freckles clustered in the hollow of Jaime's throat, my own cock was happily back on board and back to full mast as well.

Jaime's hand brushed up the back of my thigh and settled on the curve of my ass. "Mmm. I'm sorry I ruined your plan," he said.

"Nothing's ruined," I assured him. "You're naked. I'm naked. The Cup is naked." That statement earned me an amused chuckle from Jaime. "The nakedness abounds. I'm sure I can still think of something we can all do together."

I ran my tongue around a pale pink nipple, then leaned over Jaime's torso to lave the other one and lightly graze it with my teeth.

Jaime hissed in a breath, then said, "Move up here. Let me suck you."

Now why hadn't I thought of a congratulatory BJ? I had the best boyfriend ever.

I shuffled on my knees, over a few inches and closer to the head of the bed, so that my hard cock was bobbing a couple of inches above his luscious mouth. As I reached past him to grab the pillow from my side of the bed, Jaime leaned his head up and gave a teasing swipe of his tongue to the tip of my cock.

"Ungh. Here," I said. "Let's put this under your neck. Make the angle easier."

"Hmm. Thanks, Jay. Wouldn't want my neck getting tired and sore," he agreed. Jaime leaned forward and let me arrange the pillow under his head. Then he said, "Now, be a good boy and feed me your dick."

I brushed the pad of my thumb over his lush lower lip, then used it to gently nudge his mouth open. The warm exhale of his breath caressed my pre-cum-dampened slit. I brushed the head of my cock against the soft cushion of his lips, then pressed my way inside.

We groaned in unison as my dick slid into the wet recess of his mouth. "That's it, babe. Take my cock. So good," I praised him.

With his pale pink lips stretched around my dick, Jaime glanced up at me through his gold-tipped, gingery eyelashes. The way we were positioned, I was, seemingly, in complete control right now. I controlled how fast I thrust into his mouth, I controlled how far in I went, I controlled how long I'd let him suck me. But, as his tongue fluttered and flicked against the sensitive underside of my cockhead, I knew that any control I thought I had was merely an illusion.

I was nothing more than an instrument being played and mastered by a virtuoso. The magic of Jaime's mouth was going to quickly reduce me to nothing more than a quivering, salivating, mindlessly lust-drunk babbling idiot who would be begging him to get me off.

Jaime pulled off my dick long enough to take a breath and to tell me, "Fuck my mouth. Do it. Until you're coming down my throat."

Sweet, merciful fuck. I hoped he wasn't expecting this to take very long, because I was already close to desperate and aching to come.

"You sure?" I asked.

Which got me an eyeroll and a muttered, "Yes. Now, do it."

I nudged my cock back into Jaime's mouth and grabbed onto my headboard with my right hand to help with my balance as I fucked his mouth.

I was briefly tempted to wrap my arm around the Stanley Cup, but I thought that might be a little too weird. Instead, I contented myself with having my right forearm pressed up against it as I held onto the headboard.

Jaime was a superbly talented cocksucker, so I didn't take it easy on him. I thrust my cock into his mouth with firm, fast thrusts, plunging deeper and deeper, it seemed, with each pass.

One of Jaime's arms was wrapped around the backs of my thighs and his other hand gripped and squeezed my ass. I had one hand buried in Jaime's bright hair and the other was desperately still holding onto the headboard. Thankfully, it was firmly attached to the wall, but the bed beneath us creaked and groaned as the steady thrust of my hips jostled and shook the bed.

A little too hard, it turned out.

I had just closed my eyes—because it seemed impossible to keep them open with the euphoric pleasure coursing through my body—when I heard a loud, muffled thwap.

The next thing I knew, Jaime's arm was flinging me away from him and I was toppling over onto my side and onto the mattress.

"Oowww," Jaime cried out in pain. "Shit. Fuck. Son of a… Jesus Fucking Christ."

The litany of unexpected curses falling from Jaime's mouth was shocking, until I propped myself up and got a good look at him. Then my own curses filled the air.

"Holy shit. Oh my God. Jaime? Jaime? Are you okay?"

Before he could answer me, there was a loud banging on my closed bedroom door. "Hey! What's going on in there? You better not be damaging the Cup or doing something you're not supposed to with it." The Cup Keeper banged on the door some more and then the doorknob was jiggling and rattling as he attempted to open the door. "What's going on in there?" he asked again. "Why can't I open the door? You'd better open this door before you're in more trouble than you're already going to be in."

I tore my eyes off my bedroom door, which was doing an admirable job of keeping the Keeper out and unaware of what had just befallen the precious, priceless, world-renowned and highly coveted Stanley Cup.

Having been jostled off balance by the shaking of the bed as I'd fucked Jaime's mouth, the beloved Stanley Cup had clearly fallen over and landed with a hard blow against my beloved boyfriend's head. Which he was now cradling in his hands as it bled profusely all over him, the pillow underneath him, the mattress, and the Stanley Cup.

Jaime had also, apparently, relocated the bottle of lube when he'd laid down. Because once it had finished inflicting bodily injury to my dearest darling, the Stanley Cup had bounced and crash landed on top of the bottle of lube, crushing and splitting it open. So, there was now also a giant gloopy puddle of lube pooled on the mattress that the cherished holy grail of hockey was now laying in.

Yeah. There was no way I was letting the Keeper in to see the state the Cup was currently in. If he didn't outright murder me, I'd find myself banned from ever coming close to stepping a skate on ice ever again.

"Uhh... Nothing's going on in here," I blatantly and brazenly lied. "The Cup and I are merely... watching a movie before going to bed. So, there's nothing to get your knickers in a twist over."

Jamie was quietly whimpering as he muttered, "Oh God, oh God, oh God, oh God. It hurts so bad."

"Let. Me. In," the Keeper demanded.

"Not happening," I blithely called back. "I'm not wearing any clothes and I'm not putting any back on this late at night. So, you're just going to have to deal and trust that the Cup is in as pristine condition as when you handed it to me earlier today."

"It had better fucking be," he called back through the locked door. "Or you're going to be in a world of hurt."

Yeah, yeah, yeah. Whatever. He could hold his horses and wait for morning. Hopefully the blow to Jaime's head hadn't damaged the Cup badly enough that it was noticeable. And really, what were a couple extra dings and scratches? It's not like one little hardy collision with Jaime's noggin would be enough to do any real damage to it. Right? Not like the sort of damage one particular hockey team had caused when they accidentally smashed it against the ice and caved in one whole side of the bowl as they were taking their team photos on the ice just after they'd won the Cup.

I had more important things to worry about right now than the Cup Keeper's conniption tantrum and concern over the Cup. Like checking on my boyfriend and seeing just how injured he'd gotten during my, obviously ill-advised, sexual fantasy enactment.

There was no way I could assess just how bad it was— head wounds bled a lot even if they weren't serious, right?— what with Jaime clutching his head and rocking his body back and forth the way he was. I carefully crawled around his curled-up body and said, "Babe, let me see. I need to see how bad it is and if we're going to have to face the wrath of the Keeper to get you to an ER."

"Oh God."

I tenderly peeled one of his hands away from his injured head and peered closely at the wound.

There was a large lump just to the center of his forehead that was already turning a dark bluish-purple and the area around it was bright red. There was quite a bit of blood smeared all across his skin and in his hair, turning it a darker red, but it looked as though the large gash torn into his skin wasn't bleeding as profusely as it had been. There was now just a slow trickle of blood oozing out of the cut. And while the cut was several inches long, it wasn't very deep.

"I don't think you're going to need stitches," I told him. "Some butterfly bandages, some Tylenol, some ice packs, and you'll be good as new in… a couple days. And if it winds up scarring… What's one more hockey scar on a hockey player?" I asked. "And a hockey scar from the Stanley Cup? Really, you should be thanking me." I smiled at him to show I was teasing. Although…

"I hate you," Jaime muttered, narrowing his eyes in a glare. Which was a bad idea as he then flinched in pain.

"No you don't."

"Why do I go along with your idiotic ideas?"

I was pretty sure the question was rhetorical, so I didn't answer it. "And we were already going to have to wash the trophy anyway… Now we just have a little blood to scrub off of it in addition to the lube and sweat and cum that was going to end up on it."

"Oh my God," Jaime moaned. "I hadn't even… If this hadn't happened, we would've wound up desecrating the Stanley Cup."

"Yeah, we would've," I agreed with a smirk.

"Oh God," he moaned again. I liked getting those words and noises out of him in bed, but usually it was under different circumstances. "You know what this means, don't

you?" Jaime asked. "You'll never win the Cup again. And I…
I haven't won it yet and now I never will!"

"What are you talking about?"

"What we just did… The ghost of Lord Stanley probably
just put a curse on both of us and now our hockey careers
will be in the toilet. And we'll drag the rest of our teammates
down there with us," Jaime stated.

I had to scoff at that. "Yeah. 'Cause I'm sure we're the
first guys who've ever had sex in front of the Cup. Or had it
in bed with them while they did the naughty. And as for the
blood… Pfffthp. It's a hockey trophy. I'd be shocked if a
little blood had never gotten on it before. Stop stressing.
You'll just wind up psyching yourself out and then you'll be
in a self-fulfilling prophecy. I, of course, will do my best to
prove you wrong by winning the Cup again next year,
though."

That boast was a bit of a stretch. Even if I wound up
staying with the Snappers, it was difficult for any team to pull
off a back-to-back Stanley Cup run and victory. Throw in the
fact that I probably wouldn't be in Kansas City next season
and my odds went astronomically lower. There's never been
an expansion team to win the Stanley Cup in their inaugural
season.

But it's not like I could tell Jaime that, since I hadn't
exactly told him about my trade attempts yet. I figured I'd tell
him sometime after the ink was dry on my new contract.
Possibly even after I signed the lease on a new apartment in
Des Moines.

I would definitely tell him before I moved, though. After all, it was his duty as my boyfriend to help me move my shit.

"We're doomed. Doomed."

"Quit being a big baby," I told him. "Help me get the Cup into the bathroom and we'll start getting it cleaned up."

"Do you even know how to clean it properly?" he asked. "Or are you going to wind up damaging it even more."

We both sat up and looked at the Cup. It really didn't look so pretty and shiny anymore.

"Yep. Pretty sure," I told him. Jamie's groan said he didn't find much reassurance in my answer. "I did some research before you got here. Granted that was just for getting cum and lube off it, not blood. But the same principle ought to apply."

"Why? Why?" he asked. "What could I have possibly done in this life or the last to find myself in this situation?"

Jaime's head must've been hurting pretty badly; his face was all squinched up in pain and distress.

"Obviously something very, very good," I replied. "Because you got lucky enough to have me as a boyfriend."

I started to get up off the bed. I know I was acting kind of cavalierly about it, but we really should get the Cup cleaned off before it stained or something.

"I am lucky," Jaime replied as he grabbed my hand and pulled me back down to the bed.

I gave a grunt of pain, as it was my turn this time to take a glancing blow from the Cup as my hip bumped against it as I landed back down beside Jaime.

"Even though you drive me bonkers," he said. "I love you. And I am incredibly lucky that you love me, too."

"Yep. And I always will."

Jaime's hand resettled on my ass, pulling my naked body flush with his naked body. And I gave a mental apology to the Stanley Cup. Because it was going to have to wait a little—or a lot—longer to get hauled into the shower and given the scrub down it needed.

"I sort of have to, now," I added as I felt Jaime's fingertips gliding over my newest tattoo.

The one on my left butt cheek.

The one that said, "Property of Jaime Johnson."

The End

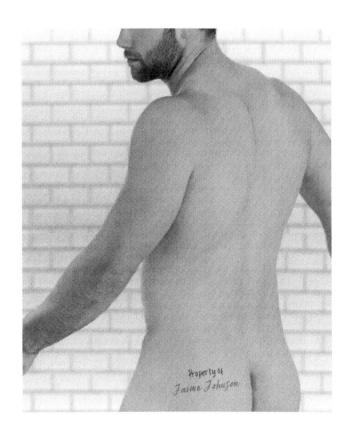

Author Notes

The NHL teams mentioned in this book are fictional. Completely, totally fictional. That being said, I did attempt to model my NHL universe after the real-world NHL, just with different team names and players. As much as I could, I adhered to the rules and regulations of NHL hockey, the structure of the NHL, and the general season and game schedule of the NHL. Any discrepancies or mistakes are my own and we'll just put them down to creative license for the sake of the story.

While this book is the first in its series, it is my second book featuring hockey players. The first, Seducing My Brother-in-Law is the fourth book of my Pine Ridge series and it tells the story of Sawyer Brzycki and his boyfriend TJ Reilly. In that book, I wrote Sawyer as the first professional hockey player in the NHL to publicly come out, although I alluded to another player who had been drafted who had come out before Sawyer—the real-life Luke Prokop, prospective NHL player who was drafted by Nashville in 2020. For timeline purposes, the events of Seducing My Brother-in-Law—and Sawyer's coming out—conclude just prior to the start of this book. That would make J.J. and Jaime the second and third NHL players to publicly come out in my NHL universe, with Carsen Appleby and Leland

Griffin following closely thereafter. Although, as also mentioned in this book, some of my other NHL players are known to be queer by their teammates, just not to the general populace.

The charity mentioned—K9s for Warriors—that J.J. and Jaime are raising money for at the celebrity golf tournament is a real charity. For more information, please visit their website K9sforwarriors.org. The Wolf Creek Golf Club is also a real and highly popular golf course located in Mesquite, Nevada. The celebrity charity golf tournament mentioned in this book, however, is fictional.

The town of What Cheer, Iowa—J.J.'s hometown and where his friends Greg and Crystal Phillipi and their children live—is a real town with just over 600 residents. Any details mentioned in this book about What Cheer and its surrounding community are based on internet Googling or otherwise made up by me. I would like to take this opportunity to apologize for my teenage-self. Whenever I drove past What Cheer on Interstate 80, teenage-me liked to routinely corrupt and intentionally mispronounce the name of this small town in order to mock it. J.J. makes no such apologies. I'd also like to point out that J.J.'s opinions regarding the entirety of Iowa and Kansas—and possibly other large portions of the midwestern US—are entirely his own.

The playlist for Johnson X 2 can be found on Spotify at:
https://open.spotify.com/playlist/7E3WhTAhnvZvY5sSwR
JydP?si=d65a95e5365b4db0

Come find me:

Website: http://www.shaemichaelswrites.com

Facebook: Shae Michaels & my reader group- ShaeMless Sinners

Instagram: @shaemichaelswrites

Goodreads:www.goodreads.com/author/show/22521736.Shae_Michaels

BookBub: @shaemichaelswrites

If you're thinking that the characters of Sawyer Brzycki and TJ Reilly seem familiar but can't quite recall why... you might want to check out Seducing My Brother-in-Law (Pine Ridge, Book Four). And don't worry, this book isn't the last we see of many of these hockey boys. There will be more Stick Handling coming soon!

Books by Shae Michaels

Pine Ridge Series

Finn's Fake Boyfriend

The Handyman's Brother

Remaking Raine

Seducing My Brother-in-Law

Stick Handling Series

Johnson x 2

Printed in Great Britain
by Amazon

29128412R00211